Christmas

at

Wynter House

Emily Harvale

ISBN 978-1-909917-47-7

Published by Crescent Gate Publishing

Print edition published worldwide 2019
E-edition published worldwide 2019

Editor Christina Harkness

Cover design by JR and Emily Harvale

To Nigel.
You're in one of my books, at last!
Thanks for getting me and my car out
of that ditch, all those years ago. We
still laugh about it.

Acknowledgements

My grateful thanks go to the following:

Christina Harkness for her patience and care in editing this book.
My webmaster, David Cleworth who does so much more than website stuff.
My cover design team, JR.
Luke Brabants. Luke is a talented artist and can be found at: www.lukebrabants.com
My wonderful friends for their friendship and love. You know I love you all.
All the fabulous members of my Readers' Club. You help and support me in so many ways and I am truly grateful for your ongoing friendship. I wouldn't be where I am today without you.
My Twitter and Facebook friends, and fans of my Facebook author page. It's great to chat with you. You help to keep me (relatively) sane!
Thank you for buying this book.

Christmas

at

Wynter House

Chapter One

Neva Grey squeezed her holdall into the boot of her Ford Fiesta estate, shifting plastic boxes filled to the brim with a variety of hair products, brushes, hairdryers, curling tongs, nail polishes and various other tools of her trade.

'You've still got to find room for all these,' Jo, her best friend and flatmate said, grinning as she handed Neva several glimmering, Christmas gift bags. 'Weren't you going to sort out this boot before you went away?'

Neva grinned back as she tried to find space for every bag, each containing presents beautifully wrapped in sparkly red and gold paper.

'I was going to do a lot of things before I went, but as usual I didn't have time.'

'You could've done it this morning if you'd gone to *Barb's Bloomers* yesterday, instead of having to dash all the way there and back at some ungodly hour today. But you insisted we had to do last minute Christmas shopping in Covent Garden.'

'Excuse me,' Neva said, throwing Jo a sarcastic smile. 'Who insisted?'

Jo shrugged. 'OK. Perhaps it was me. But you were the one who suggested we go for a Baileys Hot Chocolate in the Skate Lounge at Somerset House. And you don't even like ice skating.'

'I like watching other people ice skating. There's something special about that ice rink. The lights, the music and that massive tree make it seem so magical. Christmas wouldn't be Christmas without an evening there.'

'You say that every year.' Jo shook her head and laughed. 'You do realise that with all those poinsettias and God knows what else you've got spread all over your seats and in every footwell, your car looks like a mini, mobile Kew Gardens.'

'Oh funny. I promised Mum I'd get them. Barb has the best poinsettias and her mistletoe looks like it's just been picked off the tree. I should've put some black bin bags on the seats though. If those berries, or the holly berries get squished on the journey, I'll have stains all over my seats.'

'I think that's the least of your worries. If you brake too hard, you could well be buried under plants and presents and boxes. It'll take days to dig you out.'

Neva grinned as she jammed the final bag into a tiny space and quickly closed the tailgate, pushing against it with both hands until it locked. The sound was barely audible above the noise of the passing traffic, tooting car horns and Christmas tunes blaring from vehicles, homes and shops on the busy, south east London street, but Neva heard the satisfying click and gave her car a 'well done' pat. The lock was iffy sometimes.

'One of the things I'm looking forward to the most about this holiday,' Neva said. 'Apart from seeing my family, of course. Is having time for myself. Time to sort out this boot and all those boxes and crates. Time to relax. Time to think. Time to make a proper plan for my new business. Time to decide what else I want to do with my life and where I want to live.'

Jo raised one perfectly shaped, black-tinted eyebrow. 'You haven't sorted your life out in the last thirty-four years. What makes you think you'll do it in two weeks? That's a bit optimistic, even for you.' She laughed as she pulled Neva into her arms.

They hugged each other tight, and Neva breathed in Jo's perfume as if by doing so, she could take a small part of her best friend with her.

'Because I know I have to. I won't have you to sort things out for me anymore. I need to get my act together and concentrate on my new business.'

She eased herself away taking Jo's hand in hers and smiling at the massive diamond engagement ring neither of them had quite got used to seeing.

'You'll always have me,' Jo said, her voice cracking just a little. 'I'm only moving in with my boyfriend – sorry. My fiancé. I'm not taking a vow of silence and joining a group of monks in Outer Mongolia.'

'You're moving to Upminster. Isn't that the same?'

Neva gave Jo a playful shove; Jo did the same before giving her a serious look.

'Nothing's going to change between you and me, Neva. Friends forever, remember?'

Neva nodded. 'Friends forever. But we both know things will change. For one thing we won't be living together.'

Linking arms, they looked up at the second-floor windows, aglow with multi-coloured lights, as were all the other flats in the converted four-storey Victorian house.

'I can't believe it's been ten years since we bought that flat,' Jo said. 'I still remember what a wreck it was when we moved in.'

Neva laughed. 'I still remember the expression on my dad's face when he saw how much work there was to do, for him and his team of builders. What I can't believe is that it sold so fast. I honestly thought it would take longer. And I'll admit, I'm not looking forward to moving out in January. Or to finding somewhere else to live.'

'I told you there's a spare room at Rob's.'

Neva pulled a face. 'When Rob proposed last month and asked you to move in with him, I'm pretty sure that invitation didn't extend to me.'

Neva and Jo had put the flat on the market one week after Rob's proposal. They discussed various options first, but Neva couldn't afford to buy Jo out, and she wouldn't have done so, even if she could. Living there wouldn't be the same without Jo crashing around the place. They'd both been surprised when an offer for the asking price was received the very next day.

'He wouldn't mind.' Jo turned to face her. 'I'm serious, Neva. You're more than welcome to come and stay with us. Even if it's just until you find somewhere.'

Neva nodded. Jo would welcome her with open arms. Rob, on the other hand might not be so keen – despite what Jo thought.

'I know. And I really appreciate the offer. But it's time I stood on my own two feet. We both know you've been the grown up in our friendship. Making my own decisions without getting a second opinion from you beforehand will do me good for a while.'

Neva would miss living with Jo. They had

been friends since they were at nursery school. They'd done everything together. They even went on their first date together, with two male friends. They went to college together to study hair and beauty. Got their first job together twelve years ago and had worked together ever since, until Jo left the salon two months ago when Rob got her an interview with another well-known salon chain. The owner was a client of his. Rob was an electrician and had his own firm. Which is how he and Jo first met.

One weekend, four years ago, when Neva was at her parents' and Jo was alone in the flat, all the lights went out. Jo used her phone to search the web for local electricians, and Rob Ashford was the first on the list. That night he asked Jo out on a date – and he only charged her for parts to fix the damaged electrics, not for his labour cost, which both Jo and Neva thought was quite romantic.

Neva knew Jo wasn't sure about taking the salon job when it was offered, partly because she felt bad about moving on from *Darius May Hair & Beauty* without her best friend.

'We could look for somewhere else together,' Jo had said.

'We could. But the offer you've got is fantastic and we might not find one to match it. You shouldn't turn it down because of me. It's much better money and far better prospects. Besides, I'll get to take over some of your clients once you leave.'

Jo clearly wasn't convinced and it had taken a lot of persuading from Rob, to make Jo finally accept the offer.

But Jo's new job gave Neva the push to think about her own future career prospects. She had always wanted to run her own hair and beauty business but had never had the guts or the money.

And now she had. Well, she would once the sale completed. They had made a killing, thanks to buying their flat for a snip ten years ago and doing it up with the help of Neva's dad.

Even after paying off their joint mortgage, Neva would have more money than she ever imagined. OK, it might only be two hundred thousand pounds, but as she usually only had about ten pounds left in her account at the end of each month, the thought of suddenly being that much in the black was a heady one.

Which was why she had decided that now was the right time to pursue her dreams. Shop rents were sky-high in London and she wasn't ready to tie herself down in some other location, so she had the perfect solution: a mobile hairdressing and beauty business.

She handed in her notice at Darius May the minute she and Jo signed the contract for the sale of the flat. Some of her clients would use her if she remained in London, but the more she thought about it, the more she wondered if perhaps she should leave the bright lights and settle down somewhere closer to her family in Surrey. Or somewhere entirely new.

Now that Jo was moving in with Rob, there was nothing to keep Neva in town. Her new business was mobile. She really could go anywhere. And despite what Jo thought, Neva knew they wouldn't see each other as often. If that was the case, getting a train and meeting up with Jo in Covent Garden, or anywhere in central London wasn't much different to getting a tube to Upminster, at the end of the District line, or driving to the house Jo would be sharing with Rob.

Residential property prices in London were through the roof, so buying a place on her own would now be impossible for Neva. She didn't want to rent. She and Jo did that for a short time when they first moved to London but Neva's dad had instilled in her at a very young age the importance of owning your own property.

'Tenancies can end abruptly giving you fairly short notice to find a place to live,' he had said. 'If you buy your own home, you'll always have a roof over your head. Provided you pay the mortgage.'

But she couldn't afford to buy somewhere on her own, so she and Jo had bought the flat together.

And now it was sold, and she would have

to make a decision soon about where she was going to live. She needed a place to put her furniture and belongings when the sale completed. And she'd need to hire removers to move all her stuff. She would sort all that out over Christmas. She always left things until the last minute. Which was one of the things she was determined to change. But there was plenty of time to do that.

For now, all Neva wanted to think about was having a peaceful Christmas with her family. Not that their Christmases were ever peaceful. Especially not with her eight-year-old niece, Sasha there. But Neva had been working non-stop and once she started her own business, the hours would obviously increase. She was really hoping for some rest and relaxation and the cosy cottage her parents had rented was going to be the perfect place to do that.

'I'm only a phone call away,' Jo said. 'And I like giving my opinion on everything you do, you know that. In fact, don't think that us not being under the same roof is going to stop me, because it's not. I definitely want to hear all about this village you're going to. What's it called again?'

'Wyntersleap. It sounds idyllic.'

'It sounds tiny. Don't go into hibernation. Are you sure it's not Winter sleep?'

Neva giggled. 'I'm certain. According to the

website for the rental cottage, it got its name because the wife and teenage daughters of some old, defeated chieftain back in the day, leapt off a cliff beside a waterfall rather than end up in the hands of the invading Vikings. There was a son too but he didn't jump. He was injured in the battle and left for dead until someone saved him and nursed him back to health. That's why there're Wynters at Wyntersleap. But they don't live in the village. They live in a big house nearby.'

'Don't tell me. It was a beautiful girl and they fell in love and married. And he got his revenge on the Vikings who caused the deaths of his family.'

'How did you know that?'

Jo laughed. 'I read all the stuff on the website when you showed me the photos. I was just winding you up. I really don't get why the wife and daughters jumped to their deaths, though. Personally I'd love to be in the hands of a hunky Viking. Oh. Not now, of course.' She glanced at her engagement ring and suddenly grew serious. 'I'll only ever be in one person's hands from now on. As much as I love Rob, that's a bit frightening.'

Neva eyed her friend. 'You are sure about this, aren't you, Jo?'

'About moving in with Rob? Yes.'

'About marrying him.'

Jo sighed. 'I think so. You know me. It's

just the marriage bit. It didn't work out well for my parents.'

That was an understatement. Jo's mum and dad had possibly the worst marriage in the history of marriages and the fall-out was still affecting Jo to this day.

'But you're not your mum or your dad. In fact, you're nothing like either of them.'

Jo nodded. 'I know. That's why I used to think I must've been adopted. But those two are both far too selfish to have gone to the trouble of adopting a child. Anyway. Let's not talk about them. How did we get on to such a melancholy subject? Give me another hug, you.' She pulled Neva back into her arms. 'God, I'm going to miss you.'

They would be seeing one another again after Christmas, and they still had all their belongings to pack and move out of the flat, but this was their last Christmas as flatmates and it was different saying goodbye for the holidays when it was also the end of an era.

'But as you said, we're only a phone call away.'

'Yeah. And you'd better get going if you want to avoid the mad rush of the Christmas exodus. You know how bad it is getting out of London on a Friday. On the last one before Christmas it's going to be a stampede.' Jo wrapped her jacket more tightly around her and glanced upwards. 'The weather forecast isn't good, so you be careful. I wouldn't be surprised if it chucks it down even though there's not a cloud in the sky at the moment.'

Neva smiled. 'They always get it wrong. It's going to be a beautiful day. Cold and crisp and clear. Just the way December days should be.'

Jo didn't look convinced. 'I hope you get to Wyntersleap before it rains. Drive safely.'

'I will. And I'll call and let you know I've arrived.'

'Make sure you do. You know how I worry.'

Neva kissed Jo on the cheek before patting the roof of her car.

'Come on then my little beauty box. Let's get on the road.'

She ran her fingers over the lovingly designed art-work emblazoned across the boot and the matching signage along the side. Her logo had only been spray-painted last week by Luke – a friend who was an artist. He'd done a fantastic job, and even though it might seem foolish, Neva had an uncontrollable urge to stroke it every time she got in and out of her car.

The words, *Neva's Hair & Beauty* shimmered in the pale, morning sunlight, the holographic silver letters a kaleidoscope of colours reflecting all the Christmas lights in the windows of the surrounding shops, flats and houses overlooking the road.

'Weirdo,' Jo said, following Neva to the

driver's door.

'Heathen. It's beautiful and I want to stroke it.'

'Get a cat. Better yet. Get a man.'

'Nope. I'm off men completely, for the foreseeable future. I'm sick of being lied to, cheated on, forgotten about, or simply ignored. A man is the last thing I need. And I can't get a cat if Sasha got that puppy. But I suppose I can stroke that over the holidays.'

'I'm missing you already, you weirdo.'

Neva gave Jo a final hug before she got into her car, closed the door, switched on the engine and opened the electric window.

'Same here, you heathen. See you next year. Merry Christmas. Give Rob and his family hell. Show them all what they're in for by inviting you into the fold.' She blew Jo a kiss and winked.

'Don't worry, I will. Have the best Christmas ever with that crazy family of yours. Give them all my love. Even your annoying little niece. Tell her if she doesn't like the present I bought her, that's tough. We don't always get what we want in life. It's a lesson she needs to learn and the sooner the better.'

Neva grinned. 'Yeah right. You can tell her that yourself. I want a peaceful Christmas. Anyway, we both know she'll love it.'

She would. Sasha loved anything to do with ghosts, vampires, zombies and ghouls, so the bumper book of ghost stories Jo had bought her was the perfect present, even if the rest of the family might not agree.

Sasha was the only child of Neva's elder sister, Rowan and her husband, Nigel Lane, and she was a little odd for an eight-year-old. She had already decided to be a ghost and demon hunter when she grew up. Buffy of *Buffy The Vampire Slayer*, a series she had watched with her mum, was her role model. Her clothes, which were mainly black, had to have pockets for her to store her mini flashlight, garlic, bottle of Holy water and set of knives. The garlic, knives and bottle were plastic. The 'Holy' water was from the tap, but Sasha had a vivid imagination, so none of that mattered to her. Her footwear of choice were high top Converse trainers but her one small nod to femininity were that they were black and silver glitter, because according to Sasha, every girl needs a bit of sparkle in their lives, even vampire slayers. The family all hoped she would eventually grow out of it, but Neva wasn't so sure. And neither was Neva's dad.

'Call me!' Jo repeated, as Neva strapped on her seatbelt and put the car into first gear.

'I will. Have a fabulous time with Rob's parents, and wish Rob, Merry Christmas from me.' She hesitated for just a second. 'You're the best friend in the whole wide world, Jo Duncan. And I love you.'

Jo nodded. 'Back at ya, Neva Grey. Now get out of here before I change my mind about spending Christmas with Rob and his folks, and jump in your passenger seat instead.'

Neva laughed, turned on her indicator and closed the electric window as she headed her car into the never-ending flow of London's, morning rush hour. Glancing in her rear-view mirror, she saw Jo jumping up and down at the side of the road, ignoring all the traffic and waving her arms wildly to prolong their goodbye.

Chapter Two

Clouds bubbled up in the clear, December sky soon after Neva turned onto the M25, said to be the inspiration for Chris Rea's famous song, *The Road to Hell* – and the man wasn't wrong. It had taken her almost half an hour to travel a distance of a few miles and vehicles were bumper to bumper on every lane. At this rate she wouldn't arrive in Wyntersleap until lunchtime. Without thinking, she started singing the song over the Christmas tunes on her playlist. Chris Rea was one of her mum and dad's favourites and Neva and her sister had been brought up listening to his albums. She knew every single word to several of his songs.

As she edged her car forward to secure a place in the queue leading onto the M23, single file due to the almost obligatory roadworks on motorways at peak holiday times these days, she searched for *Driving Home for Christmas,* another Chris Rea hit, and belted out the words at the top of her lungs. It made her happier despite the curious looks from several other motorists also filtering into the queue.

No sooner had she passed the Gatwick turn-off than the rain began but at least the traffic had thinned out. Unfortunately, the rain intensified. By the time she saw the sign for Brighton and the coast, visibility was becoming a problem and half an hour later when her sat-nav informed her the turning for Merriment Bay was half a mile away, she nearly missed the sign due to the torrential rain. Luckily, she was in the left-hand lane, going far slower than her usual seventy miles an hour due to the appalling weather conditions, and as no one else was travelling in that direction, she was able to do a quick manoeuvre and veer left without causing an accident or hitting the grass verge separating the motorway and turn-off.

She breathed a sigh of relief. It couldn't be far to the tiny village of Wyntersleap now, although her sat-nav seemed uncertain. But Jo had insisted Neva check and double check the map before she left, so she knew Wyntersleap was five miles inland from the coast and Merriment Bay and her sat-nav did seem confident that Merriment Bay was fifteen miles away. Just ten more miles and Neva would step inside the cosy cottage she'd seen on the *Wyntersleap Cottage Rental* website.

The tiny village was nestled between rolling green hills and surrounded by fields and woodland. There was a burbling river passing beneath an old stone bridge at the entrance to the village and the entire place looked idyllic. And rather twee. Although the video on the website was clearly shot at the height of summer. But it looked like something you'd see on a picture postcard, or covered in snow on a Christmas tin of chocolate biscuits.

She smiled at the thought. Her mum and dad would be there waiting. They'd told her they planned to arrive first thing, which for them meant 8 a.m. even if they couldn't collect the keys until 10. Her mum would've started baking the moment she stepped into the kitchen and the smell of cinnamon, ginger and mixed spices, would be wafting around the place. Her dad would've lit the fire so that it would be roaring by the time the rest of the family arrived. He would've already hung lights around the windows, if none were there beforehand, but he'd wait to dress the tree until everyone else was there.

There'd also be a tree in the village square if the photos on the website were to be believed, although there were only nine other cottages, one tiny shop and an equally tiny pub called Wyntersleap Inn. The stately home of Wynter House, which sat high amongst the hills, looked down upon the village like a giant eagle perched at the edge of her nest overlooking her young. The website also stated that Christmas was a magical time in Wyntersleap. But magic could be good or bad, so that would remain to be seen.

Mainly, she was looking forward to spending two weeks with her family. Although two weeks with Sasha was a bit like an endurance test. Things were rarely peaceful when Sasha was around. Nevertheless, Neva couldn't wait to see her niece again, along with Rowan and Nigel. They didn't get together as a family as often as any of them would have liked because they all led busy lives, so Christmas was a special time.

And this Christmas would be even more so. Knowing that she was coming into money, Neva had splashed out on a few extra presents for her family. But it wasn't just that. They usually spent Christmas at Neva's childhood home, so renting this cottage was a first.

When her parents told her and her sister, they had done it, both she and Rowan were surprised. They were almost speechless when their dad had added that it was because they had something to tell everyone and the cottage was the perfect place to do that.

Neva immediately thought they were going to say they were selling the family home and downsizing. It made perfect sense to do so; the house was far too big for just the two of them, although the timing couldn't have been worse for Neva. She always knew she could return to her parents' house if ever she needed to, but if they moved to something smaller, that might not be possible. Hence the further indecision about where she might be living after her and Jo's flat sale completed.

And when Neva phoned her mum two nights ago, Dawn had told her that Rowan and Nigel were getting Sasha a puppy. So this Christmas definitely would be different. And certainly not as peaceful as Neva wished it might.

'Really? Is that wise?' Neva had said.

Dawn sighed dramatically. 'Nigel believes a puppy may make Sasha less interested in her obsession with the living dead. And the permanently dead, of course. Her fascination with ghosts seems to be outweighing her zombie and vampire fetishes for the time being. Your father and I aren't sure if that's a step in the right direction, or not.'

Neva laughed. 'I'll bet you anything, that puppy will become some sort of vampire slash ghost hunter's sidekick within five minutes of its arrival. I'm not sure who I feel sorrier for – Rowan and Nigel, or the puppy.'

'Can you imagine, sweetheart? I expect the puppy will have a whale of a time. Sasha will love it to bits as she does all soft fluffy creatures. Frankly, I still believe it was the death of her pet rabbit that caused this strange obsession in the first place. But your father disagrees. He says she has simply found herself a life-long interest and we have to learn to live with it. His brother is the same about trains. But trains and the living dead are not at all alike.'

Neva giggled. 'I agree with Dad. I think Sasha's in this for the duration. Of course she may grow out of it once she becomes interested in boys.'

Dawn tutted. 'Heaven forbid. That's something I'm not ready to think about. I prefer her current obsession. I remember what Rowan was like. You weren't nearly half so bad. You sort of drifted into your first relationship, and not until you were seventeen. Rowan couldn't wait. She was eleven when she brought her first boyfriend home. I'll never forget the look on your father's face when we saw him. His name was Jayden. He was thirteen, had five tattoos and he called your father, 'Mate'. We both still thank our lucky stars that he decided Rowan wasn't 'cool' enough for him to date for longer than two weeks. It took her six months of tears and tantrums to get over him.'

'Yes. I remember. But Sasha won't waste time with tears if someone dumps her. She'll probably just knock them out with a karate blow or something.'

Neva was only half joking. That's probably

what Sasha would do. Neva wished she had half the confidence and street-smarts of her eight-year-old niece.

'Turn left after one mile,' Neva's sat-nav informed her as she drove across a bridge raised high above what looked like a massive lake, but she couldn't see properly and needed to concentrate on the road because that itself was covered in water. Driving over the edge of a bridge would not be a good idea and the barriers either side didn't look that high, or as if they would stop very much at all.

Neva sighed with relief as she reached the other side and peered through the deluge. Where was this turn-off, exactly? All she could see now were fields and trees and rain.

'Take the next turning on your left.'

'I will if I can see it.' There was no point in shouting at the sat-nav, but it felt good to do it.

'You have missed the turning. It is two miles to the next turning. Take the turning on your left in—'

'Oh shut up.' Neva glanced in her rear-view mirror and braked. She turned the fan on full as the inside of the windscreen was misting up and wiped the screen with her sleeve for good measure.

There was no way she was driving an extra two miles in this weather. Two miles wasn't far but her eyes were itching and her throat was dry. The sooner she reached the cottage the happier she would be.

She looked around, to her left, her right, in front and behind before executing a careful three-point turn. The road was narrower here, more of a lane than anything, and it was bordered by trees and bushes. She didn't want to scratch her new paintwork. The sat-nav remained oddly silent, as if it held its breath, which was nonsense of course, but it made Neva smile.

'What the–?'

The squeal of brakes, the slosh of water and the thud that sent her car spinning like a ballerina, soon made Neva realise her mistake. She knew enough to turn into the spin, not try to brake, and thankfully her car came to a stop against a grassy mound.

The splash of feet running through puddles and a rapid tapping on the car window brought her back to her surroundings and she looked through the pane of glass as rivulets of rain poured down it.

She met a pair of eyes, the brightest blue she had ever seen.

'Are you OK?' The deep voice was muffled by the glass and the deluge.

Neva nodded and pressed the button to open the window. Not the wisest move as she got a face full of water so cold it sent a shiver through her body as it trickled down her neck beneath her jacket.

The man held open his weatherproof jacket to shield her and handed her a handkerchief. A cotton handkerchief.

Neva dabbed at her face. Why-oh-why hadn't she put on any make-up today? At least she had tinted her eyebrows and eyelashes two days ago. That was something. But without make-up her complexion was pale, and lipstick always did wonders for her bare, cupid's-bow lips. If only she had put some on. She licked them self-consciously as she nodded at the gorgeous hunk standing in the pouring rain.

'I'm fine thanks.'

He scanned the seats before his gaze settled on her face.

'You've got a lot of festive foliage.' He smiled as he reached out and removed a poinsettia leaf from her hair. 'What were you doing in the middle of the road? Did you hit a puddle and aquaplane?'

'What? Oh yes. Yes I did.'

She wasn't going to tell him she was doing a three-point turn. She hadn't expected any oncoming traffic even though she had checked. She had hardly seen another vehicle since she'd left the main road a couple of miles back. She darted a look in the rear-view mirror. All the presents appeared to have remained in place but one or two of the plants had tumbled over.

'But you're sure you're OK?' There was genuine concern in those unbelievably blue eyes and that deep but soft and sexy voice.

'Yes. Please don't worry. I'm just a bit shaken, that's all. Oh God! My car. Is it badly damaged?'

He glanced at the side and shook his head. 'Oddly enough, it's not. This was the side I hit and I can only see a slight dent over the wheel arch. That'll come out with a bit of hammering.'

'Hammering!'

He grinned. 'Don't worry. I'm sure they won't wreck your paintwork. Are you OK to drive?'

Neva nodded. She was shaking but that was more from the icy blast and showers of rain coming in the window. Despite his gallantry, his jacket was letting some of the rain past and each large droplet hit her hand, or face, or neck.

'I'm fine.'

'Where are you headed?' He was saturated now but it didn't seem to bother him.

'A little village called Wyntersleap. Have you heard of it? It's somewhere around here but I think I may have missed the turn-off.'

'Wyntersleap?' His large eyes grew wider and his smile doubled in size. 'You're going to Wyntersleap? To one of the rental cottages?'

Neva nodded again. 'Yes. Don't tell me you're going there too.' Her heart beat faster as hope swelled in her chest.

'Not to the village. I'm going to Wynter House.'

or two of the ones you've set her up with, she *is* far too good for.'

'Do what? They're my mates you're slagging off.'

'And Neva's my best friend. I've known her all my life and I love her more than I love you, especially right now, so be careful what you say about her or this relationship will be over.'

Neva hadn't been able to see them, just hear what they were saying and that was only because they thought she was out, but she'd cancelled her date and stayed in that night. She thought the ensuing silence meant trouble, but Rob had caved.

'Sorry, babe. You're right. Some of them I wouldn't let my sister date. I shouldn't have set Neva up with them. It's just I'm running out of guys to date her. Not everyone wants to. She's cute, but she's not as pretty as you, by a mile. She's short, too. Not all guys like short girls.'

'That's enough, Rob. Neva's gorgeous. And she's kind and loyal and loving, once she decides she likes you.'

'That's great. But she's not very sexy, is she? I'm not saying she's fat but losing a couple of pounds wouldn't hurt. And maybe if she showed a bit more of her boobs ... OK. I'll stop. But I just thought it would be nice for us to go out in a foursome. That way you wouldn't have to go out with her on your own so often.'

'I think we need to get something straight,

Rob. I'll always want to go out with Neva, on our own. Just me and her. That's what best friends do. That'll never change, no matter what. So you'd better get used to that. And as for her flaunting her body just to get one of your friends interested, well, that says more about your friends than Neva. A girl shouldn't have to show her boobs to get a guy's attention. Not if he's a decent guy.'

And to Neva's surprise, Rob had apologised and changed the subject.

But from time to time over the last four years, Neva sometimes felt that Rob resented the relationship she and Jo had. A feeling that had only intensified during the last few weeks. He'd seemed somewhat smug now that he and Jo were engaged, and he positively glowed when she and Jo got the offer on the flat and it all went through so fast to exchange of contracts. Completion was set for the 10th of January and Rob would probably come to gloat, and be grinning from ear to ear.

She didn't know why, but she had started having doubts about Rob. If he made Jo happy, that was fine, but if he didn't. Well, she would set her niece on him. Sasha would do more damage than Neva ever could.

She was being silly though. It was the mere fact that everything was changing between her and Jo that was making her feel this way. It probably had nothing at all to do with Rob.

What she saw as his smugness was probably merely him being deliriously happy that he was going to be living with the woman he loved, and one day in the future, that woman would become his wife. That would make any man in love feel smug, wouldn't it?

Adam's Range Rover drove across an old stone bridge and Neva recognised it from the website. She glanced momentarily to her right and left. The river was closer to the top of the banks and flowing much faster than it had on the video she had watched. She expected it to be more of a burbling stream than this full-blown, fast-flowing and rather fearsome looking river. The River Thames never looked like this. And that was four times the width of this one.

The River Wynter might not be burbling but her stomach was as she drove across the bridge. The huge Christmas tree right in front of her on the other side cheered her up though. Even in this inclement weather, it stood proud and the multi-coloured lights shone out through the heavy rain. The branches held up against the downfall and the baubles bounced up and down but they remained firmly fixed in place, as did the gold star at the top of the tree.

As she followed Adam's vehicle past the tree, two rows of colourful cottages came into sight, one either side of a cobbled, puddle-filled street. A sign on the front wall of one of the cottages read: *High Street*, and Neva smiled. There was only one street, so that was a bit of a misnomer.

Adam stopped and got out of his vehicle, pointing behind it for Neva to stop. As he walked towards her, the rain began to ease, but her heart beat faster and goosebumps of excitement erupted on her skin. She'd definitely been too long without a man if just watching one walk towards her had this much of an effect. But there was something about the way he walked. There was a confidence about him and an air of authority. He smiled as he reached her car and she opened her window a fraction.

'This is yours.' He pointed to the lime green painted cottage to her left in the middle of the row of five.

'How did you know which cottage my family were in?'

He raised his brows comically and grinned. 'Special powers. Do you need a hand with your stuff?'

Neva smiled. 'No thanks. We'll be fine.'

What was she thinking? Why hadn't she said yes? Too late to change her mind now without sounding foolish.

'I'll see you soon then, Neva Grey.' He winked at her and waved as he walked back to his car.

Like an idiot, she sat in hers and watched

him. There was definitely something in the way he had said those words that sent a new rush of tingles all over her body.

The front door of the cottage burst open and Neva's mum and dad dashed out, holding umbrellas above their heads and waving wildly at Neva whilst giving Adam rather odd looks but huge smiles.

As he got into his car, he smiled back as if he knew them. He was gone by the time her dad reached her side.

'What a pleasant young man,' Dennis said. 'I see you got all the plants your mother wanted. And what a lot of presents. We'll grab your things and then I'll park your car in the car park round the back of the pub. As you can see, the road's a bit too narrow to leave it here.'

He held his umbrella up so that Neva could get out without getting drenched, and she kissed him on the cheek.

'Hello sweetheart.' Her mum came and joined them, kissing Neva and hugging her with her free arm. 'Was it an awful journey? We had a smooth trip. Hardly any traffic and clear skies all the way, although it was barely light when we arrived.'

'Mine took ages, as it always does to get out of London. And the weather didn't help.'

Dawn shook her head and her damp, auburn bob swung limply around her face as she linked arms with Neva. They splashed their way to the boot, unable to avoid the large puddles amongst the cobble stones.

'Lucky for us we packed the brollies,' Dawn said. 'Always prepared. That's us. There's a lovely fire inside and I've made some mince pies.'

Neva pressed the boot release several times. 'Sorry. It sticks. I need to get it looked at.'

'Oh, darling,' Dawn said, holding the umbrella over herself and Neva. 'Is that a dent in your car? How did that happen?'

'I bumped into Adam. The man you just saw. Well. He bumped into me. But it was actually my fault.'

'Adam?' Dennis said. 'You and Adam Wynter had an accident on the first day of our holiday? Oh dear. That's not a very good start.'

'No indeed,' Dawn said. 'But he didn't seem upset or annoyed.'

'Did you say Adam Wynter? He's one of the Wynters from the big house?'

Dennis nodded. 'Yes dear. Didn't you know? We met him earlier today. He was the one who handed us the keys this morning and told us how everything in the cottage worked and where it all was. Fortunately for us, he was here when we arrived, so he let us in early. He'd come to check it was all as it should be and to give the keys to Roger Pyke, who owns the village shop. His wife works at the house.'

'Adam has a wife?'

'No, no. Roger's wife, Penny. She's the Wynter's cook. We were supposed to collect the keys from Roger at the shop.'

'I'm confused. But never mind. How odd though. When he introduced himself to me, he didn't mention he was a Wynter. But he did say he knew the Wynters intimately. I wonder why he didn't just tell me who he was.'

'I don't know, sweetheart. But he seems like a lovely young man. Will he make a claim on your insurance? Was there any damage to his vehicle?'

'None that I know of and he didn't mention making a claim.'

Was that why he had said he would see her again soon? So that they could exchange insurance details? But if so, why hadn't he just said that?

Neva hoped it was for an entirely different reason.

Damn it. Now she'd have to wait and see. Not that she was interested. Men were definitely not on her agenda. Not even for a holiday fling. Not even one as gorgeous as Adam Wynter.

Finally, the lock clicked and the tailgate popped open. Dawn took Dennis' umbrella in her other hand and held both brollies over all three of their heads while Dennis helped Neva unload her holdall and the bags of presents.

'We'll come back for the plants. But should we take all my work stuff too?' Neva asked.

Dennis shook his head. 'The village is tiny and Adam told us the pub car park is safe, so I think it's probably OK to leave it. But we can come back and get it if you'd rather.'

'No. It's fine.'

Neva wasn't sure about it but neither did she relish the prospect of unloading it all right now. There was also the small problem of where she could put it all. The boxes and crates would take up quite a bit of space, and the cottage didn't look that large from outside, or from the photos she'd seen on the website, and her sister, Rowan would be bringing everything but the kitchen sink, as usual.

'Just these bags, your holdall and the plants then, darling?' Dennis smiled at her and nodded his head towards the door. 'We can either all shuffle beneath the brollies, or we can make a dash for it.'

'Shuffle,' Neva and Dawn said simultaneously, laughing as they did so.

It took a little longer and anyone watching would probably have thought they were all barking mad but they made it to the cottage, without getting completely saturated and did the same thing again until all the presents, plants and foliage were deposited in the cottage.

Dennis took Neva's keys from her. 'I'll go

and park your car and be back in a jiffy.' He smiled at Dawn. 'Put the kettle on will you, darling, and we can have one of your mince pies, a cuppa and a catch-up when I get back.'

'I'll go, Dad.' Neva stepped forward but Dennis shook his head.

'No, no, sweetheart. You sit and relax. You've had a long journey.'

'So have you.'

'Yes, but we got here before it rained and I've been sitting on my behind for hours, waiting for you, Rowan and the rest of the family to arrive. Your mother wouldn't even let me help her in the kitchen because she says I always make a mess.'

'You do always make a mess.' Dawn smiled lovingly at her husband. 'Now off you go, and when you get back, we'll open a bottle of sherry and have that instead of tea. It is Christmas, after all.'

Dennis beamed at Neva and Dawn and headed out the door with his brolly, singing, *I'm Dreaming of a White Christmas*.

Neva smiled at her mum. 'Dad's getting into the Christmas spirit.'

'You know your father. He's been belting out Christmas songs since the beginning of December.' Dawn shook her head but her eyes and her affectionate smile showed the deep love she had for her husband. 'If only he could sing in tune. But never mind. Let's go and sit by the fire and you can tell me about the accident with Adam. How did it happen? He's a very handsome young man, isn't he? You're not dating anyone at the moment, are you, sweetheart?'

Neva gave a little laugh. 'No. And I agree. He's definitely gorgeous. But I'm putting romance on a back-burner for a while. At least until I get my business up and running and into profit. Plus, I need to decide where I'm going to live. Besides, if he's a Wynter he's obviously loaded and way out of my league. I'm no Cinderella and girls like me rarely end up with a Prince Charming. In fact, no matter how many times I kiss them, the men I date just turn into bigger frogs.'

Chapter Three

Neva opened her eyes and it took a few minutes to remember where she was. She glanced around the bedroom with its apple-white walls, wildflower printed curtains, matching bedlinen and pale green painted wood floors and smiled. The river may not have looked anything like it had on the website, and the village definitely hadn't been so appealing in the rain, but this room was exactly as it was in the gallery of photos she'd scrolled through.

She hadn't meant to fall asleep. She had only come upstairs to unpack and to try Jo again, having left a message on her voicemail shortly after she arrived. After mince pies and sherry with her mum and dad, she'd helped her mum bake cinnamon rolls, shortbread biscuits, and Christmas spiced iced biscuits for the tree. Then they'd had lunch of homemade, butternut squash soup and freshly baked wholemeal bread and afterwards had gone to the sitting room to relax and grab a few minutes of peace before Sasha arrived with her mum and dad. Neva had left her parents snoring softly in the comfy armchairs by the fire but when she came upstairs and saw the cosy room, she couldn't resist the chance to curl up on the inviting ivory-painted iron-framed bed. This time her call was answered just as the voicemail was about to kick in.

'Sorry, sorry, sorry,' Jo said. 'I missed your call because we were, well, let's just say, we were testing out our new bed. Then his mum and dad and sister arrived earlier than expected so it was a bit of a mad rush to get dressed and downstairs to greet them. And his mum wouldn't let me out of her sight. I said I needed to call my best friend and do you know what the silly woman said? "But surely Rob's your best friend now, dear. Marriage won't work unless you're the best of friends. Take it from one who knows." I thought I'd walked into an episode of some dystopian fantasy.'

Neva laughed as Jo regaled her with all the *helpful tips* Mrs Ashford had been giving her *future daughter* all morning.

'She called you her daughter, not daughter-in-law? I suppose that's a good thing.'

'It's bloody creepy is what it is. No wonder Rob's kept me away from the woman for most of the four years we've dated. Prior to today, the longest amount of time I've spent with her is about two hours. We went away last Christmas, and the one before that, I spent with you and yours. And the one before that. Oh yeah. Another disaster with my own mum. But enough about me. I'm hiding in the shed. Can you believe that? Tell me what Hibernation Central is like before Charmaine Ashford comes and finds me. Or *mother*, as the stupid woman is now insisting I call her.'

'You know you've got a lifetime of happy Christmases such as this, don't you?'

'If I get through this one. Which frankly, at this point in time, is looking doubtful. Anyway. Any good-looking guys hidden away in one of those cosy cottages?'

'I haven't seen anyone else in the village yet. But as it happens, I have met an incredibly handsome, not to mention super sexy guy.'

'W-hat! Sod it. I knew I should've come with you. Tell me, tell me, tell me.'

'His name's Adam. Adam Wynter. And he makes the word 'gorgeous' seem lame.'

'Wait. What? Wynter? As in the Wynters of Wynter House. That massive pile of luxury we saw on the website. The one you have to pay to get into just to wipe your feet on the mat.'

'The very same. He's so hot, Jo, the paintwork on my logo nearly melted. Oh. I haven't told you how we met.' Neva told Jo all about it and Jo 'ooh-ed' and 'ahh-ed' appropriately.

'Wow. Are you seeing him again?'

'I hope so. We didn't exchange insurance details so if he doesn't come and find me, I'll go to him and ask if he wants to do that. But I really hope he doesn't 'cos I don't want a claim on my insurance, especially as it's now for my business too.'

'Why don't you simply take him a Christmas card. It is the time of year to spread joy and goodwill to all men. Or invite him round for one of Dawn's mince pies. He'll never leave you after that.'

'I've got to do something. Not to be a drama queen or anything, but I'll simply die, darling, if I don't see that man again.' Neva bent backwards and placed the back of her hand on her forehead for dramatic effect, even though Jo couldn't see her. It was a routine they often did.

'What happened to your 'no men until my business is sorted' rule?'

'Adam Wynter happened. Besides, it's Christmas and as you said yourself, the time to spread joy and goodwill to all men. A holiday fling might be just what I need.'

'Wyntersleap sounds like the place to be this Christmas. You rock that man's world, Neva.'

'I'll certainly try. I can't believe a man like

41

him would be interested in me, although he was definitely flirting, I can tell you that for sure. But if he's not, it's not all bad. Mum says Rowan's definitely bringing a dog, so that's something.'

'Weirdo. Oh God. I can hear Charmaine's acid tones. I'm going to have to go. I'll call you tomorrow and I expect to hear that you've at least got a plan to get your man, even if you haven't put it into action by then. Love you. Miss you. Merry Christmas!'

'Back at ya, doubled. Speak to you tomorrow. Say hi to your new mum for me.'

'Oh very funny.'

Neva rang off and turned over. She'd close her eyes for just a minute.

But it was some time later when she stretched her arms and legs and glanced at the small sash window. It was raining hard again and the sky had grown much darker. She looked at her watch just as she heard a car pull up outside, a muffled bark and her sister shouting at someone.

'For Heaven's sake, will you stay in the car until your father and I can grab that lead.'

Neva jumped up and ran downstairs, meeting her mum and dad in the hall.

'Rowan's arrived.'

Dawn yawned and rubbed her eyes. 'Yes, sweetheart. We heard. I think the whole of Wyntersleap did.'

Dennis opened the door and a blast of bitterly cold air accompanied by a shower of rain swept into the hall, followed closely by a frazzled-looking and rather bedraggled, Rowan. Her auburn hair was plastered to her head and dripping onto the welcome mat as she dropped several bags and two holdalls on the floor.

'God, what a journey! Could you have picked a more out-of-the-way place, Mum? And this weather. I've got drenched just running from the car. Dad, will you give Nigel a hand, please? Oh hi, Neva. I didn't know you were here. Have you put on weight or is that jumper baggy?' Without taking a breath, she glanced over her shoulder. 'Sasha! How many times do I have to say it? Hold that lead tight and wait in the car until your father can take it from you. I'm not running after that dog again.' She let out a loud, exhausted sigh and gave Dawn a pleading look. 'I'm gasping for a cuppa. Is the kettle on?'

'Merry Christmas to you too, Rowan,' Neva said.

'What?' Rowan's scowl reformed into an apologetic smile. 'Oh hell, I'm sorry. Merry Christmas everyone.'

She threw one arm around Dennis and pulled Dawn into the embrace with her other, waggling her fingers at Neva to indicate that she too should join in, which Neva did.

'That's all right, sweetheart,' Dawn said. 'Come and sit beside the fire and get dry. Your dad'll help Nigel. You got the puppy then?'

Rowan rolled her eyes and sighed as Dennis kissed her cheek. 'I'm already regretting it.'

'I'll help too.' Neva grinned at Rowan as she brushed past her and gave her a playful slap on the arm. 'I could do with some fresh air to wake me up a bit. And I haven't put on weight.'

'Sorry sis.' Rowan grabbed Neva and planted a sloppy kiss on her nose. 'I get bitchy when I'm tired. But you're mad to want to go out there. I'm surprised no one's building an ark. It's like the end of the world.'

Neva laughed as she grabbed her weatherproof jacket from the rack in the hall, and shoved on her boots but Rowan was right. Both umbrellas blew inside out when Dennis opened them in the doorway, and one flew out of his hands and shot across the cobbled street, bouncing in a puddle before thumping against the façade of one of the cottages opposite.

'Oh gracious!' Dennis tossed the other broken umbrella back in the stand. 'I'd better retrieve that before we get accused of littering. Don't come out in this, Neva.'

'Don't be silly, Dad. A bit of wind and rain won't hurt me. I'll get the umbrella. You help Nigel.'

They both ran out; Dennis to the car where

Nigel was struggling, pulling cases from the boot, and Neva towards the umbrella that was off on its travels. It tumbled along the pavement, its spokes scratching against the cottage paintwork and by the time Neva grabbed it, a few seconds later, it had left a thin, squiggly black line along the length of two of the cottages.

She ran back towards the car, tossing the umbrella in the hallway as she passed. It was only then that she spotted two men standing at the edge of the stone bridge, looking in her direction. They were a couple of hundred feet away but she recognised one immediately. Why on earth was he standing outside in this rain chatting to someone?

'Adam!' She yelled and waved at him but he ignored her, and after staring at her for a second or two, he and his companion turned their attention to the river. 'Well that was bloody rude.'

'Swear jar!' Sasha's giggling voice came from Nigel's car.

Neva bent down, opened the door Sasha had previously slammed shut, and peered inside. Sasha was cuddling a large fluffy puppy that resembled a wolf and was almost the same size as her.

'Hello, horror.' Neva beamed at her. 'How are you?'

'I'm incorrigible. How are you, Neva?'

Neva raised her brows. Sasha had stopped calling her aunty Neva a long time ago and now just called her Neva, but the incorrigible bit was new.

'I'm fine, thanks, but rather wet. Who told you you're incorrigible?'

'Mrs Drummond. She's my headmistress. She told Mummy and Daddy too.'

That must have pleased Rowan and Nigel no end. Neva tried not to laugh as Nigel and Dennis hurried past with their arms and hands filled with cases and bags.

'Everything but the kitchen sink,' Nigel said, shaking his head. 'Hi Neva. Will you grab Sasha and the puppy, please?'

'Hi Nigel. Of course.' She returned her attention to Sasha. 'Let's get you inside. Is that a puppy or a wolf cub you're cuddling? It's the size of a horse.'

Sasha hugged the fluffy sable and white bundle tighter and the puppy licked Sasha's face.

'She's an Alas-kan Mal-e-mut and her name's Tempest.' Sasha struggled with the pronunciation as she fumbled with the lead, her arms still wrapped around Tempest.

'An Alaskan Malamute. She's gorgeous. Hello, Tempest. I'm Neva. I hope you won't eat me.'

Sasha giggled again. 'She won't eat you, silly. But she'll kill any vampires, or zombies, or

46

ghosts if she sees them.'

'Ghosts are already dead, sweetie, so maybe she'll just chase them away.'

'Then she'll tear them to shreds and chew them up and spit them out.'

'Good to know. Hold on to her lead as you—'

It happened so fast. One minute, Sasha was cuddling a lovable, large bundle of fur, the next four huge paws landed on Neva, almost knocking her to the ground. She tried to grab the lead but it slipped through her fingers and the puppy shot out of the car and headed down the street towards the river, seemingly chasing after something.

'Tempest!' Neva yelled. 'Sasha!' Now her niece was racing after the puppy.

'She's chasing a ghost,' Sasha yelled back, a look of sheer excitement on her angelic face.

Neva managed to catch up with Sasha fairly easily but Tempest was a different matter.

'Tempest! Come back,' Sasha screamed, trying to disengage Neva's hold on her.

'Go to the cottage and get your dad,' Neva demanded, but Sasha looked torn. 'I mean it, Sasha. Now!'

Sasha nodded reluctantly.

Neva ran towards the river, shouting, 'Adam! Help.'

As she closed the distance between her, the

puppy, the river and the two men standing beside it, she realised it wasn't Adam. The man merely resembled him.

Without a word both men looked at her, the puppy and one another as if taking stock of the situation. They both dashed forward but Tempest swerved to avoid them and headed towards the riverbank. Finally, as if realising her mistake, Tempest skidded to a halt but her paws slipped on the sodden grass and she tumbled down the bank.

Neva heard the splash above the pouring rain and her heart stopped. How could this happen? What could she do? The river had been a torrent of water this morning; by now it could only be worse. She darted a quick look backwards and saw Sasha was racing back towards her, tears streaming down her little face, her mouth open wide in horror, and behind Sasha came Dennis and Nigel. They must have come back out to get more bags and seen what was happening because Sasha was some way from the cottage. They would catch up with her. Neva must try to save the puppy.

If she could.

She ran past the cheerfully decorated Christmas tree, looking grotesquely out of place in that moment. She turned the corner beside another plain, undecorated pine tree and ran along the footpath where only one man was now visible, several feet ahead of her. She passed a safety point, the small wooden door of which was swinging to and fro and a man's jacket hung, bedraggled in the rain.

The man in front had something in his hands and as she drew nearer, she saw he held a throw-line, the other end of which was attached to a bright red life ring that bounced up and down in the rushing water. And the other man; the one she had thought was Adam, was in the water wearing that life ring.

Her heart skipped a beat as he fought against the flow and tried to swim to the bank and her heart soared when she spotted the sodden bundle of fur, with part of the line wrapped around it, that he was tugging along with him.

'Tempest,' she shouted.

The man on the path turned his head and yelled to her. 'Come and take this line. I've got to help them out.'

She dashed forwards and wrapped the throw-line around her waist as she took it from him, so that it wouldn't slip from her hands. But the pull was so strong, she almost toppled over and she was being dragged from the path onto the sodden, grassy bank. She dug her heels into the ground and leant back as far as possible. She wouldn't be able to hold it for long.

Thankfully, Dennis and Nigel arrived and after Nigel grabbed Sasha and said something to her, he and Dennis raced to Neva's aid. With all three of them pulling on the line, the man in the water was able to make it to the riverbank with Tempest, and the other man yanked first the puppy, still with the line wrapped around her, and then his friend and the life ring, from the unstoppable flow.

And, as if by some divine intervention, it finally stopped raining.

Neva caught sight of Sasha gingerly edging her way down the grassy bank towards them. The last thing they needed right now was for Sasha to slip and fall in too. She ran to her and led her back onto the stone path that ran along the length of the river, from the bridge, into the far distance. Not that you could see far into the distance now that it was getting dark.

Nigel carefully made his way to the two men and the puppy while Dennis remained where he was, the throw-line still in his hands. Tempest lay on the bank clearly exhausted but thankfully, alive. Her rescuer collapsed beside her, tugged off the ring, and rolled over onto his back, his broad chest rising and falling rapidly beneath his sodden shirt. He reached out one hand and gave Tempest's wet fur a reassuring stroke. What an incredible gesture after nearly drowning to save Tempest's life.

And when Tempest slowly raised her head and let it plop down on her rescuer's arm, Neva had tears in her eyes as she hugged Sasha tight.

This could have ended so differently. She closed her eyes momentarily and thanked all their lucky stars. This was definitely a Christmas miracle.

After a moment or two, Dennis, Nigel, the two men and Tempest scrambled up the bank to the safe ground of the path.

'Thank you so, so much,' Neva said, to the half-drowned man as he approached. Close up, he wasn't as handsome as Adam but he definitely did resemble him. Were they related?

He glowered at her with eyes a much darker blue than Adam's, and unlike Adam, there was no ready smile on his lips. 'You shouldn't have a dog if you're not going to look after it. Puppies are like children. You have to watch them all the time.' His voice was nothing like Adam's either. It was hard and cold and angry.

'Excuse me?' She couldn't really blame him, but there was no need to take it out on her.

'I said—'

'I heard what you said, thank you very much. You've got no right to be cross. I didn't ask you to jump in and rescue her. I could've done it.'

His dark brows shot up and his mouth fell open. He scanned her body from head to toe and a sudden snort of laughter escaped him. 'I think that's highly unlikely.'

'Oh really? I'll have you know—'

'What my daughter means,' Dennis began, giving Neva a pleading look, 'is that we're all dreadfully sorry about this and we'll make sure it doesn't happen again. The puppy is a new addition to the family and we've clearly got a lot to learn about how they behave. We're all so very grateful to you for your brave and selfless actions and to your friend, of course. If there's anything we can do to repay your kindness, we'll gladly do it and more.'

The man dragged his glare from Neva and gave Dennis a wan smile. 'I couldn't let the puppy die. But the only repayment I want is for you to tell your daughter that she needs to keep a tighter rein on both her child and her dog. Now if you'll excuse me, I'd rather like to go home and get dry. I'm sure I can leave one of you to rewind the line and hang it back in the box with the life ring in case they're needed in the future. Although most people are sensible enough to stay away from a flooding river. Apart from visitors, that is.'

Without another word, the man strode off and after a brief and rather feeble smile, his friend followed him. The rescuer grabbed the jacket from the safety point as they passed and threw it on.

Nigel blinked as if he had misheard and Dennis gaped, open-mouthed, one hand still holding the throw-line that was partially wrapped around Tempest, the other holding Neva's arm as if to stop her from chasing after the man and giving him a piece of her mind.

'Who the hell does he think he is?' Neva finally managed. 'And what makes him think Sasha's my daughter?'

'Ow,' Sasha said, prising her hand from Neva's. 'You're crushing my fingers.'

'Sorry. I didn't mean to. That man made me cross.'

Sasha fell to her knees and hugged the bedraggled puppy. 'Why? He saved Tempest's life. I'll love him for ever and ever. I should've told him so. I'll tell him next time I see him.'

'You do that, sweetie. I don't suppose he'll ever hear those words from anyone else.'

'What on earth is going on?' Dawn and Rowan hurried towards them.

'And who were those men?' Rowan asked. 'Oh my God! Did someone fall in the river?'

'Tempest,' Dennis said. 'And if I'm not mistaken, one of those men was Rafe Wynter.'

'Adam's elder brother?' Dawn queried. 'The one Cecil and Ronnie told you about this morning?'

Dennis nodded as Rowan bent down, grabbed Sasha and hugged her tight, gently stroking Tempest while Nigel untangled the line.

'Oh?' Neva glanced at her dad. 'I thought he looked like Adam. Who are Cecil and Ronnie and what did they say about him? And why didn't you mention it earlier?'

'They live in the cottage nearest to the pub. The one with the dark red frontage. And they said quite a bit, as it happens, but it slipped my mind. Besides, I don't like spreading gossip.'

'But telling us isn't really spreading gossip because we won't repeat it.'

Rowan stood up. 'We've got to get Tempest in the warm and get her dry. And Sasha too. All of us, for that matter. Why are we standing here chatting when we're all soaking wet? Come on. Before it chucks it down again.'

'I think we're still in a state of shock,' Dennis said, as Dawn took his hand and followed Rowan, Sasha and Nigel, who was now carrying Tempest in both arms.

'You've got to tell us, Dad,' Neva persisted as they headed back to the cottage.

'You'll have to, Dad, or Neva will pester you till you do. Or we'll start inventing stories of our own.' Rowan spoke without a backward glance.

Dennis tutted. 'Oh all right. But let's get inside and get dry. I'll tell you when we're sitting in dry clothes, beside a fire, with a glass of sherry in our hands.'

'Can I have sherry, Gramps? And Tempest, too,' Sasha asked hopefully, smiling as she turned to look at Dennis.

'No!' Rowan and Nigel agreed at once.

Chapter Four

Neva was eager to hear what their temporary neighbours had said about Adam's elder brother and she changed quickly in order to get into the sitting room in case her dad began the story without her.

The brothers were complete opposites, that much was obvious, although they did look alike from a distance. Close up though, Rafe's eyes were a much darker blue and his hair was closer to black than brown. His face was harder, his mouth nowhere near as kissable-looking, but that was perhaps because he was scowling the entire time this afternoon. He looked taller by a few inches and broader by a fraction. That should've made him sexier than Adam, instead it made him more intimidating – and not in a good or sexy way. He came across as cold, angry, obnoxious and untouchable. Adam came across as warm, friendly, approachable and oh so sexy. Neva was sure which one of the Wynter brothers she would rather bump into on a dark night – and it definitely wasn't Rafe. Even his name sounded stand-offish.

In the sitting room, the fire crackled and roared as Dennis tossed another log into the flames. Dawn sat in one of the armchairs with a glass of sherry in her hand, and Sasha was curled up on the floor beside her with her head resting on Tempest, whose large paws were gently shoving Dennis out of the way of the heat, clearly none the worse for her ordeal now that she was dry and sprawled out by the fire. And had clearly been given a bath.

'You all changed quickly.'

Neva took a seat on the sofa, and Rowan handed her a large glass of Baileys and sat beside her.

'It's a little early for this but I think we need it. And it is Christmas, after all.'

Nigel came in from the kitchen as Neva and Rowan clinked glasses. 'And Dennis and I need these.' He handed Dennis a large brandy and gave Sasha a glass of orange juice.

'I can't wait till I'm a grown up.' Sasha curled her top lip as she took the glass.

'Neither can we,' Rowan said, giving her husband a meaningful look. 'And next time I tell you to keep hold of Tempest's lead, Sasha, make sure you do. OK?'

'O-K. There's no need to keep going on about it. I didn't do it on purpose.'

'Don't answer your mother back.' Nigel shot a reprimanding look at Sasha. 'We can take Tempest back to the animal shelter if you're not going to act like a responsible person.'

'No!' Sasha sat bolt upright before throwing her arms around Tempest's neck. 'You wouldn't. I'd run away.'

Rowan whispered to Neva. 'I think that might be a bonus.'

Sasha glowered at her, bringing her brows tight together and dramatically pursing her lips. 'I heard that, Mummy.'

'Now, now,' Dawn said. 'Tempest's not going anywhere, Sasha as long as you take good care of her from now on.'

Neva looked Rowan in the eye. 'I didn't know you got her from a rescue place. The puppy, I mean. Not Sasha.' She nudged Rowan's arm and grinned.

Rowan grinned back and rolled her eyes. It was a habit of hers. 'I think that may have been our second mistake. They told us she'd been rehomed twice already and she's only eight months old. We should've asked for more details.'

Neva nodded. 'What was the first mistake?'

'Telling Sasha she could have a dog and pick any one she wanted as long as it was from an animal shelter.'

Neva laughed. 'I'm surprised they let you take Tempest. They've usually got all sorts of rules and requirements, especially where dogs like her are concerned.'

Nigel coughed. 'That was my fault. I'd had dogs all my life until Rowan and I got married. And I've known the manager of the local animal shelter all my life too, so she knew I'd know how to handle Tempest because I've had a Rottweiler, a German Shepherd and a Labrador.' He shook his head as if he had no idea what to do. 'But this little puppy is in a league of her own.'

'That's what he used to say about you, sis.' Neva laughed and nudged Rowan's arm again.

Rowan tutted. 'Oh, ha-ha. The thing is, she won't stop growing until she's at least eighteen months old. Possibly two years. I swear she's got twice as big in the two weeks since we first saw her and when we collected her two days ago.'

Neva leant closer and whispered, 'You wouldn't really take her back, would you?'

Rowan lowered her voice too. 'Don't be daft. You know us better than that. A dog's for life, not just for Christmas. It makes me so angry that she's already been returned twice. Besides, apart from the fact that Sasha would probably kill us, we've both fallen for her, as annoying as that is, and as troublesome as she may prove to be. Which I have a feeling, is very troublesome indeed.'

'I think I've fallen for her myself.'

'I just pray Mum and Dad have got plenty of this in stock.' Rowan clinked glasses with Neva again.

'Cheers to that,' Neva said.

'What are you two whispering about?' Dennis smiled at Neva and Rowan as he sat in the armchair opposite his wife.

'Nothing, Dad.' Rowan winked at him and grinned.

Neva grinned too. 'You were going to tell us what our temporary neighbours said about Adam's obnoxious brother.' She couldn't even say his name. It would make her cross again.

Nigel squeezed onto the sofa beside his wife. 'He was a bit of a grouch, wasn't he? But then he had risked his life to save our dog and I don't suppose that was easy. Those claws are sharp and I noticed blood and at least one scratch on his neck. Plus that water must've been freezing. He's a braver man than me. I hate to say it, but I'm not sure I would've dived into a raging river to save a stranger's dog, even with a safety line.'

'I didn't see any blood, or scratches.' Neva was a little shocked. Perhaps she hadn't given the man enough credit for what he did, and maybe she should've simply taken his reprimand and not answered back.

'I saw him wipe it with a handkerchief his friend handed him.'

Dennis nodded. 'He may have been a trifle brusque, but he was certainly brave. And did you see him stroke Tempest as they both lay on the ground? That almost brought a tear to my eye.'

'And to mine.' Neva twirled the Baileys in her glass. 'Perhaps I was a bit rude to him.'

'I'm sure he'll get over it,' Rowan said. 'Tell us what these neighbours told you then, Dad.'

'Oh yes. It's all rather odd. Especially now I've met Rafe. And it must have been Rafe because Adam told us he only had one brother, who was a few years older and whose name was Rafe. They look so alike they could almost be twins.'

'They don't look as alike as that,' Neva said. 'Adam's gorgeous and really friendly. His brother ... isn't.' She wasn't quite sure what Rafe Wynter was.

'Well. We must never judge a book by its cover, as your mother always says.' He winked at Dawn.

'I don't know.' Dawn shook her head. 'He did look somewhat murderous when he marched past Rowan and me on the footpath. But he also stepped onto the grass so that we could remain on the path, so I'm not sure.' She shrugged and sipped her sherry.

'Murderous?' Neva shot a look at Rowan

and twitched her eyebrows up and down. 'That sounds intriguing.'

Rowan rolled her eyes and sighed. 'Mum thinks her postman's a serial killer, so take it with a pinch of salt.'

'I do not. I simply said the man has the look of one, not that he was.'

'He's a zombie,' Sasha said. 'But next time we come to stay, Granny, Tempest will bite his leg off.'

'Thank you, my little angel. That's delightful.'

Nigel sighed loudly. 'Will you let Dennis tell us what the neighbours said or are we all going to talk nonsense all afternoon?'

'Ooo-ooh.' Neva and Rowan both stuck out their tongues and laughed.

Nigel tutted. 'And you wonder why Sasha behaves the way she does.' But he was grinning as he planted a kiss on Rowan's forehead.

'Yes. Well.' Dennis cleared his throat. 'I'd parked our car in the pub car park. Oh, that reminds me. That's where I've parked yours, in case you wonder where it is.' He nodded at Nigel.

'When?'

'When we came back from our adventure at the river.'

'I would've done that.'

'Oh shut up Nigel and let Dad get on with his story.' Again, Rowan did her eye-roll.

Dennis took a glug of brandy. 'I was strolling back here. It wasn't raining when we arrived, remember. And I was just passing the door of the red cottage when it flew open and these two rather jauntily dressed men stood in the doorway and waved at me. I wasn't quite sure what to make of it at first so I simply smiled and nodded but they introduced themselves as Cecil and Ronnie, fairly recent residents of the village, and asked how long we were staying and whether it was just the two of us or if we were expecting company.'

'The nerve of them,' Rowan said. 'I would've told them to mind their own business.'

'I'm sure you would, sweetheart. And I did, in a roundabout way. I said that we were having a quiet family Christmas and we liked to keep ourselves to ourselves.'

'Good for you.'

'Not really. I'd usually be more than happy to chat, but there was something about the way they accosted me and the way they were looking at me that gave me pause.'

'Perhaps they're vampires, Gramps.'

'I have a feeling they are. But not in the way you mean, Sasha. There are people who suck the joy out of you, and after just a few minutes in their company, I felt exceedingly deflated. I had to have several cuppas and two of Granny's mince pies before I got my cheery, Christmas spirit back.'

'I must put Cecil and Ronnie on my Christmas card list,' Rowan said, doing her usual thing with her eyes.

'But what did they say about Adam's brother?' Neva was growing a little impatient. Not that it really mattered to her. She was merely curious.

'They asked if I'd met any of the Wynters and I said that Adam had shown us around when we arrived. "He's a delight," they said. "Unlike that brother of his". I told them I hadn't met the brother and wished them a good morning, but Cecil, I think it was, grabbed my sleeve and told me there was something I should know. Before I had a chance to stop him, he'd told me that Rafe Wynter killed his wife and stole her fortune. Or the other way around. I don't recall.'

'What?' Neva almost spilt her drink. Fortunately, the glass was nearly empty.

Rowan let out a long, slow whistle. Nigel simply frowned. Dawn shook her head, and Sasha sat bolt upright.

'Is she a ghost, Gramps? Does she haunt that big house? I bet she makes his life a misery. Mr Jessop's wife does that. But she's still alive. He's our next-door neighbour.'

Rowan tutted. 'Sasha. I told you not to repeat that. Honestly. You have to be so careful what you say in front of her. She blabs it out at the most inconvenient moment.'

'That can't be true. Can it? About him killing his wife, I mean.' Neva looked from Dennis to Dawn to Rowan and Nigel. 'I know the man was rude but if he actually killed someone surely he'd be in prison?'

Sasha jumped to her feet. 'Unless he was clever. Perhaps he hid the body. Or pushed her in that river. Maybe she was swept out to sea.'

Dawn reached out and pulled Sasha onto her lap. 'I think that's quite enough about bodies, angel. Why don't you and I go and make a gingerbread house?'

'Oh Granny. I like bodies. Especially dead ones. But ... a real gingerbread house? Like the one we made last Christmas?' She fiddled with the buttons on Dawn's cardigan.

'Better. Because this year we'll make it bigger.' Dawn stretched out her arms either side and then swept Sasha into a big hug and Sasha giggled and wriggled until she slid to the floor. 'But we need to start it right away because it'll soon be time for dinner and we'll have to clear the table for that. So we've only got an hour.'

Sasha stood up and took Dawn's hand. 'Come on then, Granny. Can Tempest come too?'

Tempest raised her head an inch or two, yawned, licked her lips and closed her eyes once more.

'I think Tempest is better off where she is. She's had enough excitement for one day. She's only a puppy and she needs her sleep.'

'OK.' Sasha let go of Dawn's hand, kissed Tempest on the head and gave her a hug and a stroke before skipping off towards the kitchen.

'I'll come and help in a minute,' Rowan said. 'But I want to hear what else the horrid neighbours had to say.'

Dennis took another gulp of brandy. 'I don't believe it for one minute. And yes, Neva. If he killed his wife he'd be in prison. But they did say it was about fifteen or more years ago, so if there was any truth in it, which I doubt, he could have served his time and been out for good behaviour these days. Prison sentences are ludicrous, but I won't get on my high horse about that right now.'

'Fifteen years ago?' Neva twiddled her fingers as she mentally calculated his age. 'But that would've made him in his early twenties, wouldn't it? I have no idea how old he is but I don't think he can be older than forty, do you?'

'He's thirty-nine, according to Cecil and Ronnie. Which would make him around twenty-four or a bit younger when she died. Oh. And they also said he's into something shady with Sean Small, the owner of the pub.'

'What? Because killing your wife isn't shady?' Another eye-roll from Rowan.

Dennis shook his head. 'I'm afraid by then,

I'd had enough. I said that it was very kind of them to feel they needed to fill me in on the life history of a man I don't know and am never likely to. But that I don't hold with talking about people behind their backs so if they'd excuse me, I'd get back to my wife. Then I wished them a merry Christmas and a peaceful New Year and walked away. I could almost hear the steam rising from them as they fumed at my lack of interest in their gossip.'

'They won't be popping round for mince pies and a sherry then?' Nigel asked, grinning.

'Not if I can help it.'

'What I find amazing,' Neva said, 'is that he's supposed to have killed his wife, and not the other way around. If I was married to a man like that, I'd be tempted to kill him. Not that I'd marry a man like him in the first place. Dark, mean and moody is not a look that's ever appealed to me. Now his brother. Well, that's a different kettle of fish.'

'Don't tell me you've got the hots for that man's brother?' Rowan grinned at her.

'Yep. And if you'd seen him this morning, you'd have the hots for him too.'

Nigel threw Rowan an odd look. 'Then I'd better keep a close eye on my wife if the brother comes to call.'

'I don't expect he'll call on us,' Dennis said. 'There's no reason why he would. Unless he does want to make a claim on Neva's insurance.'

'What's this?' Rowan sat upright and darted looks at Neva and Dennis.

'Um. Adam and I were involved in a little accident which was entirely my fault. Although he thinks it was due to the weather. I'll tell you about it later.'

'Is your new paintwork damaged? Is the car OK?'

Neva nodded. 'Just a tiny dent over the wheel arch, and Adam said it will come out with a bit of hammering.'

'I'll take a look tomorrow,' Nigel said. 'I've knocked out several dents we've had in our cars, courtesy of your sister.'

'That's true,' Rowan said. 'I'd like to say it's not, but it is.'

'Thanks, Nigel.' Neva smiled gratefully. 'Well. I think we can safely say that the Grey slash Lane family has already made quite an impression on the folks of Wyntersleap, and we have yet to be here for a day. I've involved one of the Wynters in a car crash, you and your dog have nearly drowned another, and Dad's insulted two residents of the village in which we've got to spend the next two weeks. That's a pretty good start even for us.'

'Yep.' Rowan raised her glass. 'Oh. I need a refill. But here's to us. Another typical Grey slash Lane family Christmas.'

'To us,' Nigel said.

'And to the Wynters and the residents of the village,' Dennis added.

Chapter Five

Neva loved a good gossip, but the things Cecil and Ronnie had said about Rafe Wynter disturbed her and even when she and Rowan joined Dawn and Sasha in the kitchen to help make the gingerbread house, Neva couldn't shake the feeling of unease.

Of course it wasn't true. It couldn't be. According to the website, the Wynters had been renting out their cottages in the village of Wyntersleap for almost nineteen consecutive years. They would hardly do that if there had been a murder trial followed by the eldest son being thrown in prison, would they?

But that made Neva think. Who, exactly, lived at Wynter House? The website made no mention of the individual family members. It simply referred to 'the Wynters' or 'the Wynter family' and stated that, in addition to be able to pay to visit the 'open' gardens, which implied some of the gardens were closed, it was possible to take a guided tour of the main rooms in the central section of the house. That meant the rest of the house was out of bounds, and as the central section was the smallest part, you didn't get to see much for the princely sum they charged.

In addition to visiting the house and gardens, four cottages could be rented in the village. Wyntersleap only comprised of ten cottages, one small shop and an equally small pub, which meant that only six cottages, and the pub were lived in on a permanent basis. Whoever ran the shop probably lived in one. Or not. So far the only people Neva or her family had seen were Adam and Rafe Wynter, the man with Rafe at the river, whoever he was, and Cecil and Ronnie. Where were the other residents? Or was Neva now seeing mysteries where there were none?

'What're we having for dinner?' Rowan asked, once the gingerbread house was in the oven.

Dawn shrugged. 'I was going to make a chilli, but what with all the commotion, I forgot to braise the mince or put it in the slow cooker. We could have a pasta dish instead.'

'Or we could go to the pub,' Neva suggested. 'They serve food. After the day we've had it might be nice to let someone else cook and clean up.'

'But aren't we going to decorate the tree tonight?' Sasha asked.

'We'll do that in the morning when we're all rested,' Dawn said.

'We'd have to take Tempest and I'm not sure that's wise after today.' Rowan frowned and got up from her chair. 'Merriment Bay is only five miles away. I wonder if there's a takeout restaurant or one that might deliver? Were there any cards or leaflets, Mum? The ones you usually find in rental properties telling you all the local amenities and such.'

Dawn nodded. 'They're by the front door on that shelf near the coat rack, but I had a quick look earlier and I don't recall seeing any food delivery menus. It's fine. I'll throw something together.'

Neva got up, opened the fridge door and peered inside. 'There's plenty of cheese and cold meats. And you've made lots of bread. We could have a cold supper instead. And we've got crisps and stuff. That wouldn't be so bad on our first night.'

'We could make cheese and ham toasties.' There was an excited smile on Sasha's face. 'I love those.'

'So does Mummy.' Neva winked at Rowan. 'And Gramps.'

Dawn got up, tapping the table with her hands. 'That's it then. Cheese and ham toasties all round.'

Nigel sauntered into the kitchen. 'Did someone mention toasties. I could murder one of those. I'd be even happier with two.' He wrapped his arms around Rowan and kissed her on her cheek.

'Eew. Get a room,' Sasha said.

Nigel frowned before grinning at his daughter. 'Guess what we're giving you for Christmas, Neva? Our eight-year-old child!'

'I'd live with Neva. As long as Tempest could come too.' Sasha stuck out her chin and swung her blonde curls back and forth over her shoulder.

'That child's going on forty,' Neva said. 'Which reminds me. Why did Rafe Wynter assume she was mine?'

Rowan laughed. 'Did he? Maybe because you were the one with her.'

'But I could've been her big sister. Or her aunt, which I am. Or even some crazy woman who chases children. Why did he assume I was a mum?'

'Because you look worn out, frazzled to distraction, and were screaming at her at the top of your lungs, perhaps.'

Neva laughed. 'Thanks. So I look fat and haggard. I know who to turn to when I need a confidence boost.'

'You don't look fat. Just a little bigger than the last time I saw you, that's all. But you'll always look beautiful to me, sis.'

Neva pulled a face. 'And that's another thing. I was screaming, you're right. But not one of the villagers came out to see what the commotion was about, did they?'

'Ah,' Rowan said. 'But these walls are thick. If they've got their TVs or music playing, they might not have heard it. We didn't. It was only when I came back into the hall and saw the door was still open but no one was near the car, that I realised something was wrong. When I stuck my head outside, I saw Dad and Nigel disappear around the end cottage.'

'And that's when we came after you,' Dawn added, taking the large slab of cheddar cheese from Neva, together with a paper bag filled with thick slices of their favourite ham and handing both to Rowan who had sat back down, with a chopping board in front of her on the table.

Dennis joined them. 'That gingerbread smells delicious. Oh. Are we having cheese and ham?'

'Cheese and ham toasties, Gramps.'

'My favourite.' Dennis licked his lips and rubbed his stomach. He took a seat beside Sasha. 'It's raining again, by the way. Even harder than earlier, if that's possible.'

'This village doesn't look quite as beautiful as it did on the website, does it, darling?' Dawn smiled wanly at her husband.

'Nothing looks beautiful in the rain,' Nigel

said.

'Adam Wynter did.' Neva twitched her eyebrows up and down as she grabbed the bread from the breadbin, and everyone laughed or groaned or sighed accordingly.

'The other brother didn't look too shabby either,' Rowan added with a sigh. 'He reminded me of Colin Firth. You know, when Darcy came out of that lake and strode across the lawn to Elizabeth in *Pride and Prejudice*. I forget who played her.'

'I don't think anyone remembers,' Neva said, laughing. 'They only remember Colin and that shirt. That dripping hair. Those smouldering eyes. Hold on. Rafe Wynter looked nothing like that. Apart from being wet and wearing a white shirt.'

Dawn raised her brows. 'He did a little, sweetheart. Now that I think about it.'

'Then I need my eyes tested because all I saw was a rude and objectionable git. But he does have Darcy's arrogance down to perfection. I'll give him that.'

'Well, I love him,' Sasha said. 'And when I get as old as you and Mummy, I might even marry him. He did rescue Tempest, after all.'

'Rather you than me, sweetie.' Neva tossed her a thick slice of bread. 'Put lots of cheese on that and pass it to Granny.'

Rowan sliced the cheese and Sasha took three large slices and put it on the bread. Dawn took it from her and placed it under the grill while Nigel slathered butter on another thick slice of bread and slapped two slices of ham on it. He smiled at Dawn and stretched out his hands for the slice with the melted cheese. Then he stuck the two together and handed it back to Dawn to put under the grill once again. The process was repeated until each of them had at least one toastie, and Nigel and Dennis had two. Even Tempest, who had finally come to join them, clearly having caught a whiff of ham, or maybe cheese, got some, although hers was a small corner torn from Sasha's toastie.

'As we're not having a proper dinner this evening,' Rowan said, resting her elbows on the kitchen table, emphasising the point, 'and that means less washing up. Shall we decorate the tree tonight instead of tomorrow morning?'

'Yes!' Sasha bounced up and down on her chair, which creaked and moaned in protest.

'Don't break the chair, angel,' Dawn said. 'I think we've already made a rather poor impression on the owners. Let's not add breakages to the mix.'

'That's a good plan.' Neva winked at Sasha. 'If it ever stops raining, I was thinking of going for a long walk tomorrow morning. I'd like to see Wyntersleap Falls.'

'The place where that woman and her daughters leapt to their deaths back in the good old days?' Rowan queried. 'I expect Sasha would like to see those too.'

'Oh yes please. We might see their ghosts.'

'Not in daylight, sweetie.'

'We might, Neva. Ghosts are around us all the time. We just don't see them. We only see them at night because they're evereal beings.'

Rowan grinned. 'She means ethereal beings.'

Sasha drew her brows together and pouted. 'That's what I said, Mummy.'

'I know, baby, but I'm not sure Neva understood.'

'I'm not a baby, Mummy. I'm eight. I'm almost grown up.'

'Of course you are. What am I thinking?'

Neva fought back her laughter. 'You're welcome to come with me. We can even take Tempest. But I think I'd better hold her lead, just in case. We don't want her going into the pool at the foot of the Falls. From the photo on the website, it looked idyllic – like one of those pools on hair shampoo adverts. But on the website River Wynter looked like a babbling brook and as we discovered, it's not. God alone knows what the waterfall pool will be like. A swirling vortex going directly to the depths of Hell, no doubt.'

Dennis smiled. 'If the weather's good, why don't we all go?'

'I'm not traipsing through miles of mud, thanks all the same.' Rowan screwed up her face. 'I forgot my walking boots. Even if it is nice tomorrow, after all this rain the ground will be sodden.'

'Swear jar!' Sasha demanded, slapping one palm on the table.

'Mummy said "sodden", darling.' Nigel grinned at Rowan and shook his head. 'Not that other word that she knows she shouldn't use but does all the time.'

Rowan rolled her eyes. 'I've got much better. I haven't said it once since we arrived.'

'True.' Nigel nodded and nudged Neva's arm. 'We were well on our way to being able to afford a week in Barbados. We even had to buy a bigger swear jar.'

Sasha nodded as she handed Tempest her final mouthful of toastie. 'Mummy uses lots of naughty words. She said she gets them from you, Neva.'

'Oh does she?'

Rowan shrugged. 'I've got to blame someone.'

'Thanks.'

'You're very welcome.'

'I've got boots you can wear,' Dawn offered. 'I brought a couple of pairs with me, just in case. And we're the same size, aren't we?'

Rowan pulled another face. 'I knew I could count on you, Mum. It's not as if I'd like to spend the day lounging on the sofa, reading or anything. I'm not on holiday, after all. Oh wait. I am.'

Dawn laughed. 'No one's forcing you to go, sweetheart. But it would be nice if we all went together, don't you think?'

Rowan smiled like a clown with a painted face. 'Oh yes! Let's all go. I'm sure it'll be such fun. Especially having to give Tempest yet another bath, because she's covered from head to foot in mud, yet again.'

'That's tomorrow sorted then,' Dennis said, ignoring Rowan's sarcasm. 'And if the weather's really good, there's another footpath from here to Wyntersleap reservoir. It passes Little Wynter Falls. They're the baby version of the big ones and they're farther down the river.'

'Was the reservoir the thing that looked like a lake as I came across the raised bridge before the turn-off to here?' Neva stood up and began clearing the plates from the table.

'Yes, sweetheart. In good weather there's sailing, windsurfing, canoeing and virtually any other water sport you can think of on that reservoir.'

'Is there one of those banana rides?' Sasha looked hopeful.

'I'm not sure about that, angel. But there are Swan pedalos. They're in the photos on the website.' Dennis smiled at her before turning his gaze to Rowan. 'It's called *Wyntersleap Water Sports* and it's run by someone called

Amias Wells. He gives lessons in any of the water sports you fancy. It might be the perfect place for us all to learn to sail.'

'Why do we want to learn to sail?' Rowan looked confused.

'Because Merriment Bay has some of the best waters for sailing on the south coast. We could continue on the footpath tomorrow and go there. It's only five miles. And the sooner you all see the place, the better.'

'Oh? Why's that?' Neva's stomach flipped. 'Is there something you haven't told us, Dad? Are we here in this village for a reason other than "spending our family Christmas somewhere different for a change", which is what you said when you told us you and Mum had rented this cottage? Because you also said that you had something to tell us and this cottage was the perfect place to do that.'

'We were going to tell you once you'd got settled in,' Dawn said, smiling lovingly at Dennis. 'Or possibly on Christmas Eve. But now's as good a time as any and we're so excited.'

'We're moving to Merriment Bay,' Dennis and Dawn said in unison.

'You're what?' Rowan looked horrified.

'When?' Neva asked.

'As soon as the sale of our house is finalised,' Dennis said. 'Completion is set for Wednesday January 8th.'

'But that's just a few days after we leave here.' Nigel seemed as shocked as Rowan.

Now Neva was even more surprised. 'And just two days before I complete on my flat. Why didn't you tell us you were selling the house and moving? And why Merriment Bay?'

'We thought you might try to talk us out of it.' Dennis looked at Rowan.

'You were right,' she confirmed.

Neva shrugged. 'It's your house and it's your lives. You should do whatever you want. But as I said. Why there?'

'Because we've been there a few times on day trips and for weekends and we both love it. It's larger than a village but not really a town. There's fishing and sailing and lovely walks over miles of beautiful countryside. The sea. The South Downs. There's a World War Two museum and that chap I mentioned earlier, Amias Wells, flies a vintage Spitfire. You can take a flight with him but it's expensive. It's something I've longed to do. My dad was an RAF pilot and he fought in The Battle of Britain. I'd love to experience the thrill he did. Only I won't be shooting down German planes, of course. Although there is one of those simulators you can go in and that lets you shoot at enemy planes. That's a reasonable price. Sasha would enjoy it, I'm sure.'

'No doubt,' Nigel said. 'I wouldn't mind a flight in a Spitfire. How expensive is it exactly?'

Dennis patted him on the arm. 'Don't you worry about that, my boy. Once our house is sold we'll have lots of cash in the bank. We've lived in that house for so long, the value has gone through the roof, and we paid off the mortgage years ago. We'll never want for anything again, within reason. That's after taking into account the house we're buying in Merriment Bay. We'll be able to treat you all.'

'That's great, Dad,' Rowan said. 'And I'm really happy for you and Mum, but have you honestly thought this through? What about all your friends in Surrey? What about the business? Are you retiring, too? What about … us?'

'Sweetheart,' Dawn said, hugging Rowan to her. 'Merriment Bay is only about seventy miles away from Epsom. We'll still see you all the time. And think how lovely it'll be in the summer to have a few weeks at the seaside. As for the business. Well, that's something we need to discuss. I've taken a far less active role of late and you can cope quite easily without me. Your father only works part time now. You and Nigel are running it these days, to all intents and purposes. We see no reason why that should change. And we've got our private pensions, so we don't need the income.'

'We were going to wait until Christmas Day,' Dennis said, 'but what the heck? We're signing the business of Grey Building & Design over to the two of you as your Christmas gift this year.'

'What?' Rowan blinked several times and Nigel shrieked like a girl.

'Are you serious?' Nigel asked.

'Absolutely. If you want it, that is.'

'Want it? I'm bloody well over the moon.'

'Swear jar!' Sasha yelled, looking somewhat confused. She clearly didn't understand what was going on.

'And to think,' said Rowan, a blissful smile appearing on her face. 'I only got you a hamper from M&S. Oh. But what about Neva? She should get a share in it, even though she's never been keen on being involved.'

'Nope.' Neva held up her hands, grinning. 'Don't you worry about me. I'm good. I have no desire to be a partner in a building firm. No disrespect to any of you. But it's really not my scene.'

'Which is why we've got an entirely different gift for you, sweetheart,' Dennis said. 'But if you don't want it, please just say so. We won't be offended in the least. And if you don't like where it is, or want something else, we can do that instead.'

Neva darted anxious but excited looks from her mum to her dad and then to Rowan. 'What? Please don't say I've got to wait until Christmas Day because that's not fair. You know how impatient I am.'

'You can see it for yourself when we go to Merriment Bay. You've always said you would love to have your own salon and beauty place. And once you left that Darius May and said you were starting your own mobile business, we thought it might be perfect.'

'What?' Rowan snapped. 'Sorry, but I'm even more impatient than Neva.' She smiled, excitement written all over her face.

'There's a salon and beauty parlour for sale in Merriment Bay. It's called *The Mane Event*, and there's a flat above the salon. The entire building is for sale, freehold, so you wouldn't need to worry about a lease. Or a mortgage. We'd be buying it for you.'

Neva's mouth fell open. 'I can't let you do that. That's ... that's far too much.'

'Nonsense.' Dennis shook his head. 'Besides, we want to do it. Property is so much cheaper down here. You wouldn't believe it. And the owner wants a quick sale as she's moving to Spain, so it's a bit of a bargain, too. But you must see it, of course. It may not be what you want.'

'Oh, Dad. Mum. I don't know what to say. A salon of my own is a dream come true. I'm sure I'll love it. And it'll mean I'll be living close to you.' She burst into tears and hugged everyone, including Tempest.

'Why did you rent this cottage then?' Nigel asked, as Dawn opened a bottle of champagne she had taken from the fridge. 'Why not somewhere in Merriment Bay?'

'Because there are very few places to rent there. And not one was available over Christmas. This was the closest we could get. And it looked so delightful on the website.'

'Which proves yet again,' Rowan said, raising the glass of champagne Dawn poured her and waiting for everyone to do the same, 'looks can be deceiving. But this is going to be our best Christmas yet. I can feel it in my bones. Cheers one and all. Merry Christmas to us. And here's to a very happy New Year!'

They all clinked glasses.

Then all the lights went out.

'Sodding hell,' Rowan said. 'What the bloody hell caused that?'

'Swear jar!' Sasha's voice echoed Neva's, in the darkness, and they both laughed, even though a blackout wasn't funny at all.

Chapter Six

Neva pulled her phone from her pocket and used the torch to illuminate the room.

'I brought some candles,' Dawn said. 'They were for the table settings for Christmas Eve, but we'll have to get some more. Can you shine that over here, sweetheart? Now where did I put them? And where did I put my phone?'

Rowan used the torch on hers and so did Nigel and Dennis and Sasha, so by the time Dawn found hers and switched on the torch, the kitchen was almost as bright as it had been before the lights went out.

'We can check the fuse box if we can find it and see if a switch has tripped,' Nigel said. 'It may just be a bulb or something.'

'Let's do that while they look for the candles,' Dennis suggested.

They were back a few minutes later, just as Neva found the box containing the table decorations.

'I've got the candles.' She placed them on the table.

'I'm afraid we'll need more than that.' Dennis shook his head. 'It's not just a bulb. The power is out on the entire street. Even the Christmas tree lights are out. It must be a problem with the National Grid. Unless it's something more localised. Like some cables down or damage to a pylon or something.'

'I'll check the news on my phone before my battery dies,' Nigel said.

'I told you you should've charged it up earlier.' Rowan rolled her eyes. 'At least we'll have mine and Sasha's. And probably everyone else's.'

'OK. Point taken.' Nigel scrolled on his phone. 'I can't get anything. That means the communication masts are down, so it's not just this village, it's everywhere within range, or I'd be able to get a signal from one of them.'

'Does that mean we can't make calls?' Neva asked.

Why hadn't she called Jo again this evening? She was dying to tell her about Tempest and her brush with death. And about meeting the odious Rafe, the wife-killer and possibly, future brother-in-law. He would make Charmaine Ashford pale in comparison.

No. That was ridiculous. Nothing was going to happen between her and Adam

Wynter. And if it did, it would just be a holiday fling. She certainly wasn't looking for a future husband.

Although ...

'I'm afraid so,' Nigel confirmed.

Damn. Because now she also had the fantastically exciting news about the salon, to tell Jo, too.

'Is that someone at the door?' Rowan said. 'Or is that knocking a sign that the cottage is about to fall down?'

'I'll get it.'

Neva dashed past Nigel and her dad and made it to the door before anyone else had a chance. Although in her haste, and the fact that her torch wasn't directed at the floor, she did trip over the hall carpet and landed against the door with a resounding thud. And an ache in her shoulder.

It wasn't Adam, as she had hoped, but she did recognise the man who stood before her in the pouring rain, a concerned expression on his face.

'Did something just smash against the door?'

'No,' Neva lied as she rubbed her shoulder. 'You were at the river this afternoon. Sorry. I don't know your name. We weren't introduced. Have you been sent to give us another telling off?'

The man smiled and shook his head. 'No.

I've come to give you these.' He held out his hand and gave her two large bags. 'And to see if there's anything else you need. I'm Sean. Sean Small. My wife Wendy and I own the Wyntersleap Inn.'

Neva peered into the bags. One contained candles, another, torches and a third contained several lanterns.

'Thanks, Sean. I'm Neva. Neva Grey. Do you want to come in for a moment?'

'Thanks, Neva. It would be good to get out of this rain. I feel as if I've been wet through all day. But not as wet as Rafe.'

He grinned at her as she stepped aside to let him into the hall.

'A man with a sense of humour. Unlike your friend.'

His brows knit together. 'Rafe's got a sense of humour. He just doesn't have much to laugh about at the moment. In fact, he never really has. But he's a good egg, Neva. You caught him on a bad day, that's all.'

'Well, he's got a good friend in you. That's one thing. But you don't need to convince me. I couldn't care less either way.'

'The man risked his life to save your dog. You could at least give him the benefit of the doubt.'

'Sorry. I didn't mean to make you cross. I'm grateful, believe me. But it wasn't my dog. Not that that matters. The thing is, he was rather rude.'

'I'm not cross. I'm just telling it like it is. You weren't sweetness and light either.'

'True. But let's not have a discussion about it. We've got other things to worry about right now. Like this blackout. Thank you for thinking of us and bringing these. Do you know what's happened? Is the power likely to be out for long?'

Dennis appeared in the hall. 'Hello. Oh. You were—'

'Yes, Dad. We've been through that. This is Sean Small. He owns the pub and he's brought us some supplies to tide us over till whatever has happened is sorted out.'

'That's very kind of you, Sean. I'm Dennis. Dennis Grey. I expect we'll be seeing quite a bit of you. We'll no doubt be popping in and out of that pub of yours. We like a drink or two.'

Sean raised his brows. 'Good to meet you, Dennis. And you'll be more than welcome anytime, night or day.'

'We're not alcoholics,' Neva quipped. 'Although Dad's comment just now may have made you think we are.'

Sean shrugged. 'You don't need to convince me. I couldn't care less either way.' He grinned at her.

'I suppose I deserved that.' Throwing her own words back at her was rather clever. And a bit annoying. 'Thanks again for all this stuff. It really is very kind of you.'

'It isn't. It was Rafe.'

'I'm sorry?'

'Rafe asked me to bring them to you.'

Neva bristled. 'But he couldn't bring them himself? Do you usually run his errands?'

Sean glared at her and she wished she could take that back. It sounded petty-minded and insulting even to her ears. But he seemed more amused than annoyed when he responded.

'Yes. If he asks me to. And he does the same for me. That's what friends do. The reason he didn't come himself is because he's gone to meet someone from the power company. There's a tree down on his estate and it's brought a power line down with it. We think that's what's caused the problem but it should be fixed by the morning. Unless it's something more serious. Oh. And he asked me to apologise for any inconvenience and to tell you that you'll be refunded for tonight.'

'That's very kind of him,' Dennis said.

Neva frowned. 'Yes. I suppose it is.'

'Right. Unless there's anything else, I'll get back to my pub. And my wife. Give me a shout if you need anything.' He turned to go outside but threw Neva a look over his shoulder and in a lower voice added, 'I'll pass on your thanks to Rafe then, shall I? And I'll let him know you were disappointed he didn't come in person.'

Neva's mouth fell open. 'Disappointed? I've never been more thankful for anything in my life.'

'Oh? That's not the impression I got.'

He waved his hand in the air and marched off into the rain and the dark with only the beam of his torch to light his way.

Chapter Seven

Neva had the worst night's sleep, ever. Sean's words had stayed with her all evening and she had gone over and over her petty comments. And also what he had said about her being disappointed Rafe hadn't come in person. Did he think she wanted to see the obnoxious prig again? She'd just meant she was disappointed she couldn't be rude to his face. Although thinking of him as a prig made her smile. He did behave as if he were superior and he was definitely self-righteous.

But he had asked his friend to bring them the lanterns, torches and candles and he had said he'd refund them for the night. That wasn't priggish at all. In fact, that was thoughtful and kind. For some absurd reason, that annoyed her all the more.

Even when she and her family had decorated the Christmas tree by candle and lantern light, she couldn't stop thinking about how different Rafe was – or perhaps wasn't – from his brother.

The lanterns, she was surprised to discover, had battery operated faux candles inside but when they were switched on, they gave such an authentic glow that none of them could tell the difference from the real thing.

Using the playlists on her phone, they'd listened to Christmas songs while stringing the lights – which wouldn't work of course, until the power came back on, but that didn't matter. They sang along to Michael Bublé, danced to Michael Ball, who was one of Dawn's favourites, and tried to guess who half the singers were on a Christmas album from the 1990s that Neva couldn't recall downloading. By the time they had finished the tree, Neva's phone battery was as dead as they were exhausted. But it had been a lot of fun. And the tree looked beautiful even without the myriad coloured lights aglow.

She and Rowan had drunk far too many Baileys and she had definitely eaten more mince pies and Christmas spiced iced biscuits than was wise. In fact another batch of iced biscuits would have to be made to hang on the tree, because between her and Sasha and Rowan, most of the two batches had been eaten during the evening.

By 11 p.m. when they fell into their beds,

consumed. I don't think any of us should drive anywhere today. So if we're not going for a walk, I guess it's a day in front of the fire, after all. Rowan will be pleased. Is she up yet?'

'Fast asleep,' Sasha said. 'And Daddy is snoring like a piggy. Aren't we going to the waterfall?'

'Probably not today, sweetie. We'll see what the weather does, shall we?'

'We could go to the pub for lunch,' Dawn suggested. 'It may only be across the way but at least we'd technically be going out.'

'Excellent idea.' Dennis nodded, yawning again. 'And after lunch, I might take a nap.'

'I might join you,' Dawn said, rubbing her eyes.

'You sit down, Mum. I'll cook my own breakfast.'

'No, sweetheart. I'm fine. But thank you. I'm here and it'll just take a minute. You can make some more coffee though. Your father and I have drunk it all.'

Neva made coffee and smiled at Sasha. 'Have you switched on the lights on the tree?'

Sasha's head shot up. 'No.' She jumped off her chair and raced into the sitting room. Tempest chased after her.

Once Sasha was out of earshot, Neva said, 'I'd still like to go for a walk this morning, just to clear my head. I didn't sleep that well and I don't want to get a headache. Fresh air will do me good. But I don't want to take Sasha or Tempest if it's as slippery out there as you say. I'll have enough trouble staying on my own two feet without worrying about them.'

Dennis smiled. 'We'll find something to entertain Sasha. But I wouldn't recommend going far. Make sure you charge your phone. And wrap up warm. It's truly bitter out.'

'Thanks, Dad.'

Neva plugged in her phone and poured them all more coffee. Dawn placed a full English breakfast in front of her, together with a round of toast.

Neva laughed. 'If I get lost, this'll keep me going for at least a week. Thanks, Mum. And thanks again for my wonderful present. I still don't know how to thank you both.'

'You haven't seen the place yet, sweetheart.' Dawn sat beside her. 'I do hope you like it. It would be so lovely to have you living close by. And between you, me and your father, we're hoping to convince Rowan and Nigel that Merriment Bay might be the perfect place for them and Sasha. And Tempest, of course.'

'Oh Mum! That would be wonderful. But what about the business? You've just given it to them.'

Dennis nodded. 'But it doesn't have to have its office in Surrey, or even the yard. Many of our clients are scattered all over the country.

Yes, we get a lot of local work, but there's also a lot of competition these days and recently our prices have been undercut several times. If Rowan and Nigel sold their house and bought in Merriment Bay, they'd have cash in the bank for years to come. And they could generate new leads down here while continuing to work for our current clients. We're hoping that, assuming you do like the salon and are happy to move down, they'll see how lovely Merriment Bay is after a few visits and may start the ball rolling without us having to suggest it.'

'About that, Dad. I've got money coming from my share of the flat in London. I'm happy to put that towards the cost of the salon and the flat in Merriment Bay.'

'No, no. You keep that in the bank. Or use it to travel, or do the things you've always wanted. Or you may decide to rent the flat out above the salon and buy a little house. Obviously, that's your choice entirely. Seriously, thanks to the ridiculous prices of homes in Surrey, we've made more money than we ever thought possible and with that and our pensions, we'll have plenty to last us for the rest of our days.'

Sasha raced back in. 'The lights are so pretty. You must come and look!' She dashed off again.

'We'll be right there,' Dawn said. She

smiled at Neva. 'Eat your breakfast, then pop your head in and see the lights and after that, we'll distract Sasha and you can nip out the door.'

Which is exactly what Neva did. She went upstairs and put on a second jumper. If it was as cold out there as her dad had said, she'd rather be too warm than freeze to death. She headed back downstairs, popped her head around the door and admired the lights, smiling as Sasha shook one present after another from under the tree to guess what was inside. Then she crept along the hall, slipped her walking boots on, grabbed her jacket, scarf and gloves and headed quietly out the front door.

The cold hit her immediately, making her gasp. It actually made her face hurt; as if tiny arrows of ice were being shot into her cheeks. Perhaps this wasn't such a good idea. But the sky was now an icy blue with just a scattering of puffy white clouds, and a pale lemon sun fanned out its rays across the roofs. If it weren't for the cold, it would be a glorious day. Especially after all that rain yesterday.

She glanced down to the river. Was she imagining it? Were her eyes deceiving her? Was the water higher than it had been? She was sure she couldn't see the water when she stood on this very spot yesterday afternoon. But had she really looked?

Her dad was right. The pavement was icy and the cobbled street was now just like a sheet of slippery glass. She stayed on the pavement and edged her way down towards the footpath they had been on yesterday, although she would be heading in the other direction, against the flow of the river and up to Wyntersleap Falls.

The water was definitely higher. There was barely any bank visible now. Where Rafe had lain just fifteen or so hours ago, was completely under water. Should she be worried?

Yesterday, Rafe and Sean were standing on the bridge looking at the river. Were they concerned about it rising? The distance between the riverbank and the cottages wasn't very great. If there was more rain, would the river be lapping at the doors?

So much for a cosy cottage in an idyllic village setting.

She made it to the footpath and oddly enough, it wasn't nearly as icy as the pavement had been. Perhaps because the pale winter sunlight was melting the ice along here. The street was sheltered and the sun hadn't reached the ground there yet.

She turned left just before the bridge and as she walked, she grew more accustomed to the cold. Hedges, shrubs and in places, trees, separated the footpath from the bank of the river and birds darted about above her as if in a hurry to get back to somewhere warm. A robin appeared on a fence post to her left and repeated its friendly song, tipping its head from side to side and flicking its tail as she closed the gap between them. Her foot slipped from under her on an icy patch she had failed to spot and as she reached out and grabbed at the fence, the robin sounded as if it was chuckling; the loud trill now a continuous flow, until it flew off and left her alone.

Was that thunder in the distance? She steadied herself before deciding to continue. She got drenched yesterday. Why should today be any different?

She followed the path across the fields as it wound its way through gaps in the hedges and she clambered over rickety wooden stiles. All the while, the thunder grew louder. It was only when she came through one hedge out into the open and looked ahead that she discovered it wasn't thunder. Certainly not the thunder she had thought. It was the torrent of water from Wyntersleap Falls.

The sight of them took her breath away. Even from the distance of half a mile or so they were pretty impressive. And just a little frightening. She had seen waterfalls on TV but this was the first she'd seen in real life and the sheer power was mesmerising. The drop looked to be around fifty feet but it was difficult to tell from where she was.

She walked towards them and the sound was deafening; more so when she finally stopped ten feet or so from the edge of the pool, which was just a few feet below her and a frantic swirl of water – a whirlpool of currents. It was a good thing Tempest hadn't fallen in there. Even Rafe Wynter might not have been able to save her.

She was tempted to get closer but fear, or possibly common sense, held her back. Water was sloshing over the sides onto the rocky surrounds and as she glanced back along the river she saw that even that lapped at the edges of the bank, close to the hedges and greenery, the other side of which was the footpath where she had walked.

She turned and started back the way she came. It was only four more sleeps till Christmas and one day of her holiday had already gone. But her mum and dad's generosity had solved so many of her concerns and she couldn't believe her luck.

She had wondered where she was going to live. That problem was now solved. Assuming she liked the flat. And why wouldn't she? Her mum and dad had similar tastes to her and they would never choose a place for her to live that they wouldn't be more than happy to live in themselves, so she had no concerns on that score. That issue could be ticked off her list.

She had wondered whether to start her

new venture in London, or to move somewhere new. That could also be ticked off the list.

The last part was a bit tricky. She had said she needed to sort out her life and decide what else she wanted to do. She was by no means jealous of Jo. Rob was nice but she didn't fancy him and he definitely wasn't the type of man she would ever fall in love with. But in a way, she did envy Jo's steady relationship. That was something Neva wanted in the future. A stable, loving relationship with a man she could respect and trust and love with all her heart. She wanted what her sister had. But again. She didn't want a man like Nigel either.

The problem was, she didn't really know what type of man she wanted, other than one who was loyal, loving and kind. He must like animals. And children. He must have a career or at least a job he enjoyed. A sense of humour was compulsory. Good looks would be nice but weren't a necessity. And hair colour, height and physique were all negotiable. If he was a little overweight, that was fine. But he must be relatively fit. She liked walking and wanted a man to do that with. Someone to hold her hand. Someone to share a walk like this.

Someone like Adam Wynter.

Adam Wynter was definitely her type. She could happily spend a lifetime with a man like him. She knew nothing about him, that was true, but the thrill she had felt the moment she saw him was very real indeed. Had she fallen in love at first sight? Not really. But it happened to some people. It had happened to a few of her former clients.

Mrs Neva Wynter. She liked the sound of that.

A noise like the snapping of a twig made her start and she glanced around her.

Where was she? She seemed to have veered off the path and was on another one she didn't recognise from earlier.

'Please don't tell me you've lost them again.'

Her head whipped round to where the voice had come from and she tilted back her head. On a small hill, not more than twenty feet away, stood a man with broad shoulders and dark brown hair. Was it Adam? The sun was in her eyes and she couldn't see his face but the voice was familiar. Deep but soft and sexy. Her heart sank as the man stepped forward and she saw who it was.

'Who?' She stuck out her chin and shoved her shoulders back.

Rafe Wynter walked towards her, brushing a gloveless hand against the hedge as if it were an animal he was stroking.

'Your daughter and your dog.'

'As I don't have either, the answer to that is, no. Sasha's not my daughter. She's my niece. And Tempest belongs to her.'

He looked a little relieved. 'That's probably just as well.'

'What's that supposed to mean? Are you saying you don't think I'd be a good mother? Because you're wrong. As you'll see for yourself one day.'

'Oh? And how will I do that? Are you planning on moving to Wyntersleap?'

The beginnings of what looked a little like a grin twitched at the corner of his mouth and his dark eyes sparkled. He was obviously making fun of her but there was something in his eyes that unnerved her.

'Um.' She looked away and shrugged. She could hardly tell him she had just been daydreaming about marrying his brother, could she?

'Please don't tell me you're going to include me in the Neva Grey annual Christmas newsletter. I despise those things.'

She glared at him. 'No I'm not. And so do I, as it happens. Especially as they're always about how fabulously everyone is doing and what fantastic places they've all been to on holiday. Fabulous doesn't often figure in my life, and no one wants to hear about my summer in Bognor, or some equally unexotic place. Wait a minute. How do you know my name?'

'Sean told me.'

'Great.' What else had Sean told him? 'Oh.

Thank you for the candles, torches and lanterns last night. That was very thoughtful.'

He shrugged. 'Not really. You've paid to stay in the cottage. I didn't really have a choice. I couldn't expect you all to sit in the dark.'

She hadn't expected that. She thought he would say it was his pleasure, or milk the fact he'd been thoughtful and kind. At least he was honest.

'I suppose not. But it didn't stop you from being rude and frankly rather insulting yesterday afternoon.'

To her surprise, the twitch turned into a grin.

'Ah. But I didn't know you were paying guests at the time. You could've just been passing through the village.'

'I'm beginning to wish I was.'

He raised his brows. 'You don't like Wyntersleap? Or are you saying there's a problem with the cottage?'

'Apart from having no electricity for several hours yesterday evening, you mean? No. The cottage is lovely. The village probably looks quaint on a hot summer day, but in the middle of winter in the pouring rain. Not so much, if I'm honest.'

'I suppose that's fair. There's not much I can do about the weather, I'm afraid. If I could give you sunshine and warm and gentle breezes, I would.' The grin broadened.

'Although they'd cost extra.'

'I don't doubt that for a minute. Tell me. Were the photos on the website photoshopped?'

The grin vanished and the sparkle left his eyes. Perhaps she'd gone too far.

'No. They weren't. You may find this hard to believe, and given the present situation, I can accept that, but Wyntersleap is beautiful. Especially in the summer. But it's glorious at any time of year. If you look for the best, you'll see that. On the other hand, if you're only looking for the worst, then you'll rarely see beauty in anything. Even in a stunning place like this.'

'I do see the best in things. I was simply saying that nothing looked as I expected. For example, I expected a gently burbling river, not the raging torrent that almost drowned my niece's puppy. I expected a friendly welcome from the locals, not a mini ghost town where the only people my dad met were two gossips who had nothing pleasant to say. I expected a warm and cosy cottage, not a power cut on our first night.'

'I get the picture. I'm sorry you're disappointed. If you and your family want to go home, I'll refund your money. The power cut was out of my hands. And it's the first we've had for years. You'll get a friendly welcome from most of the residents when you meet them. Yesterday wasn't a day for doing that. As for the gossips. I know who you mean and I can imagine exactly what they had to say. There's not much I can do about that. I don't listen to gossip. I can only suggest you don't either. And the river is as much of a surprise to me as it was to you, believe me. Sean and I were worried about it which was why we were at the river yesterday. Although given what happened, it was just as well we were.'

'And I'm grateful for that. We all are.'

'I don't want your gratitude. In fact, you may have to go home anyway, if the river rises any higher. The cottage will be even less cosy with water pouring under the door.'

'Has that happened before? Perhaps you should say so on your website. And perhaps you should have some photos taken in the winter, too, not just the sunny, summery ones.'

'If you're suggesting I hide things to make the cottages more attractive, you're wrong. As I said, I can't recall the last time we had a power cut. The tree coming down on the line was a complete surprise. We check them regularly for broken branches or disease, but it's a fairly large estate. I can hardly say on the website that there are gossips in the village. I don't want to be tied up in litigation. The river has never flooded in my lifetime. But we've never had rain like we seem to be having this year. Blame global warming if you want to blame something. I'm hoping the levels will drop if the weather stays like this but I'll keep a close eye on it, I assure you. As I said. I'll give you a full refund if you want to leave.'

'We don't. But neither do we want to have to wade through inches of water to eat breakfast. Or find our Christmas presents floating down the street. I'll talk to my family and see what they want to do.'

'Let me know. Or tell Sean and he'll make all the arrangements.'

'Thank you. Have a lovely day.'

'And you.'

Neva turned away and looked from left to right.

'Is there something else you want to say?'

She coughed and sucked in a breath as she twisted round to face him. 'Um. I seem to have wandered off the path.'

The grin returned for a split second before it was gone again. It was a shame. Smiling, he looked completely different. It was probably something he didn't do often as the grin was a little lopsided. As if he were uncertain how to smile.

'Of righteousness? Or the footpath back to the hideous village of Wyntersleap?'

'Both, as it happens.'

'Then allow me to show you the way.'

'No need. Just point me in the right direction.'

'And risk losing you by the wayside. No. I was going that way in any event. I need to discuss something with Sean. If you can tolerate ten more minutes in my company, that is.'

She tipped her head to one side and rubbed her chin, keeping a straight face.

'Ten minutes? Are you sure that's all it'll take? Or is this like your website?'

She finally smiled at him and saw the doubt flickering across his face replaced by a lightness and that hint of a grin.

'That depends on how fast you walk.'

'I can run pretty fast.'

'Not on this icy ground. Unless you want to add a broken ankle to your list of Wyntersleap woes.'

'Absolutely not. I'd need to start another notebook to add that.'

'Perhaps we should take it slow.'

She smiled again. 'Are we still talking about the walk back to the village? Or are you flirting with me?'

Why in God's name had she just said that? It wasn't as if she wanted the man to flirt with her. He wasn't Adam, after all. Adam could flirt with her every day of the week, and twice on Sundays.

He didn't respond at first, just furrowed his brows and pointed in the direction they needed to go. Neva fell into step beside him, hanging her head with embarrassment. But a moment or two later he spoke, although he didn't look at her.

'I wasn't flirting with you, Neva. It's been a very long time since I've done that with anyone. I'm not sure I still know how. These days I just say what I mean.'

'Sorry. It was just a silly quip. I didn't mean it. I don't think you'd flirt with me for a second.'

'I wouldn't.'

'Well, I'm glad we sorted that out.'

'So am I.'

'How's Adam?'

He shot a look at her. 'He's fine.'

'Did he tell you about our accident?' She needed to change the subject and that was the first thing that popped into her head.

'Accident? No. When was this?' He looked annoyed again.

'The morning I arrived. I was ... Um. I think my car hit a pool of water and aquaplaned. Adam came around the corner and hit my car. But there was only a slight dent in my wheel arch so no real harm was done.'

'He didn't mention it.'

'Sadly, I haven't seen him since. I mean. I'm not sure if he wants to make a claim or anything and I'd like to know because I don't like to leave things like that outstanding.'

'I'll speak to him.'

'Or I can. I don't want him to think I've

gone running to his elder brother.'

'He wouldn't think you had. But if you'd rather I didn't get involved, that's fine. I'll leave it to the two of you to sort out.'

He didn't sound pleased and he looked straight ahead as if he had something important on his mind.

'Thanks.'

'For what?'

'Err. For not getting involved.'

'I never get involved, Neva. At least, not if I can help it.'

What an odd thing to say.

'You got involved yesterday when you leapt into the river to save Tempest.'

'That was different.'

'In what way?'

'In every way. Let's just leave it at that, shall we? Look. There's the village. You can make your own way from here.'

'Aren't you coming? I thought you said you were going to see Sean?'

'I was. I am. But there's something else I need to do first. I've only just remembered. Talk to your family about the river. The more I think about it, the more I think it's best if you go home.'

Without another word or as much as a smile, he turned and walked back the way they had come.

'Bye then. Thank you,' she yelled after him

in a slightly sarcastic tone, but he didn't turn around, or wave or even acknowledge her words.

What on earth was wrong with that man?

She let out a sigh and marched towards the village in a bit of a mood.

There was nothing else for it. She'd have to call Jo.

She was going to call her anyway to tell her about her fabulous present from her mum and dad. And about Tempest and the river. And the power cut, of course. She may as well tell her about this morning too and get a little advice. Jo was so much better at understanding men than Neva would ever be. Besides, Jo would probably be grateful for the interruption. Even if it meant she would have to go and hide in the shed to get away from Charmaine Ashford.

Chapter Eight

Neva opened the door to the cottage and was met by a sulky-looking Sasha. Her arms were crossed in front of her and she had the usual tight-knit brows and familiar pursed and pouty lips. But she was wearing the zombie princess outfit that was part of the present Neva had bought her for Christmas.

'You went to the waterfall without us, didn't you? I'm never going to speak to you again.' She turned and flounced off along the hall, stomping her feet as she went.

'I'm sorry, Sasha. It was slippery and I didn't want Tempest to get hurt. You look beautiful in that dress.'

'Don't care. I hate you.'

'OK then. But I still love you. I promise I'll take you both when it's not so icy.'

'Not listening.'

Sasha hesitated when she reached the foot

of the stairs, clearly undecided whether to race up to her room, or turn and face Neva so that she could go back to the sitting room or kitchen. Dawn, coming out of the kitchen, made the decision for her.

'Let's go and decorate that gingerbread house we made yesterday.'

Dawn eased one of Sasha's hands out of the tight cross and led her back into the kitchen and Sasha kept her head turned sideways so that she didn't look at Neva.

'You gave her an early present then, Dad?' Neva tried not to laugh as she popped her head around the sitting room door.

Dennis grinned over the rim of his teacup. He looked very relaxed in the chair beside the fire, his feet on a padded footstool and Tempest stretched out in front of him, both taking full advantage of the warmth of the blaze.

'It was the price we had to pay. Once she discovered you'd gone out, she had a bit of a tirade about how unfair life was when you're eight and how everyone got a present yesterday except her. So we gave in. But she insisted it must be one of the presents from you that she opened. We didn't think you'd mind. Especially as you seem to have bought so many presents for us all this year.'

'I don't mind at all. But you and Mum didn't get presents yesterday.'

'That's what we said. She told us we should

have and that each of us could open one too.'

Neva laughed. 'You can't argue with that logic.'

Dennis shook his head. 'You can't argue with Sasha. You'll never win. Did you enjoy your walk? Are the Falls as beautiful as they look on the website?'

'Yes. They're spectacular. But when we do take Tempest, we must definitely hold on tight. They look a bit dangerous. I need to talk to you actually. Well, to everyone really. The river's much higher today and I met Rafe Wynter who's rather concerned about it. He thinks it may flood.'

Dennis sat upright. 'Flood? Really?'

'Yep. He says if we want to go home, he'll give us a full refund.'

'Oh. That's very good of him.'

'No, it's not. We paid for a cosy cottage in an idyllic setting. We got the house from Hell. OK. That's a bit of an exaggeration but it hasn't exactly been what any of us expected so far, has it?'

'He can't be held responsible for the weather, sweetheart. Or the power cut. And he promptly provided us with lighting, didn't he? You seem to have taken an immediate dislike to the man, which is very unlike you. You're usually friendly and goodhearted, like your mum.'

'He was rude.'

'So were you. He had just saved Tempest's life. And he did have a point. It was our fault she was running wild.'

'My fault, you mean.'

'No. Rowan, Nigel or I could have easily grabbed the lead and got the dog inside. We didn't. It was just one of those things. But let's not worry about that anymore. Was he rude to you today?'

Neva hung her head. 'No. He was actually quite pleasant. Although he did say he thought it was best if we went home. That wasn't very nice, was it?'

'It was if he thinks the river may flood. Offering to give us a full refund means he's not only putting our safety ahead of his profits, he's paying for an 'Act of God', as such incidents are called, which he doesn't need to do. No one's automatically entitled to a refund due to bad weather. I have to say, all things considered, Rafe Wynter seems a very decent sort of chap. Do you want to go home? We could move Christmas back to our house, as usual.'

'I'm not sure. We're sort of settled here now, aren't we? The tree's up. The presents are piled around it. Mum's made enough mince pies and shortbread, and other biscuits – and also the gingerbread house, to feed the entire village. And if it doesn't rain again the water should recede. On the other hand, we could wake up one morning and find the presents floating in an indoor pool.'

'We'll discuss it over lunch. Perhaps Sean will have more information.'

'We're still going to the pub?'

'Yes. Unless you'd rather not.'

'No. That's fine.'

She didn't relish the prospect of seeing Rafe again. But perhaps he would have been and gone by then. And there was always the possibility that Adam might pop into the pub for a drink. She was disappointed she hadn't seen him again. She thought he might call round to see how they were doing after the power cut. Or to ask after Tempest. Although perhaps Rafe hadn't told him about that. Adam hadn't told Rafe about the accident. Not that there was much to tell.

And Jo had been no help. She was excited about Neva's news and thrilled that Neva's long-held dream was finally coming true, although not quite so pleased to learn that her best friend would be moving so far away. But as Neva explained, Upminster isn't exactly close to anything much, unless you live in Essex. And Neva didn't want to do that. She had nothing against Essex but it was the wrong side of London as far as she was concerned. South of the river was the place for her. And Merriment Bay was south. Just a little farther south than she had initially planned.

Jo also said she rather liked the sound of

Rafe Wynter. Which annoyed Neva quite a bit.

'How can you like the sound of him? He's rude. Even when you think he's being nice, he's rude.'

'I like strong men. You know that. And he sounds strong in more ways than one. Is he tall and hunky?'

Neva cleared her throat. 'He's tall, yes, and I suppose you'd call him hunky. But not in an overly muscular way. Just ... firm and broad-chested.'

'When he got out of the river after saving Tempest, was it like that scene from Pride and—'

'Don't you start! I had all that with Rowan and Mum yesterday.'

'Oh God. I so-o-o wish I had come with you. He sounds divine. The dark and moody hero only the heroine can change. You should see this as a challenge. Perhaps Adam's not the one for you. Perhaps it's Rafe instead.'

'OK, that's it. I'm going to hang up. I phoned you for advice because you're always the sensible one of us, but if all you're going to do is make ridiculous comments like that, then there's no point in talking to you. You can go and chat with your new mum.'

'Oooooh. Get you.' Jo laughed loudly down the phone. 'I was joking, Neva. Although ... why does the thought of being with Rafe make you so cross?'

'That wasn't funny. And it's not the thought of being with him that makes me cross – because I haven't thought about being with him. It's *him* that makes me cross. There's something about him. I can't explain it. But he's nothing like Adam, I can tell you that.'

'Maybe not. But I'll tell you one thing, Neva. I have a feeling I'm going to be hearing a lot more about Rafe Wynter than I am about his brother, Adam.'

'Oh go away. I love you, Jo, but sometimes you're a pain in the bum.'

'I love you too. And so are you. Call me tomorrow and fill me in.'

Chapter Nine

Neva put on her new red dress. She was going to wear it on Christmas Day, but lunch at the pub was a good enough reason. She tonged a few waves into her hair, put on the sheerest touch of foundation and checked her lipstick twice. Despite her eyelashes being tinted, she topped them up with some mascara and even wore the merest slash of 'morning sunrise' – a pale, glistening, golden beige that brought out the colour in her eyes. She wanted to look her best, just in case Adam was there.

'Wow,' Rowan said, as Neva came downstairs. 'You look good. Are we hoping to see someone special?' She winked at Neva.

'It's Christmas. I want to look nice. You look good too.'

Nigel wrapped his arms around his wife. 'She always looks good. But so do you, Neva. And you, Dawn.'

'What about me, Daddy?' Sasha tugged his sleeve.

'No, angel. You don't look good. You look fabulous.' He lifted Sasha in the air and spun her around. No mean feat in the fairly narrow hall. 'Although you might want to change out of that zombie princess outfit. You don't want to get it ruined before Christmas Day.'

'I'll be careful.' Sasha smoothed down her knee-length black satin dress and the strategically torn, deep pink ruffles of the net overlay, and readjusted her cobweb-covered, diamanté tiara.

'Perhaps we could leave the festering blister at home,' he suggested.

'No way,' Neva said. 'I'm coming with you.' That at least made Sasha laugh.

'Funny,' Nigel said. 'I'm trying to stop my daughter going out in public, and for lunch no less, with a rather realistic-looking, puss-oozing, silicone blister stuck on her face and you make jokes about it.'

'Well, she is a zombie princess, Nigel. And she can't be a zombie princess without a festering blister or two.'

'Then she's sitting next to you. I thought the idea was for her to kill the zombies. Not turn into one.'

He threw Neva her jacket but he was smiling so she knew he wasn't cross.

'But if you can't beat them, it's best to join

them. Besides, it's a cunning plan to get the zombies to think she's one of them, when really, she isn't at all. That way she can catch them with their guards down and kill them all at once.'

Rowan shook her head. 'Sometimes I wonder exactly who the eight-year-old is in this family. My daughter or my sister.' But she was smiling too.

The pavements weren't as icy now as they headed towards the pub and the temperature seemed to have warmed up just a touch. As they passed the red house, chattering loudly, the door flew open and two men, dressed in somewhat clashing tartans, stood in the doorway.

'How wonderful to see you again, Dennis. How did you manage during that frightful power outage? We were going to come and check but it was as black as pitch. I assume the lovely Sean brought you ample supplies. I'll say one thing for Rafe Wynter, he may have an ugly past but he's clearly trying to make amends. He even asked Sean to bring us some lanterns, and he didn't need to do that at all. But this must be your delightful family. Hello all.'

'Hello,' they all replied as they hurried past.

Neva stopped and grabbed Sasha's hood, pulling her back and wrapping an arm around her to pin her in place. She smiled as the two men's lips curled upwards in horrified looks.

'This is my niece, Sasha. We're hoping this country air will help her condition. Oh. Don't worry. It's not contagious. At least we hope not. Wasn't that power cut frightening? But not as frightening as it'll be when the river floods later and comes crashing through all our front doors. Lovely to meet you. Have a super day.'

'What? Good heavens! You can't be serious!' Cecil shrieked.

She glanced over her shoulder as she and Sasha walked across the cobbles, now drowning in puddles again, and no longer covered in ice.

'About the river? I'm deadly serious. Ask Sean. I'm sure he'll confirm it. Bye-ee.'

Sasha giggled. 'They think I'm a real zombie, don't they?'

'I think they're the zombies, sweetie. But yes. I think they do.'

Dennis grinned as he held open the door to the tiny, Wyntersleap Inn where the others had already gone inside. Sasha smiled up at Neva before she dashed in to join them.

'Sean may not thank you for that, and neither will Rowan and Nigel if those two men start telling the locals Sasha is diseased, but at least she's speaking to you again. The expressions on their faces were priceless.'

'I couldn't help myself. And no one will believe them about Sasha.'

She glanced around as she stepped inside. The pub really was tiny. Only room enough for five small tables and chairs, a couple of padded seats by the windows and two more beside the fireplace in which there was a roaring log fire. The bar ran the length of one wall, with stalls in front of it here and there and the long mirror on the wall behind, made the place look a little bigger than it was. Tinsel of various colours glistened between every bottle and glass and were reflected in the mirror, while nets of twinkling lights hung like stars from the low, blackened ceiling. Jugs of holly, ivy and mistletoe sat on every table and the small Christmas tree in one corner of the room was dressed with so many colourful decorations that hardly any pine was visible.

Apart from Neva and her family, the only other person inside was a pretty blonde woman in early forties if Neva had correctly judged the woman's age. Perhaps this was Sean's wife, Wendy. But just as Dennis was about to close the door behind him, someone called out to him.

'Hold the door please if you don't mind, young man.'

Dennis pushed it open again and two elderly women stepped inside, arm in arm.

'Thank you, handsome.' The one with tight grey curls and what appeared to be a knitted tea cosy on top of them, gave him a huge, toothless smile and a wink. Her multi-coloured coat was about three sizes too big and almost touched the floor. And she was wearing fluffy boots that looked more like slippers than outdoor wear.

Her friend, who looked as if she shared the Queen's dressmaker, patted him on the arm, adjusted her three-stringed pearl necklace and pushed her mistletoe festooned tiara back in place on a head of tight and perfectly coiffed, silver-white curls.

'Boris and Duchess are right behind me, if you don't mind, my good man.'

She wafted into the pub and two corgis trotted behind, both wearing blue and gold, majestic-looking dog coats and little matching hats in the shape of tiny crowns.

'And we thought Sasha would get strange looks,' Rowan whispered to Neva as both women walked towards them.

'Oh my dear, you were positively marvellous. I'm Queenie and this is my dearest friend, Ethel. Cecil and Ronnie were beside themselves with fear.'

'Yes, dear,' Ethel added, with another toothless grin. 'Well done. It's about time someone stood up to those two.'

'You heard? It was a bit mean of me really. I'm Neva. Neva Grey. And this is my sister, Rowan. You've met my dad, Dennis.'

'He can't be your dad,' Ethel said. 'He's far too young. But I can see where you get your good looks from.'

'Thank you,' Dennis mumbled, squeezing past and hurrying towards his wife.

Neva tried not to giggle. 'This is my mum, Dawn.'

'Oh yes. I can see the likeness,' Ethel said. 'Another beauty.'

Dawn's cheeks flushed as she smiled at the women and said, 'Hello.'

'I'm Sasha and I'm a zombie princess. And that's my puppy, Tempest. She nearly drowned yesterday.' Sasha came and grabbed Neva's hand. She pointed to Tempest who had found a spot by the fire and curled herself into a ball of sable and white fur, resembling a large, plump cushion.

'So you are,' said Queenie. 'And your puppy looks exceedingly cute. We heard about your little adventure. You're so lucky young Rafe was there. He's such a dear.'

Ethel nodded. 'And you're a very lucky girl.'

'Where are your teeth?' Sasha asked. Neva tried to shush her.

Ethel shrieked with laughter. 'At home in a jar, princess. I can't get on with the things.'

Neva gave Ethel an apologetic look but the woman didn't seem at all bothered or embarrassed.

'I like your tiara,' Sasha said to Queenie. 'Is that mistletoe? I wish I'd put some of our mistletoe in mine. May I have a little bit of it, please? You can have some of ours tomorrow.'

'Sasha.' Nigel stepped forward and took her gently by the arm. 'That was rude.'

'Why? I said please.'

'Sorry. I'm Nigel. Her dad. Sometimes she forgets her manners.'

Queenie tapped his arm. 'No cause for concern, my good man. And of course you can, Princess Sasha.' She took several sprigs of mistletoe and fixed them under Sasha's tiara.

'Thank you, Your Majesty.'

Sasha made the most polished curtsey Neva had ever seen. Not that she had seen many, other than on TV.

'Hello, Wendy,' Ethel waved to the barmaid. 'The usual, please.'

'Hi Ethel. Hi Queenie. Coming up.'

'Oh I do apologise,' said Queenie. 'You were here before us.'

'It's not a problem, ladies,' Dennis said. 'We don't know what we want yet anyway.'

'You live in the village?' Neva asked.

Ethel nodded. 'All my life. I was the cook up at the house until I got too old. Now my daughter, Penny's replaced me and I'm a lady of leisure. My dear departed Norman worked there too. But he's long gone. Butler, he was. Now that stuffed shirt, Archibald Carruthers rules the roost.'

'Have you met the Wynters?' Queenie

asked.

'Adam and Rafe, yes.' Neva unbuttoned her coat to cool herself down. She was suddenly feeling rather warm.

'Not Olivia? She's their grandmother.'

'And tough as old boots.'

'Ethel, dear. We shouldn't criticise or we'll be no better than Cecil and Ronnie.'

'Hmm. You're right. Let's just say the old boot and I didn't see eye to eye. I must sit down. My arthritis is giving me gyp.'

'It was lovely to meet you, ladies.' Neva smiled at them and stood aside to let them pass.

'Rafe! You young devil. Looking as handsome as ever I see.' Ethel hurried towards the bar, her arthritis apparently forgotten.

Neva's head shot round and her eyes met Rafe's. How long had he been standing in the doorway at the end of the bar? He hadn't been there when she had first looked around.

'And you are more lovely every day, Ethel.'

He smiled at her as she tugged his shirt collar, pulling him down so that she could plant a kiss on his cheek.

He wasn't wearing his coat, just the casual pale blue shirt Neva had noticed earlier, and a navy-blue jumper and jeans, so he must've been here for a while.

'Get away with you. I bet you say that to all the girls.' Ethel giggled loudly.

'I can promise you I don't. Hello, Queenie. You look wonderful as always.'

'Thank you, Rafe. And thank you again for popping in to check on us this morning.' She looked at Wendy. 'Without those lanterns, I'm not sure what either of us would've done on Friday night. I rushed next door to Ethel's as soon as it happened and nearly took a tumble, but your lovely Sean came to my rescue, and brought us the lights from Rafe.' She smiled at Rafe again. 'Bringing light into our lives. As you always have. And then to come and check that we survived the night, was above and beyond, dear boy.'

To Neva's surprise, he coughed and appeared to be somewhat flustered, and her heart skipped a beat when he shot a look in her direction. It almost stopped when Sasha raced over to him and threw her arms around him. Due to his height, she only came up to his waist.

'You're the lovely man who saved Tempest. I should've said thank you then but I didn't.'

'Er. It was my pleasure.'

Rafe's face was a picture. A mixture of surprise, amusement and embarrassment.

'I'll love you forever,' Sasha added. 'Neva said it's OK for me to tell you that.'

'I said no such thing!' Neva's was as hot as the fire.

Sasha did her pouty and knit brows look, as she turned her head in Neva's direction, still clinging to Rafe's waist.

'Yes, you did. You said it was OK for me to say it because he'd probably never hear it from anyone else. I remember exactly—'

'That's enough, Sasha,' Rowan said. 'Leave the poor man alone.'

Now Rafe's face was a completely different picture. And not a happy one. His voice was soft but his eyes were cold when he replied to Sasha; his gaze fixed firmly on Neva.

'She's probably right. Now if you'll excuse me, someone's waiting for me.'

He gently prised himself free and went to another doorway, this one behind the bar, at one end of the mirrored wall. He ducked his head so as not to hit the beam above the door.

'That was awkward,' Rowan said, as Ethel, Queenie and Wendy all gave Neva somewhat cooler looks than earlier, and Sasha skipped back to give Tempest a hug.

'Come and sit down, sweetheart.' Dawn patted the chair next to hers. 'And don't worry about it. I'm sure he'll understand.'

'I wouldn't bet on it,' Neva said, dropping onto the chair and suddenly feeling deflated. 'Not that I care. But I think I'm now in the same book as Cecil and Ronnie as far as our new friends are concerned.'

'What's everyone having?' Wendy asked, having given Ethel and Queenie two large glasses of sherry. She smiled broadly at Sasha, a little less so at everyone else and positively glowered at Neva.

'A hole in the ground to swallow me,' Neva whispered to Rowan who was sitting the other side of her.

'I think she'll dig that for you,' Rowan whispered back.

Everyone gave their drinks orders and Wendy handed over a pile of menus, although as there were only four choices, she probably could have simply told them what was on offer.

'I'll have the cottage pie,' Dennis said, the moment he saw it, and Dawn and Nigel ordered the same.

'Macaroni cheese for me, please,' Neva said. 'It sounds delicious.'

'It is,' Wendy replied, a small smile breaking onto her face.

Sasha jumped up as Dennis handed her a menu and her face lit up.

'Burger and chips, please.' Sasha beamed at Wendy.

'What the hell,' Rowan said, handing back her menu. 'I'll have that too. Sod the bloody diet. It's Christmas.'`

'Swear jar!'

Rowan rolled her eyes at Sasha. 'You and that bloody swear jar. Oh s—damn it!'

'What is the matter with you today?' Dawn asked, frowning slightly as Wendy strolled off towards the doorway Rafe had gone through.

'I got about an hour's sleep, that's what. I had the most dreadful nightmares. Add those to Nigel's snoring and a restful night's sleep was a far-off dream.'

'You had a lie-in though,' Neva said.

'I stayed in bed. Tossed and turned. Had more nightmares. Or daymares, or whatever they're called and got up feeling even worse. I thought I'd be fine, but suddenly I feel a bit grumpy. Nothing some food and a glass or two of wine won't cure.'

'Have a sleep this afternoon,' Dennis said. 'Your mother and I intend to.'

'Me too,' said Nigel. 'It's always the same with me and holidays. I feel shattered the moment I leave work for a break.'

'Well, that's that then. I'll have to look after Sasha, won't I? And someone needs to take Tempest for a walk.'

'I'll do it,' Neva said. 'I'll take Sasha and Tempest in the opposite direction to the way I went this morning. There's a smaller waterfall down there, so I won't be quite so concerned about anyone falling in. And it's no longer that icy, so we'll be fine.'

'But I thought you had a bad night too?' Rowan queried.

'I did. But I can have a nap before supper. Or an early night.'

'We need to discuss whether or not we're going home,' Dennis said.

He and Neva had mentioned it to the others earlier but said they would see what Sean or any of the locals felt about the prospect of a flood.

'Let's ask Wendy,' Neva said, as the pretty blonde brought their drinks on a tray.

'Ask Wendy what?' Her tone was still a trifle cool.

Rowan smiled at her. 'About the river. We hear there's a very real chance it may flood.'

Wendy looked annoyed. 'Who told you that? Those two in Ruby Cottage, I don't doubt. It's never flooded in my lifetime. And I've lived here for forty years. I don't know why they want to scare away our tourists.'

'Actually,' said Dennis, 'Rafe told my daughter, Neva this very morning.'

Wendy blinked several times. 'He did? Oh. As it happens, that's one of the things he and my Sean are discussing right now. They're in the back. You can ask for an update after you've had lunch.' She looked Neva up and down and opened her mouth as if she intended to say something else, but she turned and walked away.

'That was helpful,' Rowan said, before taking a large gulp of wine.

'We may as well do as she says,' said Dennis. 'If they're discussing it, they might have more information for us later.'

A little bell tinkled over the door at the end

of the bar and Neva's heart pounded as Adam Wynter walked in. He spotted Ethel and Queenie, gave them each a friendly wave and headed towards Wendy, but he did a double take as he spotted the group of Neva's family. He smiled broadly as his gaze rested on Neva and instead of going to the bar, he turned and came towards her.

'Hello again. How are you all doing? I hope last night wasn't too awful for you. We got it sorted as fast as we could.' He stretched out his hand towards Nigel who shook it. 'We haven't met. I'm Adam.'

'Hi. I'm Nigel. Last night was a surprise but it ended up being fun.'

'I'm pleased to hear it. And who is this lovely lady?'

'I'm Rowan. Nigel's wife and Neva's sister.'

'A pleasure to meet you.' He smiled at Neva and his eyes sparkled. They definitely weren't as dark as Rafe's. 'Yes. I can see the resemblance.'

'I'm Sasha. No one ever asks about me.'

For a split second, Adam flinched, but his smile was quick to return.

'No one ever asks to be introduced to the most beautiful girl in a group, especially if she's clearly a princess. It's too hard to pluck up the courage.'

He gave a little bow and Sasha clapped her hands with delight.

'Would you like to join us?' Neva asked, blushing profusely.

His eyes scanned her from head to toe and his smile grew wider.

'Nothing would give me more pleasure but sadly, I'm here to meet my brother. Have you seen him? He's tall, grumpy and domineering. I'm only joking. He's the best brother in the world.'

'He went that way.' Neva nodded towards the door behind the bar.

'Then if you'll excuse me, I'd better go. He doesn't like to be kept waiting. Lovely to see you again.'

'Adam?'

'Yes, Neva.'

'Um. I was thinking of going for a walk to Little Wynter Falls this afternoon. I just wondered if you thought it was safe to take my niece and her dog. I went out walking earlier and it was rather icy.'

'Did you? Where did you go?'

'To Wyntersleap Falls.'

'Really? They're quite impressive at the moment.'

'They were a little frightening.'

'Did you all go?'

'No,' Dennis said. 'Just Neva. She bumped into your brother who told her there's a chance the river may flood. Do you know if that's a possibility? Wendy says Rafe and Sean are discussing it now, so we're hoping to get an update because Rafe suggested we might want to leave. He very kindly offered to give us a full refund if we choose to do so.'

Adam gave Neva an odd look. 'Did he indeed? That's interesting. I'm hoping it won't but it's hard to tell. Two days before you arrived, it was only an inch above its usual level for this time of year, so we weren't at all concerned. If it had been as high as it was yesterday, we'd have given you the option to cancel before you set out. But it rained here all of Wednesday night and all day and night on Thursday. And not just rain. It was a deluge. I've never seen the water rise so fast. By the time Rafe checked on Friday, you were already here, of course, and as you saw for yourselves, it rained again.'

'But it's a gorgeous day today,' Neva said.

'Yes. And we're hoping the levels will lower but I'm afraid the forecast isn't good, hence the little powwow.' He nodded his head towards the door.

'I really want to stay,' Neva said, possibly a touch too eagerly. 'Unless of course, you think it might actually happen. I don't relish being swept away. At least, not by water.'

He clearly picked up on her veiled hint because his huge smile reached his eyes.

'I would save you, don't worry, but you're right. A flood is not an exciting prospect. I'll come and give you an update as soon as we've finished. If you've left by then, I'll call round to the cottage. And Neva, if you do go for that walk, perhaps I could come with you. Just to show you the way and to point out one or two areas of interest.'

'I'd love that, Adam. Thank you.'

'I'll see you later then. Enjoy your lunch. The food here is excellent.'

He smiled at each of them and gave Sasha another formal bow before walking behind the bar. As he opened the door, he glanced back at Neva and winked.

'Nigel,' Rowan said. 'I don't think you'll be getting your nap this afternoon. It sounds as if Neva's got a date, and Sasha and Tempest would seriously cramp her style. You'll have to take them out instead. And please don't argue. It's about time Neva had some fun in the romance department. And it's Christmas. The season of good will to all men and sisters-in-law.'

'OK,' mumbled Nigel.

And he didn't even look cross.

Chapter Ten

About three quarters of an hour later, as Neva and her family were finishing their lunch, Adam, Rafe and Sean appeared behind the bar. Rafe didn't look in Neva's direction and nor did Sean, but Adam couldn't seem to take his eyes off her and Neva smiled as tingles of excitement ran up and down her spine. The three men continued talking and Wendy had to squeeze past them twice. Once to take Ethel and Queenie more drinks and again to come and clear the plates from Neva and her family's table. Wendy frowned at Sean as she tried to balance several plates and he soon come rushing over.

'Let me help with these, love.' He beamed at her as he cleared the remaining plates and put them on a tray.

'What's the news about the river?' Dennis asked.

'I'll let Rafe and Adam fill you in,' he replied, 'but we think it should be OK.'

Neva sighed with relief. Apart from wanting to go to Merriment Bay in the next day or two to see the salon and to get a feel for the place, she wasn't ready to lose the chance of seeing more of Adam. It was unlikely that it would lead to anything, but a kiss or two, or maybe something more, would be good. And who knows, if she moved to Merriment Bay, she might get to see him again in the future.

She watched as Rafe and Adam talked to Ethel and Queenie. Both women shook their heads, or nodded, as appropriate it seemed, to whatever Rafe was telling them.

She smiled at Adam as he approached. She even smiled at Rafe but he merely gave her a cursory glance, although as he came closer, she was sure he became more attentive. He definitely gave her a full once over when he reached the table and she stood up to hand Sean the last two empty glasses. As she sat back down, she was very glad she had worn her red dress and put on make-up. But more so for Adam's admiration than for Rafe's.

'After a lot of debate, we think the river may hold,' Rafe said, looking away from Neva and giving Dennis his full attention. 'But the forecast is changeable and it could go either way. The Environment Agency and the Met Office are both issuing flood warnings for several areas but the Merriment District Council are of the opinion that the river won't breach its banks and Wyntersleap reservoir can cope with any excess water. That's great for Merriment Bay, but what they seem to be forgetting is that the bank narrows as it passes Wyntersleap village. There's more water coming over Wyntersleap Falls than I've ever seen before. If I were you, I think I would leave.'

'Are you telling everyone to leave?' Neva asked.

'Excuse me?' Rafe's brows furrowed as if he didn't understand the question.

'What about Ethel and Queenie? And Wendy and Sean. Not forgetting the other villagers we haven't met and any other holidaymakers in your additional rental cottages. Oh, and the terrible twosome, Cecil and Ronnie. Are you suggesting they all go elsewhere?'

'Not yet, no.'

'Then why are you telling us to go? Especially if the other holidaymakers are staying.'

He took a deep breath. 'You're the only ones in the rental cottages at the moment. One family cancelled on Friday morning and the others weren't due until today. I advised them not to come.'

'Oh. But Ethel and the others? They're all staying put?'

'For now. Yes.'

'Then I think we should stay too. If the local council says there's nothing to worry about, and you said yourself it's never flooded before, then I don't see any reason for us to leave.' She looked at the rest of her family. 'What does everyone want to do? Stay or go?'

'Stay!' yelled Sasha. Tempest barked but that could have meant stay or go.

'Stay,' said Rowan. 'I'm too knackered to pack up and drive all the way back to Surrey today.'

'Whatever my wife and daughter say,' said Nigel.

'Mum? Dad?'

'It seems we're outnumbered anyway.' Dennis smiled at Dawn. 'But what do you think, darling?'

'I was so looking forward showing everyone Merriment Bay. It seems a shame to leave now that we've settled in. And surely if there was a real risk of it happening, the local authority would be issuing sandbags or something or telling people to leave their homes. Isn't that what they usually do?'

'Has the council issued sandbags or warnings?' Rowan asked.

Rafe shook his head.

'It looks like we're going to stay then,' Dennis said.

Rafe didn't look at all pleased.

'Then I hope you've got holiday insurance that covers flood damage to your belongings, because now that I've warned you, our insurance probably won't extend to you.'

'We can make sure all our things are out of harm's way, just in case,' Neva said. Even if it floods, it won't go higher than a few inches, will it?'

'As it's never flooded before, I have no idea.' Rafe glared at her.

Adam had remained oddly silent but now he spoke. 'That's the point, Rafe. It never has flooded. Not since records began. So if they want to stay, what's the problem?'

'The problem, Adam, is I'll have enough to do if the river breaches. I don't want to have to worry about holidaymakers too. No offence to you and your family, Dennis.'

'None taken. As we've decided to stay, we wouldn't expect you to. We'll set our phones for weather updates and the local news alerts, and if it sounds like it may become an issue, we'll leave, I promise you that.'

'Yes,' Neva said. 'We're not idiots.'

Judging by the look Rafe gave her, he clearly didn't agree.

'Fine.' Rafe glanced across at Sean who was leaning on the bar. 'They're staying. Will you keep an eye on things down here?'

Sean nodded. 'You know I will.'

Rafe gave Dennis and Neva a perfunctory

smile. 'Good bye then.' He turned to walk away. 'Adam? Are you coming?'

'Right behind you.' Adam smiled apologetically at Neva. 'I'm sorry but Rafe needs me to help him on the estate. I'm afraid I won't be able to join you on your walk. But can I have a rain check? Sorry. Not a good choice of phrase given the situation. Can we do it another day?'

'Any time you want. You know where I am.' Neva smiled at him, and glared at Rafe's back as he and Adam left the pub via the door at the end of the bar.

'Well', said Nigel, 'this is all very exciting. And the best bit is, I get to have my sleep this afternoon because now Neva can take Sasha and Tempest for that walk as originally planned.'

'Yay!' Sasha jumped up and down.

'Yay,' said Neva, despondently.

Did Rafe Wynter have the slightest idea that he had just ruined her day? And not just hers, but possibly also his brother's.

And would he give a damn if he did?

Chapter Eleven

Neva woke with a start and opened her eyes. Despite having an early night, she was exhausted, but that was only to be expected. She had had another restless night. This time she had dreamt of thunder storms so loud she was sure the cottage shook, and lightning bright enough to light up her room like day. In her dream, the rain had been so heavy that it sounded as if a dance troupe, all wearing clogs had held a performance on the roof. She glanced at her phone and groaned. It was 5.30 a.m. and still dark outside. Pitch black, in fact. But it would be twilight in half an hour. She turned over to go back to sleep, knowing precisely what had caused her strange dreams.

After the pub, yesterday afternoon, she had gone for her walk with Sasha and Tempest. They'd seen Little Wynter Falls, which were nowhere near as impressive as Wyntersleap

Falls. From there they'd walked to Wyntersleap reservoir and Neva had been relieved to see that there was certainly room for a lot more water in there. But that of course, was way past the village. Having seen the amount of water gushing over Wyntersleap Falls that morning, and the height of the river between them and Little Wynter Falls, she began to wonder if she and her family had made the right decision.

But Rafe was the only one who seemed to be especially worried. The local authorities were clearly not concerned enough to give out more than warnings. They weren't telling people to leave their homes. How awful that would be; even more so at this time of year.

Sasha was as tired as Neva when they returned to the cottage and after a late afternoon nap, followed by a supper of Dawn's homemade, hot sausage rolls, and later, warm mince pies and cream, then a few games of scrabble, monopoly and charades, every member of the family, including Tempest was in bed by 10 p.m.

But someone was up early. Who would be running a bath at this time in the morning? And taking a shower. And now something was hammering on the roof.

A crack of thunder brought her to her senses and she leapt out of bed and raced to the window, peering through the darkness. That wasn't the bath or the shower. That was rain.

The Christmas tree lights gave some illumination and shock set in immediately. The river had breached and water was already at the door of the cottage closest to it.

'Mum! Dad! Everyone! Get up! The river's flooding the village!'

She raced to each room, banging on the doors and within seconds everyone was up and running around like headless chickens.

'What should we do?' Rowan shrieked. 'Sasha! Sasha where are you?'

'I'm here, Mummy. And Tempest too. Are we all going to drown?'

'No,' Neva said, trying to regain her composure. 'No one's going to drown. I think the water's only reached the first cottage but we need to get our things together and get to our cars. We can't go over the bridge so we must make our way to higher ground. I've got to let the rest of the village know. I don't think anyone else is up.'

She dashed downstairs and grabbed her jacket, slipping her bare feet into her walking boots but not stopping to tie up the laces. She ran outside. Which cottages were empty and which ones were occupied? Sean would know. She ran to the pub, banging on Cecil and Ronnie's door as she passed and shouting as loud as she could above the storm.

She banged on the door of the pub and screamed Sean and Wendy's names. The door was opened within seconds.

'I know,' Sean said, pulling her into the doorway even though she was already saturated. 'I've seen it. I've called Rafe, and he and Adam are on their way.'

'I've told my family we must get everything into our cars and get to higher ground. Where does the road lead from your car park? We can't cross the bridge.'

'To Wynter House. And beyond that, there's nothing but fields and hills for several miles.'

'Then we'll have to go to Wynter House for now. I'm sure there must be room on their drive or whatever. But we need to tell the other villagers. Who lives where, Sean?'

'Don't worry about that. You go back to your family and get yourselves to safety. The water's just flooding right now. It's not a torrent. But I can see it's rising quickly and if this storm continues, it won't be long before we're up to our knees or worse. Wendy and I will deal with the villagers, and Rafe and Adam will be here any minute.'

A screech of brakes and tyres proved Sean right. Rafe and Adam appeared in two Range Rovers which they drove right in front of the pub. Rafe leapt out and shot a look at Neva through the rain.

'Are you OK?'

'Yes.'

'I told you to leave.'

'It's a bit late for that, isn't it? Sean says you and Adam will help get everyone out. Can we go to your house and park outside until we know what's happening?'

'Of course,' said Adam. 'You must come and stay with us. You all must.'

Rafe glanced at Adam and seemed to hesitate for a second before nodding to Sean, but neither of them looked pleased.

'Thank you. I'll go and get dressed and tell my family.'

Dennis was rushing towards her. 'I'll get the car and park outside the cottage. That'll be quicker.' He ran on towards the car park.

'Don't waste time dressing,' Rafe said. 'Just grab your things and get out of here. I don't think the water will reach dangerous levels but I'd rather not take that chance.'

Neva dashed back out into the rain and bolted to the cottage. She grabbed a towel from the kitchen, dried her hands and then whizzed around unplugging everything electrical, especially the Christmas tree lights. She checked around to see if there was anything of theirs on the ground level but they'd all taken everything upstairs last night, just in case. Now they had to bring it all down again.

Rowan was tossing suitcases and bags down the stairs and one nearly hit Neva.

'No breakables, don't worry,' Rowan said.

'This is faster. Sasha? Bring your things, and don't leave anything behind.'

Neva moved all the cases and bags to the door and Dennis charged back in, and began ferrying everything out to his car.

'We'll use ours for as much of the luggage and presents etc. as we can. Nigel's gone to get his. Does anyone else in the village need to move anything because if so, is there any room in yours?'

Dennis was half way to the kitchen as Neva replied, 'Yes. I'll find out who needs what.'

Rafe appeared at the door. 'We need to get things moving. How many cars do you have?'

'Three,' Neva said. 'I can fit some stuff in mine and some people. We're going to put all our belongings in Dad's and some in Nigel's but there may still be some room for other people's things. I've turned everything electrical off but not at the mains. I'll do that as we leave.'

Rafe looked both surprised and impressed.

'Builder's daughter,' she added.

'Well. Thank you. But don't worry about that. I'll deal with it. Can you take Ethel and Queenie and the dogs in your car? They'll struggle to get in and out of the Range Rovers.'

'Yes. What about Cecil and Ronnie? Do they have a car? If not, I can fit them in at a push.'

'Thanks. That'll leave more room in Penny and Roger's car. Gavin and Archie are on their way too, so that will help.'

'No idea who they are, but is there anyone else you need us to take?'

'No. I think that's it. Just follow the road until you see a fork ahead. The gates to Wynter House are on your left. They're open of course so just drive in and continue on until you see the house. Park anywhere. We'll worry about that later. And Neva.'

'Yes.'

'Drive safely. Even the roads are like rivers today and just before the gates where two roads lead into one, there's a large pool of water. Go slow there or you'll aquaplane again.'

'Again?' She'd forgotten her lie. 'Oh yes. Right. I'll be careful. And I'll tell the others.'

People rushed to and fro, several of whom Neva had not seen before. They must be the ones Rafe mentioned. By the time she went to get her car, the water was creeping along the cobbles, getting nearer all the time, but even though the river was a torrent, the overspill was like a gentle brook trickling over the cobbles.

'Have you got everything, Neva?' This time it was Adam asking as she got out of her car to pick up Ethel, Queenie and the dogs.

'Yes. I just need to get Cecil and Ronnie after I've got Ethel and Queenie in my car.'

'You go and get the men. I'll deal with the ladies. They may be a bit unsteady on their feet.'

He was right. They were. As Neva banged on the door of Ruby Cottage, she watched Adam help the ladies to her car and get them settled in the back, together with the corgis, Boris and Duchess.

'We're not coming,' Cecil said, opening the door the merest fraction.

'What? The village is flooding. We don't know how high the water may get.'

Ronnie peered around Cecil. 'It's a worry, I'll admit. But it doesn't look too bad. We've been moving everything upstairs. We'll be fine.'

'Not without heat, hot water, or electricity you won't. You can't light a fire in a pool of water. And the water will fuse the electrics if it reaches the sockets. Come with us. We're going to go to Wynter House until we know the situation.'

Cecil and Ronnie exchanged anxious looks. 'We'll be fine.'

'No you won't.'

'We've got a cat. We can't leave Persephone. We can't. We won't.'

'No one expects you to. Bring her with you.'

Again the looks. 'But Rafe Wynter hates us.'

She burst out laughing. 'Sorry. But I don't think he likes me much either. I'm still going to his house though. And I need you to get a move on. Apart from the fact I'm drowning in the rain out here, I've got two little old ladies freezing to death in my car.'

'Persephone doesn't like dogs.'

'Persephone won't have to sit with them. She can sit in the boot.' The look of horror on their faces made her realise how awful that sounded. 'She can sit on the front seat with one of you and we can cover her basket with a towel. That should comfort her.'

Rafe's voice suddenly boomed out and Cecil and Ronnie quivered as he charged towards them.

'What's the delay?'

'They think you hate them.'

He blinked as a look of disbelief swept across his face. 'Seriously?'

She shrugged.

'You do,' they said.

'I don't. I don't hate anyone. But even if I did, this is hardly the time to debate it.'

'Well, you don't like us much.'

'So what? Look guys. I really don't have time for this. Can we discuss it when we're all safely away from here, in the warm and dry? Or do you want this lovely young woman to die of pneumonia?'

Had he just called her lovely? Neva smiled at him but he wasn't looking at her.

'We've got a cat.'

'And?'

'You don't like cats.'

He sucked in a breath. 'I love cats. Now

please guys, let's move.'

'Please!' Neva pleaded. 'I'm freezing. Look. I've only got my PJs on under this jacket and I'm soaked.'

Rafe looked her up and down, and the lopsided grin briefly appeared.

He'd obviously just spotted the giant snowmen on her PJs. How embarrassing was that?

'Well, if you're sure we'll be welcome,' Cecil said to Rafe.

'I'm sure. Have you packed a bag?'

'We'll be two seconds.'

'Do you need any help?' Rafe asked, and he left when they shook their heads.

A few minutes later, they and Persephone were in Neva's car and heading towards Wynter House.

Chapter Twelve

Neva had seen from the photos on the website that Wynter House was a grand, stately home. But as she drove up the winding lane and reached the fork in the road, which as Rafe had said was a pool of swirling water where the two roads above merged into one narrow lane, the glimpse she got of Wynter House took her by surprise. It was like something out of *Downton Abbey*, a series she had watched on TV and one that had been made into a movie very recently.

She turned into the long drive bordered either side by massive oak trees; bare-leaved at this time of year but dressed from top to bottom with white static fairy lights. The second glimpse took her breath away.

As she got closer and the house came into full view, she was speechless. Ethel and Queenie were chattering away in the back, each with a corgi on their lap and Ronnie was leaning forward giving commands to Cecil who was mumbling comforting words to a hissing and spitting Persephone, in a basket on his lap in the front passenger seat.

'Why have we stopped here?' Cecil asked, looking up from his ministrations. 'We're in the middle of the drive.'

'I'm well aware of that,' Neva said, staring straight ahead. 'But I had to stop for just a second and take this in. It's magnificent!'

'What did you expect, sweet cheeks?' Ronnie slapped her lightly on the shoulder. 'You didn't think the county's two most eligible single men would be living in a hovel, did you?'

The two most eligible single men in the county? Is that how people thought of Adam and Rafe?

'I hadn't really thought about it. I'd seen the photos on the website but nothing prepared me for this.'

The house was built of red stone and exuded a warmth that was both welcoming and intimidating at the same time. She didn't know if she'd like to reach out and touch it or bow down before it. It consisted of a central portion, guarded by two protruding towers; one on each side, both with onion-shaped, lead roofs which glistened even in the rain. To the left and right of those, an east wing and a west wing, both larger than the central portion, stood proud. There were large, mullioned windows everywhere. The house must be bathed in light, no matter what the season, or the weather. There were more white fairy lights trailing along the holly bushes at the front and across the frontage of the house and the large portico.

'Well take a good look and then get moving,' Ronnie added. 'There are two cars racing up the drive behind us.'

Neva glanced in the rear-view mirror then put her foot on the accelerator.

'It is a magnificent house, you're right,' Ethel said, a trace of emotion evident in her voice. 'Inside and out. There used to be such grand parties. Even more so when I was a girl. I came to work here when I was twelve and I loved every day of it. Apart from my run-ins with Olivia Wynter. I liked her when we first met, but she changed.'

'Twelve? That was young to start work.'

'Not in my day. Lots of girls went into service even younger than that. I'm eighty-eight you know. Things were different way back then. Everything changed after the war. And not necessarily for the better, I say.'

'I agree,' said Queenie. 'Life at Wynter House was hard work but we were a family.'

'Oh. I didn't realise you worked there too.'

'I was lady's maid to Olivia. I came here with her when she married Sebastian. He was Rafe and Adam's grandfather, and such a lovely man. It was a few years after the war and they were so in love even though he was almost fifteen years her senior. She was nineteen when she married him. Olivia was different then. Young, carefree, kind and most of all, blissfully happy.'

'What happened to change that?'

'Life.' Queenie sighed loudly. 'Or more to the point, death. She lost two children. One to a miscarriage and one to illness. Phillip was her third time lucky. But he wasn't very lucky, and neither was she. Phillip was just two when Sebastian died. They said it was from the wounds he sustained in the war. It broke Olivia's heart. It was as if a veil came down and everything changed. No more parties. No more laughter. The entire house went into mourning.'

'And it never really came out,' Ethel added, with a sigh. 'But we all made the best of it, and we managed to have some fun. It was Phillip I felt sorry for. Olivia couldn't bear to look at him. He reminded her too much of what she had lost. And when he died, she had no time for his sons, Rafe or Adam, either.'

'That's so sad. But it looks really festive and cheerful with all the lights in the trees and bushes and over the entrance.'

'That's just for the paying visitors,' Queenie said. 'People coming for the tour expect to see all that at this time of year. There'll be a marvellous tree in the grand entrance hall and one in the dining room, a smaller but rather splendid tree in the library and two trees which are identical, one in the drawing room and one in the morning room. All richly decorated and each with myriad lights. There'll also be an abundance of greenery everywhere. It's what the visitors want. But in the private parts of the house, you'll be lucky if you can spot a sprig of holly.'

Even Cecil and Ronnie sighed.

'It's not a happy house, that much is for sure,' Cecil said. 'You can feel it the moment you walk in. We've done the tour. It's as if the place is haunted.'

'Haunted? Please don't tell my niece, Sasha that. We'll never hear the last of it. She's into ghosts, vampires and zombies in a very big way and she'll cause all sorts of offence by offering to chase out the ghosts. She'll definitely want to hear all the gory details. From the sound of Olivia, that wouldn't go down too well.'

'That's an understatement,' Ronnie said. 'I've only met her once. It's not an experience I particularly relish repeating.'

'Was that why your niece was wearing that horrid thing on her face?' Cecil asked. 'It was so realistic. But we noticed it wasn't there when you went out for a walk in the afternoon.'

'Yes.' Neva pulled up to one side of the spectacular, red stone portico festooned with fairy lights. 'Please don't take this the wrong way, but do you two spend all day looking out over the street?'

'Not *all* day,' Cecil said. 'But people-watching is a bit of a hobby of ours. Your niece is into dead people, vampires and ghouls. We prefer the living. They're so much fun to watch.'

Neva couldn't argue with that.

Chapter Thirteen

A stream of vehicles formed a remarkably orderly row alongside Neva's car. Rafe and Adam were the first to get out of theirs and Adam approached Neva while Rafe strode towards the front door of the house. It shot open before he reached it and a tall, straight-backed man in a charcoal grey suit, matching tie and white shirt stood to one side to let him pass. Rafe said something to him but he didn't move until Rafe was out of sight.

'That's the butler, Archibald Carruthers,' Ethel said, following Neva's gaze as the man dashed back inside. 'My Norman could knock him into a cocked hat, both in looks and manners, but he takes his post seriously, I'll give him that.'

Adam smiled and Neva opened her window an inch or two. The rain was sheeting in the other direction so only a few spatters found their way inside.

'Rafe's gone to break the news to Olivia,' Adam said, with something between a frown and a grin on his face. 'She wasn't up when we came out.'

'She'll be pleased.' Ethel smacked her lips together and sniggered.

'You call your gran, Olivia?' It was a ridiculous question, given the situation but it popped into Neva's head right away.

'She insists upon it.' Adam smiled. 'Ah, Here's Carruthers.'

The man, who now wore a black coat over his suit, strode towards them as if he were a sergeant on a drill parade. He held one umbrella aloft and carried several more under his arm, deftly handing one to Adam without getting himself wet. It was a bit late for Adam; he was saturated.

'I think we should get everyone into the drawing room, Carruthers.'

'The drawing room, sir?' One eyebrow went up, the other went down.

'Yes. Is that a problem?'

'Indeed not, sir. But if I may, Mr Rafe instructed me before he went out this morning, to light a fire in the morning room.'

'Oh. Well, the morning room it is then. I'm not sure how many bedrooms we'll need aired. You or Judith will have to count them up. I can leave that with you, can't I?'

'It's already underway, sir. Mr Rafe gave us a rough idea of numbers before he left this morning and he texted us an update a short time ago.'

It seemed Rafe had already decided everyone would be coming to Wynter House, long before Adam suggested it. So why had Rafe looked so displeased? Was it because he wanted to be the one to say it? That seemed unlikely. Or was it because although he knew there was little choice, it was an invitation he would rather not have had to make?

'Did he? That's perfect. Let's get everyone inside then. I see Judith has more umbrellas. Thank you, Carruthers. You may get on.'

Neva couldn't help but giggle. She'd stepped into a real-life, *Downton Abbey*. Were they for real?

'What's funny?' Adam asked, in a pleasant manner as he opened the car door for her.

'Nothing. Nothing at all.' She turned and looked at Ethel. 'I think we should get Ethel and Queenie in first, don't you?'

A woman in her mid to late thirties rushed up and smiled at Adam.

'I've got more brollies.'

'Thanks, Judith. This is Neva, but I think we'll save the introductions until everyone is inside.'

'Of course, Adam.' She smiled at Neva and handed her a brolly.

'Thank you, Judith.'

Adam turned and opened the rear door to help Ethel and Queenie, while Cecil and Ronnie got out and sheltered beneath the brolly Judith handed them.

'Who's Judith?' Neva asked when the woman ran to Dennis' car. 'She's very pretty.'

Adam grinned. 'Is she? I hadn't really noticed. She's Rafe and Olivia's PA, the housekeeper, visitor co-ordinator and anything else Rafe or Olivia need her to be. You've got no need to be jealous. She's not my type.'

'Who says I'm jealous?'

'I hate to say this, Neva, but it's written all over your face.'

Ethel chuckled as Adam helped her out of the car. 'He's not wrong, dear. You've got very expressive eyes. I noticed that yesterday when I saw you look at Rafe.'

'Rafe?' Adam and Neva said in unison and looked at one another.

Ethel chuckled louder and slapped Adam's arm. 'Now who's jealous, Adam?'

'I am, actually.'

Adam made a foolish, pouty face before smiling provocatively at Neva. He oozed such sex appeal that she almost jumped on him then and there.

'I'm not interested in Rafe, Adam. I think Ethel's just winding you up.'

'Am I?' Ethel looked doubtful.

'Let's get you inside,' Neva said, linking an arm through hers. 'Will you help Queenie, Adam?'

'Of course.'

'Is this the first time you'll have been back to this house since you stopped working here?' Neva asked Ethel.

'Gracious, no. I come back several times a year. We all do. There's a party on Christmas Eve, for staff, both current and former. Rafe reinstated it many years ago. And also the Summer Fête. That's a hoot, especially with Olivia playing the lady of the manor in recent years. But it's fun for other reasons. They have side shows and rides, games and displays, stalls selling produce and craft items from people from all the towns and villages within twenty or so miles. And there's music and dancing into the wee small hours. Outside, under the stars, weather permitting, or in the ballroom if it's bad.'

'There's a ballroom?' Neva had seen it in the photos but it was obvious that Ethel was enjoying sharing her memories.

'Oh yes, dear. There's a grand ballroom. I doubt you'll see better in all the fine houses in the land. Of course, these days it's hired out for conferences and weddings, which is lovely for those involved, but such a shame to see it not being used as it once was. When I saw my first ball here, I thought I'd stepped into a fairy tale.

165

I was only six and I sneaked up from downstairs. My mother was working late into the night, so she had brought me with her. There was enough champagne flowing that night to fill the River Wynter. And the gowns! It brings tears to my old eyes just remembering the beauty swirling around that floor. The men weren't bad to look at either.' She chuckled loudly.

'What are you laughing about, Ethel?' Queenie asked, from a little way behind as Boris and Duchess trotted at her heels, making sure they were sheltered by Adam's umbrella.

'I'm telling Neva about the balls they held here when I was a child.'

Neva lowered her voice so that Adam wouldn't hear. 'Life was hard for so many, back then, but if you were rich, it must've been magical.'

'It seemed that way. Certainly as a 'below stairs' child looking in. But life wasn't that magical for Olivia, was it? Or her husband and son. And it's not for Rafe, either. As the youngest son, it doesn't affect Adam quite so much, but Rafe has to keep this place going. That's a mammoth task. But Life's hard for many people these days, dear. Sometimes I think we forget that. And in the end, we're all human and we all have happiness and sadness. Perhaps money makes the sadness a little easier to bear. Although Olivia would disagree with me on that.'

'That's very true, Ethel. You're right. Oh!'

She careered headlong into Rafe as they entered the house. He was walking so fast that he was in front of her before she knew it. He grabbed her arm and reached out for Ethel to stop them both from falling.

'I'm so sorry. I didn't see you. I ... Are you both OK?' An expression of genuine concern replaced the look of surprise on his face.

'I am. Ethel?'

Ethel nodded. 'It'll take more than a bump from a handsome young man to knock me off my feet, Rafe Wynter.'

He grinned at her. 'Come inside and let me take your coats.'

It was then that Neva realised she was still wearing her pyjamas. Rafe had been the one who told her not to waste time getting dressed, but as she looked around and everyone else came into the impressive, wood panelled hall, she seemed to be the only one who hadn't done so. Her three-quarter-length waterproof jacket covered most of her, but there was no way she was taking that off and parading around in her snowmen-dotted pyjamas.

'I think I'll keep mine on for the time being, thanks.'

He frowned, looked her up and down, and the grin reappeared. 'Ah,' he said.

'You were the one who told me not to put

my clothes on.'

He raised his brows as several pairs of eyes, including Adam's turned to him and Neva.

'Sorry. That came out louder than I expected.' She glanced around. 'He told me not to get dressed because–'

'I think you should stop now.' He looked as if he was trying not to laugh. 'Judith will take you upstairs in a moment and you can have a hot shower and get changed. Are your bags in your father's car? I'll get them for you.'

'I've got one of them here.' Dennis stepped forward. He had holdalls slung across his body, bags under both arms, and cases in his hands. 'Where's a good donkey when you need one?'

'Forgive me, sir.' Carruthers darted forward, laden with bags himself. 'Let me take those from you.'

'Oh. No, it's fine. I didn't mean it. I'm not complaining. It's so good of you to have us here.'

Rafe and Carruthers relieved him of his burdens.

'Don't mention it,' Rafe said, smiling at Dennis, as Nigel, Rowan, Dawn and Sasha appeared, all carrying bags.

Tempest came charging in behind them, sliding across the wooden floor when she tried to stop, and almost careering into the exceptionally large and resplendent Christmas tree. Queenie's corgis, Boris and Duchess, tugged at their leads, and Adam, who wasn't really paying attention to the fact he had Queenie on one arm and the leads in his other hand, let the leads slip from his fingers. Suddenly, the imposing hall was filled with skidding, barking and saturated dogs. Fortunately, Persephone, Cecil and Ronnie's cat, was still safely ensconced in her basket but she hissed and spat and growled almost as loudly as the dogs. And a cacophony of voices all talked over one another.

Carruthers looked as if he was about to have an apoplexy.

'What *is* the commotion?' A commanding voice boomed out from the top of the intricately carved oak staircase at the end of the hall, and all eyes turned to Olivia Wynter. She took one stair at a time, using a large ebony cane in her right hand to help her balance and resting her left hand on the banister. But even so, she gave the impression of sweeping down the stairs like Royalty. She was dressed like Royalty too. 'Carruthers! Are you going to let those animals run wild?'

'Apologies, ma'am.' He quickly but quietly deposited the luggage on the floor.

'I think he has enough to do at the moment, Olivia,' Rafe said, turning to try to catch Boris. 'We can all benefit from some leeway in circumstances such as these.'

Neva tried to help, as did Adam, Sasha and Nigel, but the dogs thought it was a good game and bounded around more wildly. It took a few minutes to catch them and all the while, Olivia made her way down until she reached the bottom stair, where she stood, chin raised, as if she were watching a peasant's revolt or something equally unpleasant. Rafe managed to grab Tempest just as the puppy seemed intent on going to introduce herself to Olivia, who backed away against the newel post as if the dog had rabies.

Neva ran forward to take Tempest's lead from Rafe. 'Sorry. That's the second time you've saved her from impending death.'

Rafe glanced up at Olivia. He clearly understood Neva's meaning, and Olivia looked Neva up and down as if she thought Neva might be rabid too. But who could blame her for that? Neva was wearing PJs, walking boots, and a saturated jacket. No doubt her hair was also a complete mess.

'Olivia, this is Neva. She and her family were guests at one of the cottages.'

'Did you not tell them to go home?'

'He did,' Neva said. 'We decided to stay. It's very kind of you to welcome us into your home.'

'I had no say in the matter.' She looked down her nose at Neva, but Rafe gave her a quelling look and suddenly she smiled. 'You're most welcome, at such a dreadful time. I'm sure Rafe and the staff will ensure you have everything you need. I have a headache. Please excuse me.'

'Of course. It's lovely to meet you.'

'Indeed.' Olivia turned her back and made her way up the stairs.

It was really rather pointless of her making all that effort to come down.

'I apologise,' Rafe said.

'Rudeness seems to run in the family.'

Had she said that out loud? Judging by the look on his face, she had.

'Oh God. I'm so sorry, Rafe. It's me who's being rude. I didn't mean that. You've been nothing but kind today.'

'It's fine.' He turned away. 'Judith? Would you show Neva and her family to their rooms, please?' He walked off without another word and started leading the others into what Neva assumed must be the morning room.

'Of course, Rafe.' Judith deposited several umbrellas into a large iron stand and hurried forward, picking up one of the bags from the floor. 'If you'll follow me, Mr and Mrs Grey and family.'

'It's Dennis and Dawn,' Dennis said, as Neva walked back towards her family to pick up her own bag. 'Neva, Rowan and Nigel, and Sasha. And Tempest, of course. Who can forget Tempest?'

'I'm Judith. Please let me know if there is anything you need. I can't promise we'll have it but we'll do our best to get it, whatever it is.'

She had obviously worked in the hospitality industry prior to coming to Wynter House. Perhaps a luxury hotel. She also clearly had a bit of a thing for both Adam and Rafe.

Or perhaps Neva was being ridiculous.

'I don't know what the plan is,' Dawn said, 'but we emptied our fridge and brought all our food and drink. Most of it can stay in the car for now, but I don't suppose there's room in your fridge to pop our perishables in, is there? Everything is in these two bags.' She nodded to two large cool bags at her feet.

'Oh. Yes of course. We can put the bags in the walk-in chiller. Just give me one moment, please.' She grabbed the bags, dashed along the hall, disappeared through a door and was back in less than a minute, a huge smile on her face. 'All safe and sound and waiting for you when you need them. Now if you'd like to follow me, I'll show you to your rooms.'

Chapter Fourteen

Neva stretched out on the huge four-poster bed. It looked as if it could have been slept in by someone from the court of King Henry VIII, or even the man himself, it was so ancient and grand. If the Wynters ever decided to move, it would take an army of removal men to lift it. But that was something that would never happen.

What must it feel like to live in a house in which generations of your family have lived for centuries? Would it be a comfort, or a chain around the neck to know this would be your home for life?

A fire roared in an impressive fireplace, where lions rampant held the fire basket aloft and hot ash fell onto a red-brick hearth. It would cost a fortune just to heat this room. No wonder the Wynters needed visitors to pay to walk around a few rooms and a garden.

Judith had told Neva and her family that they could get some rest after their ordeal and large, fluffy towels were deposited on each bed, so that they could all take hot showers. Then breakfast would be served in the dining room at 10 a.m. It was 6.30 a.m. by the time they arrived so that didn't give them long, but it also meant they wouldn't have long to wait to eat. Neva was starving.

She showered as soon as Judith had left and then jumped into bed, setting the alarm on her phone to wake her promptly at 9.30, but she didn't sleep. Her mind was replaying everything that had happened since coming to Wyntersleap on Friday. It was only Sunday and yet it was as if she had been in the village far longer.

She washed and dressed and ran to the room Judith had allocated to her parents.

'Come in,' Dawn said. 'Ah, Neva. Isn't this something?'

'You're not kidding.' Neva collapsed onto their bed. It was similar to hers and felt just as comfy. 'I feel we should be paying extra just to be experiencing such luxury.'

'Do you think we should?' Dennis asked. 'Offer to pay extra, I mean. After all, we were the ones who decided to stay. They didn't have to invite us here. They could've told us to find alternative accommodation.'

'They still might. Adam only said we

should come here today. He didn't actually invite us to stay for Christmas and the New Year. Once we've had breakfast, they might ask us to be on our way. Especially now that we're packed and ready to go.'

Dawn's face fell. 'Do you think so? Oh, I do hope not. Wouldn't it be wonderful to spend Christmas here? But of course we would have to pay something. This is like staying in one of those posh country-house hotels and they charge an absolute fortune. Much more than we paid for the cottage.'

'Let's wait and see.' Neva scrambled off the bed and strolled towards the door. 'Didn't Judith say something about Rafe having a chat with us all over breakfast?'

'She did,' Dennis said. 'And if they do say we can stay, I'll have a word with him about it. I think at the very least, we should offer to pay for our food and a little bit more towards the accommodation.'

'Who knows, Dad. He may give us a price list over scrambled eggs on toast. And if it's based on the prices they charge for the tour, we'll have to rethink the move to Merriment Bay, and possibly take out another mortgage.'

Neva was only half joking. It would be lovely to spend Christmas here. Even with the Ice Queen, Olivia Wynter. But they couldn't expect the Wynters to let everybody stay, and the villagers would rightly take precedence.

Rowan, Nigel, and Sasha were coming out of their room. Judith had offered Sasha a room of her own but Rowan wanted her with them for now. That was probably because Rowan was concerned about how much trouble Sasha could get into in a house like this if given free rein. She had already said it would be fun to slide down the banister of the main staircase. The only thing she wasn't happy about was the fact that she hadn't been allowed to bring Tempest upstairs. Judith said that everyone's pets would be taken by a member of staff to be towel-dried, or bathed first if necessary, which in Tempest's case it was. Her mass of fur seemed to have collected every bit of dirt in the street as they'd bundled her into the car. The pets would also be fed, and returned to their owners later.

Carruthers was at the foot of the stairs, as if standing to attention, when Neva and her family came down. He no longer wore a suit but was far more formally dressed in a white, wing collar dress shirt, black morning coat and matching tie, grey waistcoat and grey pinstriped trousers. He also now wore white gloves.

'Good morning,' Dawn said, beaming at him. 'Thank you for all your help earlier. I'm sorry but I didn't catch your name. I'm Dawn. This is Dennis, Neva, Rowan, Nigel and Sasha.'

One eyebrow went up, one went down.

'Good morning, Mrs Grey, Mr Grey, Miss Grey–'

'Whoa. Stop there,' Neva said. 'I don't mean to be rude by interrupting but please don't call us by such formal names.'

'I beg your pardon, Miss Grey. But by what else should I call you?'

'Mum just told you.'

He looked as if she had asked him to run naked across the hall.

'I couldn't possibly do that, Miss Grey.'

'Hmm. As a butler, isn't it part of your job to ensure all the guests have what they need, or is that Judith's role?'

'Miss Thorn and I share that function.'

'Well, at the moment, we're your employer's guests, and what we want is for you to call us by our Christian names, please. If it makes you uncomfortable, I'll clear it with your boss.'

'No need.' Rafe appeared from one of the wood panelled walls as if by magic.

'He just walked through a wall, Daddy!' Sasha jumped up and down with excitement.

Rafe smiled. 'It's a secret passage which was originally a priest's hole. I'll show it to you later. It leads to the east wing and it's a short cut from my bedroom.'

'Wow! I love this place.'

'Me too,' he said, and it was obvious from the look in his eyes, he did. He gave the butler a quick once over and frowned, as if displeased by what the man was wearing. 'Olivia?'

The butler gave a slight nod and Rafe sighed and shook his head.

Had Olivia told the butler to change his clothes?

Rafe shot a look at Neva, coughed as though he had been caught off-guard, and added: 'Archie, I know it will be difficult for you, but if our guests wish you to call them by their Christian, or given names, please do so.'

Again the butler did the thing with his eyebrows. One up, one down. He was as bad as Rowan with her eye-rolling. But he gave a little bow of his head.

'Of course, Mr Rafe.'

Neva smiled. 'Thank you. And may we call you, Archie?'

He threw Rafe a pleading look and Rafe grinned. 'I think that might be asking too much. He prefers to be called Carruthers. The dining room is the first door to your left. Please go ahead.'

'Carruthers it is then,' Dennis said, grabbing Neva's elbow. 'Leave it, Neva. We're guests, remember.'

But Neva couldn't, and she hung back to speak to Rafe.

'Is there something you need?'

His voice was cool and he wouldn't meet her eyes. Was he still cross about her saying rudeness ran in his family?

'Yes. First, I want to apologise again for my earlier comment. I didn't mean it, honestly. Please don't be cross.'

'I'm not.'

'OK. Second. Thank you so much for this. The rooms are magnificent and it's really very kind.'

'It's nothing. I couldn't leave you all to drown.' There was a hint of a grin on his lips, but only very slight.

'Third. How come you call him Archie and we can't?'

He looked surprised. 'Er. Because apart from the fact that he works for me, I've known him for most of my life. You've only just met him.'

'Fair enough. But Adam calls him Carruthers?'

'He does. Is that a question?'

'Yes. Why doesn't he call him Archie, too?'

'You're asking the wrong person.'

'OK. Fine. Is there any news about the river? Did it flood the village completely? It's stopped raining. Will the water recede now? And if so, will we be able to go back?'

Rafe shook his head. 'There's a few inches of water in the cottages closest to the river, and just a covering in the rest. If it doesn't rain anymore and the water levels drop, the water will recede. But it'll be some time before anyone can go back. The cottages will have to dry out and be checked for other damage, especially to the electrical supply.'

'Oh. So will you expect me and my family to go home then?'

He hesitated for a second. 'I'm not sure there's an alternative.'

'Isn't there?' She looked up into his eyes and saw confusion. 'Where is everyone from the village going to stay?'

Again the hesitation. 'Some may have relatives they can go to. But for those who don't, as most of them are either former or current employees of this estate, they will stay here until other arrangements can be made.'

'But not us?'

'I don't understand. Why would you stay here? You have homes to go to.'

'So that's that then. Thank you, Rafe.'

She hurried into the dining room without another word and sat beside her dad.

'It seems we won't be staying. Rafe's made it pretty clear he expects us to go home.'

Dennis sighed. 'Oh, what a shame. But it's probably just as well. It might be odd spending Christmas with so many strangers, and in someone else's home, especially one like this. We can take a day trip down to Merriment Bay between Christmas and the New Year. It won't be quite the same, but no one can do anything about Mother Nature and we'll all still have fun. I'll tell the others.' He leant to his side and spoke to Dawn, who passed the news along after a moment or two, to Rowan seated beside her, and Rowan passed it on to Nigel.

'What are you all whispering about?' Sasha asked Nigel, rather loudly.

He quietly broke the news and she didn't take it well. She jumped to her feet and yelled, 'But why can't we stay here? I don't want to go home. Rafe said he'd show me the secret passage.'

'Sit down and behave,' Rowan snapped. 'You can't just invite yourself to stay at someone else's house. They've made plans for Christmas and those plans didn't include us.'

Sasha sat down but sulked until Rafe asked for a moment of everyone's time. He stood at the head of the long dining table and apologised for the slight delay in the arrival of breakfast.

'It'll be here shortly, but as you can imagine, the kitchen is somewhat busy at the moment. Penny and Taryn weren't expecting to be catering for so many today.'

'I'll go and help,' Ethel said, slowly getting to her feet.

'No need, Ethel,' Rafe said. 'Judith, Wendy and Sean are lending us a hand.'

Ethel sat down again and a second or two later, a door at the other end of the room opened and Judith, Wendy, Sean and

Carruthers, who seemed to be able to flit from one place to another as if he had some futuristic transportation device, wheeled in large silver-plated, or possibly solid silver trolleys, one stacked with plates over a warming rack, one with juices and glasses, one with pots of coffee and tea, and one with cups, saucers and cutlery. A young girl of about eighteen came in with a plump woman and two more trolleys and, together with the others, they laid crockery and cutlery in front of each guest, filled glasses with juices, and cups with tea or coffee. They offered cereal, eggs, bacon, sausages and mushrooms, and rounds of toast, butter and marmalade. For people who weren't expecting to cater for so many, they did a pretty spectacular job. And then, to Neva's continued surprise, they sat down at the table and joined the guests. Because, of course, given the situation, they were also guests right now.

'I hope they don't ask us to do the washing up,' Rowan said.

'I'd be happy to help,' said Dawn.

Rafe gave a short speech about everyone being welcome, and was only briefly interrupted by Sasha.

'Not everyone. Weren't not.'

'Sasha!' Rowan glowered at her and so did Nigel and the rest of the family. They immediately apologised to Rafe.

He seemed a little distracted but he soon

got back into his flow, especially when Adam came in and whispered in his ear.

'For those of you with pets,' Rafe continued, 'George has kindly fed and watered them. I know one or two of you were a little concerned to be separated from them in the hall, but you'll be reunited now they're clean and dry. I'm sure you'll appreciate that some of the furnishings here are irreplaceable and whilst we realise how much your pets mean to you, we can't allow wet animals upstairs or in the main rooms of the house, I'm afraid.'

One of the men Neva had seen in the village earlier came in with Tempest, Boris and Duchess, all on their leads and all clean and dry and rather well-behaved. An elderly man with a warm smile and a stooped back, brought in Persephone, purring happily in his arms.

'We've put temporary beds for the dogs, in the servants' hall, and a dry blanket in Persephone's basket. Gavin and George will look after them until you've finished breakfast. I want you all to know that those of you who don't have relatives or other homes to go to, are welcome to stay with us for as long as necessary, or until other arrangements can be made. We'll keep you apprised of the current situation and we'll do everything we can to make your stay here comfortable. Are there any questions?'

'Why do we have to leave?' Sasha yelled.

She clearly wasn't going to let this drop.

'You don't,' Adam said, but Rafe scowled at him and he quickly added: 'Not yet. Not until you're completely rested and we're sure the roads aren't flooded.'

Nigel grabbed Sasha's arm. 'If you say another word, you won't be getting any Christmas presents. You're being extremely rude.'

But no sooner had he finished than a crack of thunder made everyone jump and rain lashed at the floor to ceiling mullioned windows, bringing a smile to Sasha's face.

'The roads might flood now, Daddy.'

And as awful as that was, it made Neva smile too.

Chapter Fifteen

Neva needed something to do. The house was palatial and she would love to look around, but as ridiculous as it was, she didn't want to do that. Not yet anyway. She didn't want to see what she would be missing if they had to go home today. Her parents had no such qualms, and nor did Rowan and Nigel.

Neither did Cecil and Ronnie, who seemed to have completely forgotten the fact that they were in Rafe Wynter's home, the man they had accused of killing his wife. They were plumping cushions on the sofas in the drawing room and even discussing rearranging the furniture. Neva didn't want to be involved in that. Rafe was obviously still cross with her even though he had said he wasn't. She didn't want to exacerbate the situation by suggesting his home interior style needed work.

Sasha was busy trying to find the panel

through which Rafe had appeared in the hall, and Neva had not seen Ethel and Queenie since breakfast.

Adam and Rafe, and Wendy and Sean, dashed here, there and everywhere, but when Neva asked Judith if there was anything she could do to help, she was reassured there wasn't.

She couldn't go for a walk outside; the rain was once again, torrential. Instead, she wandered into the library. And what a library it was. It was the size of the entire cottage they had rented, with floor to ceiling shelves crammed with leather-bound books.

A fire crackled cheerfully in the large hearth with yet another impressively carved surround. This was obviously one of the rooms open to the public, and a mass of holly, ivy and mistletoe, interspersed with flickering faux candles, dressed the mantle. A tree, much smaller than the one in the hall but adorned with similarly beautiful decorations and candle-shaped fairy lights, stood majestically in one corner. But when she shook one of the presents piled beneath, it was obvious it was empty and merely for decorative purposes, which was somehow disappointing.

She scanned the bookshelves and was surprised to see a copy of one of her favourite books, Mrs Gaskell's, *Wives and Daughters*. She was even more surprised to find it was a first edition and astonished to see what appeared to be the author's signature inside. Of course that could have been a forgery, but would Rafe Wynter condone such a thing? Unless he didn't know.

She walked to the window seat and sat on the sumptuous cushion. The view from here was idyllic. It overlooked the drive to one side, still aglow with the fairy light-hung trees and the gardens to the other. Were the lights left on all day? And what about at night? Perhaps they were switched off once the paying visitors had gone. But there weren't any paying visitors at the moment. Ethel had told her that the house was closed from December the 20th until the second weekend of the New Year. Perhaps the lights had been left on to cheer everyone up after having to evacuate the village.

There was a long length of immaculately mown lawn leading to a copse of trees. To the side of the lawn sat formal gardens; the ones open to the public, no doubt. Beyond those were rows of fruit trees and, as she peered around the window frame, she caught a glimpse of an ancient brick wall, probably part of the kitchen garden she had seen on the website.

She removed her boots; although why she had put those on and not a pair of shoes, she had no idea. It wasn't as if she would be going out anywhere for a while. She twisted on the seat so that her feet were on the cushion and her back was against the wooden frame and gingerly turned the pages, breathing in the smell that only such an aged book has. For one moment she could imagine Molly Gibson, the novel's heroine, sitting opposite.

She read for quite some time before her eyes felt tired and she laid the book to one side and closed them. Surely she would sleep tonight, no matter in which bed that might be. Her mind wandered. If only it could be in Adam Wynter's. But there was no chance of that. Especially as Rafe seemed so intent on her and her family going home.

She opened her eyes, hugged her knees to her chest and leant her head on them as she watched rivulets of water cascade down the mullioned windows, running off the red stone sills like mini waterfalls. She shouldn't have, but she couldn't help it. She wished the rain would continue so that Rafe couldn't ask them to leave.

A shadow caught her eye and as she turned her head, Rafe was standing in the doorway, and as usual, he didn't look pleased.

'You look very comfortable.'

She smiled at him. 'I am. I was watching the rain. And I was thinking how beautiful it is.'

'Beautiful? People have had to leave their homes. They may lose much of their furniture and some of their possessions and you think this rain is beautiful?'

'I wasn't talking about the rain. I was talking about your house and the view, so there's no need to get all high and mighty. But I do think the rain is beautiful, actually. Sometimes beautiful things can be destructive. That's just the way it is.'

'That part, you're right about.'

For some reason, she didn't think he was talking about the rain.

'You're so lucky to live here. It must have been wonderful growing up in a place like this.'

His snort of laughter was derisive. 'Wonderful? I certainly wouldn't call it that.'

Neva met his eyes. 'You don't think it's wonderful to be rich? To have servants at your beck and call. To know you'll always have a roof over your head, no matter what. To own a magnificent stately home and to live a life of privilege.'

She hadn't meant to say that and from the look on his face, she shouldn't have.

'A life of privilege. Is that what you think I've had?'

'Well, haven't you?'

He let out an almost inaudible sigh. 'Yes, Neva. Very privileged. I spent my early years in the company of just my nanny. Not Olivia. A paid nanny, who frankly, didn't seem to like me very much.'

'I wonder why.'

Why couldn't she shut up?

His eyes narrowed. 'She didn't like anyone. It wasn't just me. From the age of four, when Adam was born, I had a tutor, and when I was seven, I was shipped off to boarding school in Scotland. Which is where all the Wynter boys for generations have boarded. Adam joined me on his seventh birthday, but we were kept apart, as per Olivia and also our father's wishes. All Wynters must learn to stand on their own two feet. Mother ran off with a count when I was nine, and we haven't seen her since. Shortly after that, our father decided he'd had enough of life's 'privileges' as you call them, and by the time I was ten, he had drunk and drugged himself to death. Yes, Neva, I've had a very privileged life.'

'I'm sorry. I didn't know.'

'Why would you? But perhaps it's best not to assume.'

'At least you inherited this place. And you have Olivia and Adam and a good friend in Sean. That's something, isn't it? Friends and family help get us through anything.'

He ran a hand through his hair and nodded. 'I'm grateful every day for Sean, and Adam and Olivia too. But I inherited my father's mortgages, and his father's before that. I have to open our home to the public and charge them to look around. If my bank balance ever gets into the black, even by a pound, it'll be the first time the Wynters have had money in their account since before the second World War. Gavin, our estate manager has more disposable income than I do. This house may be beautiful but it's a money pit. Something always needs repairing, replacing or rebuilding. Every day, I worry that I may not be able to keep up with it all. So many other families like ours have had to sell. I can't even do that. Not that I would. But the house is tied up in a trust which can't be broken by us. The only way it can be sold is if the banks repossess it and sell it to some foreign investor who'll turn it into a luxury retreat, or worse still, a luxury hotel.' He shook his head and screwed up his eyes as if he had just realised what he'd said. 'Forgive me. I have no idea why I told you that. Self-pity is not a trait I admire. Excuse me. I have things to do.' He turned to walk away.

'Rafe!'

His entire back stiffened noticeably and he drew in a loud, deep breath.

'Yes.'

As he turned around, Neva saw the sadness in his eyes and her heart went out to him for a moment.

'You're right. I shouldn't have assumed. I'm sorry. I can't imagine how awful that must've been, or how hard it must be to deal with all that now. But thank you for sharing it with me. This doesn't help you, but we all have our crosses to bear. Sometimes we need to get things off our chest. It's not self-pity to tell someone that you've been unhappy or that you have worries and fears. And despite everything, you're keeping this place going. You're renting out the cottages. You're opening your home and gardens. You're keeping the wolf from the door. You should be proud of that. I'm sure Adam and Olivia are proud of you.'

He met her look and held it, and there was something in his eyes that sent a strange sensation coursing through her, but his voice was devoid of emotion.

'Are they? That's good to know.'

She had to say something to lighten the mood.

'What you need is a wife. Someone to support you and–'

'A wife is the last thing I need.' His face darkened and so did his tone. 'I had one once. Haven't you heard? I killed her.'

'Did you? I mean I don't believe that for one minute. But ... are you saying it's true?'

He gave another derisive snort. 'You don't believe it, but you're asking if it's true. Thank you for the vote of confidence.'

'Oh, don't be so bloody melodramatic. Either you did or you didn't. If you did, there must've been a reason. You're grumpy and moody and rude, but you're not a maniac and you're definitely not a serial killer. If you didn't, then why on earth would you let people think you did? That's just stupid. And you're not a stupid man, Rafe Wynter. You're arrogant and stubborn and pig-headed but stupid you're definitely not. So get a grip and tell the truth. And no. I don't believe you did. Not even for her money.'

He raised his brows and burst out laughing. 'Money? I wish. If Pippa had had money, I might have been tempted to kill her. But she didn't. She thought I had. That's why she married me. I was in love and I thought she loved me in return. That's why I married her. I was young. I was foolish. I was wrong. It's something I'm trying not to repeat.'

'What happened to her? Is she really dead?'

'She's dead to me. We got married when I was twenty and still at uni. She worked in a local bar. I'm not sure why I fell in love with her. I am sure that she never really loved me. It was a whirlwind romance. Something I'm also trying not to repeat. After uni, we moved back here. Three years later, she'd had an affair and we were discussing divorce. I have no idea where she is now, or if she's alive or not. Although I have no reason to believe she isn't.'

'So ... you're still married?'

Why did that matter? And yet it did.

'No. She was definitely alive five years after she left. She sent me divorce papers which I was more than happy to sign, especially as she made no claims on my estate. Not that there is anything to claim. As I said, the house is tied up in a trust, and there wasn't any cash then either.'

'So how can anyone possibly say you killed her?'

'Because some people like to invent stories about others. Some say I pushed her over the Falls.'

'The Falls? Wyntersleap Falls?'

'Yes.'

'But why would they say that?'

He shrugged. 'Who knows. Perhaps I did. Perhaps everything I just told you is a lie. People do lie, Neva. Especially if there's something that they want.'

'That's utter nonsense. Not the bit about people lying. I know they do. I've had one or two boyfriends who've been very good at that. But the bit about your wife. If I ever hear anyone say that from now on, I'll soon put them in their place. I can't believe you've let this continue.'

'People will always find something to talk about if they've got nothing better to do. It doesn't bother me. As long as the people I care about don't believe it. That's all that matters to me.'

'Well, I don't believe it. Not that I'm suggesting you care about me. I know you don't, of course.'

'What makes you think I don't care about you, Neva?'

There was a strange intonation in his voice and it sent a little quiver through her.

'Yeah right. We both know there's no way you'd ever do that. And if you did, you wouldn't be in such a hurry to get rid of me. You'd want to keep me here for as long as you possibly could.'

His brows knit together. 'Or perhaps I'd want you to leave as quickly as possible because I thought there was a very real danger that I could fall in love with you.'

Had her heart just stopped? She definitely couldn't breathe. She stared at him and he stared right back.

'Ah, there you are!' It was Ethel and Queenie. They tugged Rafe's sleeve, but it was several seconds before he dragged his gaze from Neva.

Chapter Sixteen

Neva had never been more disappointed, and yet at the same time, more relieved, to see anyone as she had been to see Ethel and Queenie at that moment. And as they dragged him off, and he took a final look at Neva, she wasn't sure if she should stay where she was in the hope he might return, or run away as fast as she could and avoid him at all costs.

Had he really just said what she thought he had? That he could easily fall in love with her. But why was that a danger? Because of what happened with Pippa? Or because he didn't think she could feel the same way about him? Which of course, she couldn't.

Could she?

Or was it because he knew that she liked Adam? Ethel had said Neva's eyes were very expressive. Had he seen the way she looked at his younger brother?

And what was she supposed to do now? Could they simply carry on as if he hadn't said that? Would he say anything else? Would he – God forbid – ask her on a date?

He would hardly do that, would he? He'd just told her that his estate manager had more money than he did. If he asked her on a date, it would have to be to somewhere that was free.

But why was she thinking about that? She wouldn't go on a date with him, even if he did pay. It was Adam she was interested in. Adam she wanted to kiss. Adam she rather hoped she might possibly get a chance to do even more than simply kiss. Especially now that they were under the same roof and she could easily go with him to his bedroom and jump into his bed.

The thought of that sent waves of excitement over her. It had been a while since she'd been in anybody's bed other than her own. Alone. Or the bed in the cottage. Alone. Being in Adam's bed would be her Christmas wish come true.

But not if Rafe had his way and sent her home.

And then, before she knew it, she was thinking of Rafe, 'having his way', but it had nothing to do with sending her home. And strangely enough, the thought of being in Rafe's bed made her even more excited.

She pulled out her phone and called Jo.

'Perfecting timing,' Jo said. 'I hope your

Christmas is going better than mine so far. I love Rob. You know I do. But I honestly don't think I can marry him unless we move at least ten thousand miles away from his mum. The damn woman won't give me a minute's peace. And you'll never believe this, Neva, in a million years. The bloody woman has knitted us matching jumpers with, 'I belong to Robert' on mine and 'I belong to Joanna' on his. Let's forget for one moment that no one, and I mean, *no one*, ever calls me Joanna, apart from my own mum, which is one of the reasons I hate Joanna. But also, I'm sorry to burst the bubble, but the only person I belong to, or ever will, is me!'

Neva burst out laughing.

'It's not funny, Neva. That woman needs help.'

'I shouldn't laugh. I'm sorry. But perhaps it was just a joke. You know. One of those awful Christmas jokes that always falls flat or that makes people groan. Maybe she simply has a strange sense of humour. And perhaps Rob hasn't told her about your relationship with your mum. Or that you hate being called Joanna. Why don't you have a word with him and get him to put her straight?'

'That's the other problem. I've been dating this guy for four years. Four years, Neva. And you'd think you'd know a person after spending four years with them, especially as we spend a lot of time together and almost every night. But since his parents have been here, the man has changed.'

'In what way?'

'Well for a start, he's become bone idle. He sits on his arse and Charmaine rushes around after him like a bloody servant. He even asked me to go and get him a beer out of the fridge last night and when I told him, politely, to get up and get the bloody thing himself, he actually looked surprised. And surprise was definitely not the look Charmaine gave me. Then she got up and got it for him. And now his sister has arrived and it was as if she had a personality transformation, the minute she hugged her mum. I'm beginning to think this family is a little weird. I'm telling you now, if this goes on, this is going to be a very short engagement.'

'Are you serious? Are you really saying you're thinking of breaking up with him?'

'Oh, I don't know. It's really hard. On the one hand, I do love him, but on the other, there's my mum and dad. They were in love and look what happened. I'm terrified that'll happen to me. To us.'

'But you're not like them, Jo. And neither is Rob. Although ...'

'Although what?'

'I wasn't going to say anything. And I may be completely wrong. I'm hardly that experienced when it comes to serious relationships. But. Well. He does seem a bit on the possessive side. Just a bit. I get the distinct impression that he's glad we're not living together anymore.'

'It's funny you should say that. I got that impression too. He's even been saying that it's good we won't be seeing so much of one another from now on. I don't know where he got that idea from but it certainly wasn't me.'

'He's right though. We won't. Especially now you're living in Upminster, and I may be living in Merriment Bay.'

'I suppose so. But we'll chat every day, and text and stuff. And we'll see each other regularly. At least once or twice a week, won't we? Which reminds me. Here's me going on about my problems and I haven't asked about you. Have you seen the salon and the flat and are they fab? Are you having a wonderful time in Wyntersleap? Has Tempest caused more havoc? And more importantly, have you got Adam or the lovely Rafe into bed yet?'

'You'll never believe what's been happening here. Since I spoke to you yesterday morning, I almost went on a sort of date with Adam but his brother got in the way. I've insulted Rafe several more times. Met some of the other villagers. Woken up to find the river was flooding the village and been involved in the evacuation.'

'What? The village has flooded? Are you

OK? Was anyone hurt?'

'We're all fine. The water was surprisingly calm, which was odd seeing as the river is a raging torrent. It just sort of crept over the bank and trickled into the village like an incoming tide on a summer's day. It was a really weird experience to say the least. But also a bit frightening because although the flow was gentle, the water was rising pretty fast.'

'Where are you now then? Are you at your parents'?'

'No. Adam told us all to come to Wynter House and Rafe reluctantly agreed even though he didn't seem happy about it. But that was odd too, because when we got here, Rafe had already instructed the butler and other staff to prepare rooms for us all and to light fires etc.'

'Butler? Staff? It sounds like *Downton Abbey*. Is it as grand as it looks in the photos?'

'It's magnificent. The photos don't do it justice. I've met Olivia Wynter, who I think could give Charmaine a run for her money. I've spent a couple of hours in a bed that dates back to Tudor times, but sadly, alone. I've been served breakfast by the staff and I'm currently sitting on a window seat in the library where I've been reading a copy of *Wives and Daughters* that I think has actually been signed by Mrs Gaskell herself. Oh, and I think, but I'm not entirely sure, that Rafe Wynter may have just told me that he thinks he could easily be in danger of falling in love with me.'

'W-what? He said that? When? Why? What were you doing at the time? Tell me everything. Wait. You said "danger". I know you're a bit of a weirdo sometimes, but why would falling in love with you be a danger?'

'Because he doesn't want to fall in love ever again, it seems. He was married when he was twenty and it was a big mistake. She had an affair soon after, and left. They got divorced but some people think he killed her. Don't ask. It's all rather silly. But anyway, marriage is definitely not on his radar.'

'Wow! That's so romantic.'

'Romantic? What's romantic about him not wanting to fall in love and get married? I think it's rather sad.'

'It is sad. But that's what makes it romantic. He's fighting his feelings. But he'll be overcome and he'll pull you into his arms and kiss you passionately and tell you that he can't live without you and beg you to be his wife and have his children and live happily ever after.'

'Yeah, right. I don't think so. Besides, I'm not sure he's the passionate type. Or romantic. Angry? Yes. Rude? Yes. Passionate and romantic? Hmm. I'm not so sure. Although he did say he fell in love with his wife pretty fast. But he also said it was a mistake and one he won't make again.'

'He sounds like he's putting up barriers.

Like he's trying to be tough and he doesn't want to risk getting hurt again. Maybe deep down there's a soft side to him.'

'He did tell me things I think he later wished he hadn't. I assumed he'd had a fantastic childhood, living here in the lap of luxury. It seems he didn't. I may be wrong, but I think he's very sad. And lonely in a way. I had no idea how hard it is to keep a place like this going and he's burdened with so many responsibilities that, in my opinion, are crushing him. I'm not sure he knows how to just have fun. He spends his days and probably his nights, worrying about this place and I hadn't realised, but it must be awful to have to open your home, no matter how huge it may be, to paying guests when you clearly don't want to. Anyway, my problem is I'm not interested in him. It's Adam I fancy. Although there's something about Rafe that makes me think he'd be bloody fantastic in bed. But if Rafe really was saying he likes me, and I now go and jump in bed with his younger brother, which I will given half a chance, that's only going to make Rafe even sadder.'

'I hate to break this to you, Neva, but I don't think that's your problem. From what you've just told me, your problem is that there's a very real possibility you might be falling in love with the other brother. And I don't mean Adam.'

'Rafe? Are you suggesting I might be falling for Rafe? You're crazy, Jo. I can assure you I'm not.'

'Can you? I wouldn't be so sure.'

'Well, I *am* sure. But it doesn't make much difference because as Rafe wants us to leave, I won't get a chance to do anything with either brother, let alone fall in love.'

'So you're leaving?'

'Once the rain eventually stops and providing the roads are OK, we'll be leaving later today.'

'Oh no. I hope you don't. I hope you get to stay. I believe that you going to Wyntersleap might be the best thing that's ever happened. And after a few more days, I think Rafe Wynter will feel the same.'

'Adam Wynter, Jo. Adam's the one I like. Not Rafe. Rafe's nice in his way, but he's not the man for me.'

'OK. You keep telling yourself that. Oh hell. Charmaine is on her way. She's like a bloody guided missile and she's definitely got me permanently in her sights. Call me again tomorrow or tonight if you do have to go home. I need to know what's happening. And Neva?'

'Yes, Jo.'

'I know you think you fancy Adam. But sometimes we fall in love with the last person we ever thought we would. Plus, lust and love are two completely different things. Remember that. As you've always asked my advice, even if you don't always take it, listen to this piece of Jo's dating wisdom. Give poor Rafe a chance. He sounds like he could do with a woman like you, and from the way you talk about him, he could well be the man for you.'

Chapter Seventeen

By 1.p.m. the temperature had dropped and the torrential rain had turned to hailstones. Lumps of ice the size of golf balls pelted the windows and bounced on the lawns. Within the space of half an hour, the ground was covered with a layer of lumpy white ice.

'Ah, there you are, sweetheart,' Dennis said, as Neva gingerly came down the stairs into the hall.

Since speaking to Jo she had hidden herself in the bedroom she'd had earlier. She hadn't wanted to bump into Rafe again and she didn't know where else to go.

'Hi, Dad. Have you seen the weather? It sounds like a herd of reindeer are stampeding around the grounds.'

'I don't think I've ever seen anything like this. But I do have one bit of good news. I saw Rafe a short time ago and, due to the worsening weather, he thinks it's best if we stay. At least for tonight. Although he didn't look as if the prospect pleased him.'

Neva's stomach did an odd little flip. It was probably because she was hungry.

'I don't suppose it did. Um. Did you offer to pay extra?'

Dennis frowned. 'I did. But that seemed to make him even more irritable and he said the strangest thing.'

Her stomach flipped again. 'Oh.' She cleared her throat. 'What was that?'

'That he didn't know what you had told me, but he didn't take advantage of people just because he could. What do you think he meant by that?'

Neva flushed and her heart thumped in her chest. Oh great. Now the bloody man thought she'd run off and told her family everything he had said.

'I have no idea. Where're Mum and the others?'

'In the dining room. Apparently there's soup and fresh bread for lunch. Although it doesn't seem five minutes since we all sat down to breakfast.'

'Tell my tummy that. It's doing the strangest things. Aren't you having any?'

'Yes. I came out to look for Sasha. Have you seen her?'

'Not since shortly after breakfast. She was

here, searching for the secret panel the last time I saw her.'

'Oh dear. I wonder what mischief she's getting up to now. At least she doesn't have Tempest with her.'

'Where's Tempest then?'

Dennis grinned. 'Having puppy training. You remember that man George we saw this morning?'

'The one who'd turned Persephone from a hissing, spitting, wild thing into a ball of contented fluff?'

Dennis laughed. 'That's the one. It seems he has a way with animals. We were chatting to him earlier and he offered to give Tempest some training. It was far too good an opportunity to miss.'

'Wow.' Neva nudged his arm. 'Maybe he can do something with Sasha too. I wonder where she is then?'

'At least we know she's nowhere near the river. She won't have gone outside because of the weather. This house is huge. She must be wandering the corridors.'

'She'll come back when she smells food, or when she gets hungry. I wouldn't worry about her. I don't think she can come to much harm here.'

'It's not her I'm worried about. It's the house. Some of these antiques are priceless.'

Neva laughed. 'Should we send out a

search party then?'

Dennis glanced along the hall and then towards the dining room. 'If she was going to do any damage, she probably would've done it by now. You're right. She'll come back when she gets hungry. Besides,' Dennis added, with a laugh, 'she's not my child. Rowan and Nigel can foot the bill.'

'That's the spirit, Dad.'

They walked arm in arm into the dining room and joined the rest of the family who were seated across from one another on the chairs closest to the door. Nigel sat opposite Rowan and Dawn, so Neva sat beside her sister and Dennis sat next to Nigel.

'Where's everyone else?' Neva asked.

'They've already eaten,' Nigel said. 'We're the last ones.'

Rowan beamed at Neva. 'Have you heard the good news?'

'Yes. Tempest is being trained. And we've lost Sasha.'

'Oh very funny.' Rowan rolled her eyes. 'We can stay.'

'Oh that. Yes. Can life get any better?'

'What's up with you?'

'Sorry. I'm a bit out of sorts. Nothing a Baileys or three won't cure, but I suppose it's a bit early for that.' She looked at her family in mock horror. 'Please tell me we saved the Baileys from the flood.'

'Now who sounds like an alcoholic?' Dennis said.

'It's wonderful though, isn't it?' Dawn ladled soup into bowls for Dennis and Neva, from the large tureen sitting on a hot plate on the table. 'That we can stay here, I mean. Even if it's only for tonight. You should see this place, sweetheart. Why didn't you want to take a look around? It's most unlike you not to want to take advantage of such an opportunity.'

Neva shrugged. 'I just wanted some time alone.'

'I think you spend far too much time alone. What you need is to find yourself a nice young man.'

Rowan laughed. 'Men aren't the answer to everything, you know, Mum. Although she has got her eyes on the delectable Adam. And if she's plays her cards right, she could be staying here for more than just one—'

'Rafe!' Dennis leapt to his feet, his face redder than the tomato soup in the bowl his wife held out to him. 'Anything we can help you with?'

Neva closed her eyes, praying the ground would open up and swallow her. He might not have been there long but knowing her luck, he probably heard every word of Rowan's comment. She could imagine the expression on his face.

'I think you already have.' His voice held a

cold, hard, sarcastic note. 'I wanted to check that you have everything you need because we're going to the village, so there won't be anyone around to assist you.'

'No. We're fine, thanks. There's nothing we need. But you said you're going to the village? In this weather? Is that to move more of people's belongings?'

'No. We've finished moving those. At least as many as we can. That's been going on all morning. Now, despite these hailstones, we're going to move the remaining stock from Roger's shop and the barrels from Sean's pub. We were hoping the water wouldn't reach that far, but it's almost there, so I've got to dash. Please make yourselves at home.'

'We can help,' Dennis offered.

'Yeah.' Nigel got up. 'I'll grab my coat.'

'I can't expect you to do that. This weather's horrendous and the barrels are heavy.'

'We're builders,' Nigel said. 'We're used to bad weather and lifting heavy things. It's the least we can do after what you've done for us.'

'Grab my coat too please, Nigel,' Neva said, getting to her feet. 'There's room in my car. I can't fit a barrel in it but I can help with the stock from the shop. Although not fresh food because I've got chemicals in my boot.'

Rafe gave her an odd look as he was turning to leave.

'I'm a hairdresser,' she added.

'I know.' He looked away. 'I think it's best if you stay here.'

'Why? I'm a builder's daughter. I'm stronger than I look.'

'I don't doubt it.' He didn't turn to check.

'Me too,' said Rowan. 'And here's a newsflash, Rafe. Women are just as capable as men.'

'True. Then join us when you're ready.' He was halfway to the door. 'But please be careful, and make sure you each take one of our umbrellas. They're heavy but they're made from stronger fabric.'

Dawn got to her feet but Rowan shook her head. 'Will you stay here please, Mum? I don't want Sasha to panic when she finally reappears and finds we're not around.'

'Of course. And perhaps I'd better go and see if I can find her.'

Neva suggested that Rowan should go with her, as they would both be helping at the shop and they, together with Dennis and Nigel in their cars, weren't far behind Rafe and the rest of the vehicles returning to the village.

The water had risen, but not as much as Neva had expected, although it was creeping along the street and trickling into the cottages and, as Rafe had said, getting very close to the pub. If the barrels were in a cellar, surely it would be too late? But perhaps the pub didn't have a cellar. They wouldn't be trying to save them unless they thought they could.

'Aren't barrels sealed?' Rowan asked as they pulled up in front of the shop.

'Yes. But I think they need to be kept at a certain temperature and I expect there're probably regulations that state if barrels are submerged in water the beer can't be drunk, or some such ludicrous thing.'

A tall man, possibly in his fifties and holding an umbrella, came out from the shop doorway to meet them. Once they were all inside the rather bijou shop, he smiled.

'You must be Neva. And Rowan. Rafe's just told me you've offered to lend a hand. I'm Roger. Penny's husband. You might have met her earlier. She's the cook up at the house.'

'I saw her, I think,' Neva said. 'But we weren't introduced. Sorry we're meeting under such circumstances, Roger. What can we do to help?'

'I've packed up most of the boxes and got as many as I can in my car, so it's just ferrying the remaining ones to yours, if that's OK.'

Neva explained about the chemicals and he said that it was just as well he'd taken all the perishables first. It was only tinned foods left.

They took it in turns for one of them to hold the umbrella over another who carried a box out to the car, while the other moved the remaining boxes nearer to the door. It took less than half an hour to clear the entire shop. But that was only because Roger, and no doubt some of the others, had cleared so many boxes earlier.

'I'll be back in a second,' Neva said, grabbing one of the umbrellas they'd brought with them from Wynter House, and dashing back to their rental cottage, splashing through a couple of inches of water on the way. The door was still unlocked and when she pushed it open, the beautiful wood floors were beneath an inch or so of water too, but to her surprise the thing that she was looking for, had gone.

'If you're looking for your tree,' a voice said from behind her, 'we took it earlier.'

She turned and smiled at Adam. 'You did? In all the rush, we completely forgot about it. I came and unplugged the lights and I meant to come back and pack the decorations. Some of them are old and have a sentimental value.'

'That's what we thought.' He returned her smile. 'We went through all the properties just after breakfast to see what else could be moved out of harm's way. We managed to save a few more items of furniture for Ethel and Queenie and one or two of the others, and also a few Christmas trees. Although I'm not sure we know whose is whose.'

'Dad picked up the tree from B&Q on his way here, so we're not attached to that. It's really just the decorations, and we'll recognise those as soon as we see them. But did you really stand here and take them all off?'

He nodded. 'We did. And nothing was broken, you'll be pleased to hear.'

'We? You had some help? Please say thank you to whoever it was. It was really very kind.'

'I shall. But unless there's anything else here we missed, I think we should get back.'

'There's nothing else.'

He stood aside to let her pass and she reopened her umbrella and held it over both of them as Adam locked the door.

'I don't think we need to worry about vandalism here in Wyntersleap, but it's better to be safe than sorry. Now that we've moved everything we possibly can, I don't think we'll be back until the water eventually recedes. If this weather continues, that may not be for some time.'

'I can't believe these hailstones.'

'I know. But at least one good thing has come out of it.' He carefully took the umbrella from her, making sure it sheltered her the entire time. Then he linked her arm through his and smiled down at her. 'It means you're going to be staying. And I'm very pleased about that.'

He wasn't the only one.

Chapter Eighteen

'We can't find Sasha anywhere.' Dawn looked terrified as Neva and Rowan carried boxes into the hall. 'We know she can't have gone far, but we have no idea where else to look.' She glanced at Judith, and the woman and teenage girl, Neva had seen at breakfast.

'Well, she must be somewhere.' Rowan dumped her boxes on the floor and hurried over to Dawn. 'She definitely didn't go out. The house is huge. Perhaps you just kept missing her. You know, while she was in one corridor, you were in another.'

'That's what we thought, but we've called and called. George even brought Tempest in to see if she could sniff her out, but all she wanted to do was chase around in here and scratch at the wood panelling. And we couldn't let her do that, so he's taken her into the staff sitting room with Boris and Duchess.'

'Mum. You're rambling,' Rowan said.

'You're right, sweetheart. I'm sorry. I'm all of a dither today.'

Judith stepped forward and smiled. 'I'm sure there's nothing to worry about. We'll find her very soon, you'll see. And now that all the others are returning, we can enlist their help. I know it's easy for me to say, but please try not to panic. She can't come to serious harm here.'

'Unless she's fallen down a flight of stairs. Or out of a window. Or off the roof!' Rowan's pitch increased with each syllable.

Neva took Rowan's hand in hers. 'She won't have done any of those things. But what she might be doing, is hiding.'

'Hiding? Why would she be hiding?'

'What's wrong?' Nigel dumped what he was carrying and ran to Rowan the second he walked through the door.

'We can't find Sasha. Mum and these people have been searching for her and she's nowhere to be found. But Neva thinks she's hiding.'

'What's this?' Rafe strode towards them, a serious expression on his face.

'It's Sasha,' Nigel said. 'She's vanished.'

Rafe shot a look at Judith. 'Is this true?'

Judith nodded. 'We've searched every room in the house and she's nowhere to be seen.'

'The attics?'

Judith nodded. 'Everywhere.'

'I think she may be hiding,' Neva said.

Rafe frowned at her. 'Why would she do that?'

'Because for one thing, she's eight. And for another, she made it pretty clear she didn't want to leave today.'

'But you're not leaving.'

'No. But Sasha doesn't know that.'

His brows knit together. 'I told your father before lunch.'

'But no one's seen Sasha since just after breakfast.'

The frown turned into a scowl. 'You mean the child's been missing for several hours and no one thought to mention it?'

'Look. This hasn't exactly been a normal day. We thought she'd be safe here.'

'You said yourself, she's eight.'

'Stop arguing and do something!' Rowan yelled. 'My baby's missing and we need to find her.'

'We'll find her. I assure you.' Rafe turned on his heel and marched towards the front door. 'Archie!' He boomed out commands while he waited. 'Judith. Get everyone together and search the house again from top to bottom. The attics, the cellars. Would she have ventured outside in this weather? No? But check anyway. Search the gardens. The sheds. She may have gone to see the chickens or the ducks. What would interest an eight-year-old?'

'Sasha's not your average eight-year-old,' Neva said, 'so I wouldn't go by that.'

Panic shot over Rafe's face. 'There's one place she might ...' His voice trailed off as he dashed towards the front door, bumping into Carruthers on the way. 'There you are. The child's missing. Find her, will you? I'm going to the old barn, just in case she went there.'

'The old barn. Oh I do hope not.' One eyebrow went up and one went down, much farther than they had before, Neva couldn't help but notice.

What on earth was in the old barn? A vicious dog? A wild animal? Dangerous machinery?

'Wait for me. I'm coming with you.'

Rafe spun round. 'No, you're not! No one goes to the old barn except me. It's off-limits.'

Neva grabbed a brolly and ran after him but the hail suddenly stopped. 'May I remind you, there's a missing eight-year-old? Nowhere should be off-limits.'

He stopped so abruptly, she ran past him, and she skidded to a halt and turned to face him. He was scowling so hard, she thought he might actually growl.

'And may I remind *you* that this is *my* house and you're a guest. If she's in the old barn, I'll find her. Go back to the house right now.'

Neva's mouth fell open as he marched off, but although she wanted to chase after him, there was something about his tone and his entire demeanour that made her do as he said. She ran back to the house as fast as she could.

Inside it was now pandemonium. Even more so than when they evacuated the village earlier. People were dashing everywhere, calling Sasha's name. Neva ran upstairs and searched their bedrooms. Perhaps she was under the bed, or was hiding in a wardrobe. Or ... 'Oh. My. God!' She said out loud. That was it. It must be.

She ran back downstairs, yelling George's name. 'George? George? Ah, Ethel. Have you seen George? Where's the staff sitting room? He may be there. I need to find him and Tempest.'

'It's along the corridor and down the back stairs and ... oh there he is. And he's got the puppy.'

'Sorry it took me so long,' George said, hurrying in a lopsided fashion. 'I'm not as fast as I was.'

'Don't worry. I just need Tempest. Thank you,' she said as he handed her the lead. 'And Carruthers. I need Carruthers. Or better still, Adam or Rafe.'

'Adam's out searching the grounds with Gavin and Sean,' Ethel said. 'I saw Carruthers going to the cellars.'

'I'll get Carruthers, miss,' George said. 'And if I see Mr Adam or Mr Rafe I'll tell them you need them.'

Neva let Tempest off the lead. The puppy belted over to the walls and started scratching the panelling, just as Neva expected. She grabbed the lead and hugged the puppy tight.

'You're such a clever puppy. Ah! There you are!' She jumped up as Rafe strode back in, at the same time as Carruthers, but from opposite directions. 'She's in the wall. Don't look at me as if I'm mad. Watch this.'

She let go of the lead and once more, Tempest ran and scratched the wood. Rafe didn't look pleased at all, but suddenly, he smiled and Neva grabbed Tempest again.

'But how did she find the release?'

Neva shrugged. 'No idea. But I bet you that's where she is.'

He dashed to the panelling, reached up high and pressed a delicately carved rose. A panel clicked open and Rafe stepped inside, flicking a switch so that a light came on. Neva and Carruthers followed him in.

'Watch your step,' Rafe said. 'The ground's a bit uneven and the ceiling is low in places.'

'That's more of a problem for you two. I'm only five-foot-four. But what I don't understand is why she couldn't hear them all calling her. And you said this is a short cut to your bedroom. If that's the case, why didn't she come out the other side? Unless she stayed in here on purpose.'

'What I don't understand is how she reached that rose. Hopefully, we'll soon find out. But there's more than one passage in here, and only lighting in one of them. If she's in one of the others we'll need a torch. I've got my phone. Have you got yours?'

'Yes,' Neva said.

'As do I,' said Carruthers.

They reached a fork in the passageway and Rafe pointed ahead.

'Archie, you take that one. We'll go this way. Yell, if you find her.'

Carruthers veered off to the left and Neva followed Rafe as the passage sloped downwards.

'It forks again a little farther on. You take the one that leads up to my bedroom and I'll take the other one.'

'Where does that one lead?'

'That doesn't matter. She can't have gone out there because there's a gate and it's locked. I'm the only one with a key. Apart from Archie.'

Why was he being so secretive about the other passageway? She wasn't sure she wanted to go to his bedroom. Perhaps she should ask to stay with him. But that was silly. It was only a room for goodness sake.

'Right. You go that way. The lights go all the way up, but you may still need your torch. I know the way like the back of my hand but as someone who's never been here before, it may be difficult to keep your footing. Yell, if she's there and I'll do the same if I find her.'

'Rafe!'

'Yes, Neva.'

'What if I'm wrong? What if she's not here? She would've had to climb on a chair to reach that rose.'

He reached out suddenly and touched her cheek. 'I'm sure she's here. But if she isn't, we'll find her, Neva. Wherever she is.'

And then he was gone and all she could see was the beam of the torch on his phone.

She followed the passageway and began calling Sasha's name, her heart sinking more with every step. Even if Sasha was hiding, she would've come out by now. She'd been gone for several hours. And then, as she turned a corner in the passage, her heart skipped a beat.

'Sasha! Sasha!'

Oh God. Her niece was dead. She was curled up in what looked like a wooden chair set in the wall to one side of the passage.

Sasha's eyes shot open as Neva shook her. 'Neva!' Sasha yawned and stretched. 'What time is it? I'm hungry.' She pulled her ear buds from her ears and smiled.

Neva didn't know whether to laugh or cry; so she did both. And she cuddled her niece so tight that Sasha yelled to be let go.

'Oh,' Sasha said, glancing around her. 'I'm still in here.'

'Yes. And everyone is worried sick. What the hell were you doing? Why didn't you answer when they called?'

'I had my ear buds in.' She yawned again. 'I found the catch by poking the walls with an umbrella, and got in. But then I couldn't get out because I left the umbrella outside and the catch was too high for me to reach. I walked all over the place but one gate was locked, and this one must have another secret catch thing but I can't find it and can't reach up high. I did call out but no one heard so I came back up here because this part has this sort of chair in the wall. And then I suppose I fell asleep. I did try to call and text but I couldn't get a signal.'

'Weren't you scared?'

Sasha shrugged. 'No. I knew someone would find me. But I need to pee, and I'm cold. And I really am hungry. Can we get out now please?'

'Yes. Yes of course. Rafe! Carruthers! She's here. She's safe!'

Chapter Nineteen

Neva smiled as Rafe marched Sasha into his bedroom and showed her to his en suite, closing the door behind her and informing her that Neva would wait for her and that he would be outside in the hall, to show them the way downstairs. Neva was about to say she was perfectly capable of finding her own way, but in a house the size of this, she probably wasn't. He wouldn't be pleased if he had to send out a search party for her too.

Carruthers had been sent to tell Rowan and Nigel and everyone else that Sasha was safe and sound, and as soon as Rafe closed his bedroom door behind him, Neva took the opportunity to have a look around. She couldn't wait to tell Jo she had been in Rafe Wynter's bedroom – even if it wasn't to have sex.

It was similar to her room in a way, but

more masculine with dark wood furniture, and the bed coverings and matching soft furnishings were all a deep midnight blue. The wood panelling was also dark as was the wood floor but when she crept over to his bed and gingerly sat on the edge, she glanced up at the ceiling which was ablaze with beauty and colour.

Like Rafe's, her own bedroom ceiling had once been a mass of stars and planets, but she was twelve at the time and into astronomy, and hers were nothing like his. Her planets and stars were stick on, peel off; these were painted, and by the detail and sheer beauty of the workmanship, possibly by Michelangelo, or someone of a similar ilk. Imagine going to bed each night and looking up at something as beautiful as this. Except would you see it properly with the four-poster canopy in the way?

She couldn't help herself. She laid back on his bed, and almost shrieked with delight. Instead of swathes of silk which were on the underneath of the canopy over the bed she had been given to sleep in, this one had the same painting as the ceiling, only scaled down to size. She lay there mesmerised and only heard Sasha's voice as if in the distance.

'I'm ready, Neva. Let's go downstairs. I'm starving. Are you coming?'

'Yes. Just give me a second.'

But she heard Rafe's voice loud and clear when Sasha opened his bedroom door and he obviously saw Neva lying on his bed.

'Are you quite comfortable?'

Neva sat bolt upright, nearly tumbling off the high mattress, and scrambled to her feet in a most ungainly fashion, her face burning and her heart pounding.

'I'm so, so sorry. I was looking at the ceiling and when I saw how beautiful it was, I had to lie down to see if you could see it from the bed. The canopy blew me away. I'd love to sleep in that bed every night and wake up to that every morning.'

He raised one eyebrow and a slight curve appeared on his lips but it was gone in a second and a grim line took its place.

'Adam's bed has one similar. Now if you don't mind, we should go downstairs. Please close the door behind you.'

He didn't wait for her but he clearly expected her to follow immediately and she hurried to the door, taking one final look around as she closed it. That would no doubt be the last look she would ever get of Rafe Wynter's bedroom. And what was pretty obvious by his comment was that he had definitely heard what Rowan had said about Neva fancying Adam.

She followed behind him and Sasha as if she were a servant. For someone who had been locked in a dimly lit secret passage for several hours, Sasha was full of beans, bouncing up and down as she skipped along the hall trying to keep apace with Rafe.

'Will you show me where all the catches are, please so that next time I can get out by myself.'

'No. Because there won't be a next time. Those passages may look like fun but they were there for a serious reason. And they're dangerous if you're not sure of your footing. Please don't go in there again unless you're with me or Archie.'

'Who's Archie?'

'The butler. You should call him Carruthers.'

'Why? If his name's Archie, I'll call him that.'

'No. He would rather you called him Carruthers.'

'That's silly. Why's that gate at the end of the long passageway locked? Is there secret treasure behind it?'

'Not the type you mean. But it is off-limits, so I'd rather not discuss it.'

'Why? Ooh! Is that where you buried your wife?'

He stopped so abruptly that Neva almost crashed into his back. He darted a look at her before narrowing his eyes at Sasha.

'Who told you I buried my wife

somewhere?'

'Gramps. Cecil and Ronnie told him but he doesn't like gossip so he was rude to them. And Neva told them I had a disease.' She giggled. 'Did you kill her? Did she scream? Does her ghost haunt this house? I'd love to see a ghost. Is she mean or does she weep all the time? I'm going to be a ghost hunter when I grow up. And I'm going to kill vampires and zombies too.'

A sudden burst of laughter escaped him and he made a growling sound and held out his arms from his sides.

'Well, little one. I'm a vampire and I bet you can't kill me.'

He swept Sasha up and marched down the hall as she twisted and turned and screamed with delight in his arms.

Rowan appeared at the end of the hall with Nigel and Carruthers and gave Rafe a look of abject horror.

'What are you doing to my child!'

'He's a vampire, Mummy and he thinks I can't kill him, but I can. Just you wait and see.' Sasha laughed so loud that even Rowan burst into a smile.

Rafe immediately set her on her feet. 'I apologise. I don't think I frightened her, but I'm sorry if I worried you.'

Rowan let out a sigh 'No, Rafe. It's me who should apologise. When I heard her scream, I thought ... Well, you know. I was worried to death we'd never find her. I'm so sorry we've put you all through this. Carruthers says she had got herself locked in the secret passage.' She frowned at Sasha who had grabbed Rafe's hand. 'You're so naughty. Do you know the trouble you've caused? Come here at once and apologise to Rafe.'

Sasha shot a look at Rafe. 'Are you cross with me? I didn't get locked in on purpose. I'm sorry. Please let us stay. I love it here. I'll be good from now on, I promise.'

He smiled at her. 'You are going to stay. At least for tonight. But please remember what I said. Next time, ask me or Carruthers.'

Sasha's eyes were the size of saucers. 'We're staying? Yippee!' She jumped up and down and her curls danced around her face as she ran to Rowan. 'Mummy we're staying. I'm very hungry. May I have something to eat?'

'If I may,' Carruthers said, his back straight, his face deadly serious. 'Afternoon tea will be served in the drawing room shortly, now that Miss Sasha is safe.'

Neva couldn't help herself. She suddenly burst out laughing.

Carruthers did the usual thing with his brows and looked from her to Rafe as if wondering what was so funny.

'I'm sorry. It's been a very strange day.'

'You're not kidding,' said Rowan, hugging Sasha tight. 'That's the understatement of the year.'

Neva walked past Rafe, briefly meeting his eyes, and went downstairs with Rowan and the others. Rafe and Carruthers followed close behind. She couldn't hear what they were saying but they were whispering intently about something.

Judith was waiting at the foot of the main staircase and she showed them to the drawing room where Dawn and Dennis and everyone else were all seated on chairs and sofas, some of which had clearly been brought in from another room to allow for the additional seating required.

There was a roaring fire in the hearth; another grand fireplace and a mantle decorated with Christmas greenery. A tree as large as the one in the grand hall and as equally stunning was positioned near the window. Were those presents also fake? The ones beneath the other trees were. Where did the Wynters have their own tree and were there real presents piled beneath that? But hadn't Ethel said the only decorations were the ones on display for the paying visitors?

Neva perched on the arm of a sofa, next to her mum but when she saw the look Olivia Wynter gave her, she squeezed in beside Dawn instead, Dennis and the others shifting along to make room for her. She was surprised to see Olivia there, sitting in an armchair close to the fire, looking every bit the matriarch. She hadn't seen her since they had arrived, even with all the commotion going on.

The woman and the teenager who always seemed to appear with food, apart from when they were searching for Sasha, brought two trolleys in, piled high with cakes and sandwiches, exceedingly well displayed. There were pots of coffee, tea and hot chocolate. No wonder Rafe Wynter didn't have any money in the bank. If he continued catering for everyone like this, he'd increase his chances of losing Wynter House tenfold. Or perhaps it was compulsory for families such as the Wynters to go overboard when entertaining guests. Except none of the people here were really guests; they were here as a result of circumstance, not a friendly invitation to spend the Christmas holidays.

'It's time I made some introductions,' Rafe said, 'now that we've done everything we can in the village, and Sasha is safe and well.' He threw Sasha a small but friendly smile. 'Would you all be good enough to give a little wave when I say your name so that anyone who doesn't know who you are can at least put a name to a face? First, our holidaymakers, Dawn and Dennis, their daughters, Neva and Rowan. Rowan's husband Nigel and their daughter, Sasha.' He held out a hand to indicate who each of them was as he said their names and they each waved as he had asked. 'Olivia, Adam and I, you all know. Judith, our right-hand woman, even though she's currently standing to my left.'

Everyone chuckled appropriately, even more so when Judith hurried around him, stood to his right, waved like the Queen and gave a beaming and over-the-top smile.

Rafe grinned. 'I think you can see why we value her so. Carruthers, our butler without whom Wynter House couldn't function. And who's giving us a small bow instead of a wave, as any self-respecting butler would. Gavin, our estate manager and so much more besides. George, who lives in the village but formerly held Gavin's position and still comes to help out whenever we need him. Ethel and Queenie, both treasured former employees and now residents of Wyntersleap. Penny, our excellent cook, whom I thank wholeheartedly for rising to the challenge and keeping us fed and watered so wonderfully today.'

Applause stopped Rafe in his flow and everyone cheered until Penny gave a little curtsy, blushing profusely at such adoration.

'Her husband, Roger,' Rafe continued, 'who owns the village shop and stocks such a variety of goods that we seldom need to go elsewhere. Wendy and Sean who own the Wyntersleap Inn, one of our favourite places. Their exceptional daughter, Taryn, who helps with anything we need around this house, entertaining us with her sensational singing in the process. Today, she has been even more invaluable by pitching in and helping Penny.'

More applause, together with encouragement for Taryn to 'give us a tune' from Ethel and Queenie. Taryn smiled, glanced at Rafe, and when he nodded, she burst into the most beautiful rendition of 'Good King Wenceslas' which given the circumstances was rather appropriate in a way. Rafe was right. Taryn had a sensational voice. She should audition for the X-Factor. She'd knock it out of the park.

'And last but not least, Cecil and Ronnie, fairly new additions to Wyntersleap, but nevertheless, most welcome. I hope I haven't forgotten anyone.'

'He does go on, doesn't he?' Adam teased, strolling towards Rafe and giving him a pat on the back.

Rafe smiled good-naturedly. 'And I haven't finished yet. Drinks will be served in here at 8 p.m. this evening, and dinner in the dining room at 8.30 p.m. As it's not a formal affair, please don't feel the need to dress for dinner, unless you wish to of course. And now that we've all been properly introduced, Olivia, Adam, the staff and I will start planning how we're going to be spending Christmas. It's Christmas Eve the day after tomorrow, and as you all know, other than the Christmas Eve staff party, we usually spend the holiday quietly. With so many people staying here, we'll need to sort a few things out. If you have any thoughts or suggestions, please tell Judith, Carruthers, Adam or myself. Right. Now I've finished.'

More applause, above which Ethel yelled, 'You may regret saying that, young Rafe.' She smacked her toothless gums together and chuckled so hard her tea slopped into her saucer.

Chapter Twenty

Neva was surprised when Adam came and sat beside her at dinner. Once again, she had made a bit of an effort and she had seen him cast an admiring glance in her direction over his cocktail glass during drinks in the drawing room. She was fairly certain he'd say hello at the very least but until now, he hadn't done so.

'You're looking lovely this evening. May I sit beside you?'

'It's your house,' she said with a smile. 'But yes. I'd like that very much.'

He grinned at her. 'Legally it's not. But that's unimportant. I wanted to come over earlier but Cecil and Ronnie looked so intense, I'm afraid I chickened out. Were they telling you some awful story about the things we Wynters get up to?'

'No,' she lied. 'We were discussing how generous and thoughtful you've all been.' She was hardly going to tell him that, despite the fact they had been given shelter in Wynter House, they still thought Rafe was 'shady'.

'How else could he afford to do all this?' Cecil had said. 'And have you seen these decorations? The Ritz wouldn't turn their noses up at these.' He flicked his finger against a beautiful glass bauble hanging on the Christmas tree.

'They have tours of the house and gardens,' Neva said, bristling at their ungracious behaviour. 'And they let the cottages.'

'And charge an arm and a leg for the privilege,' Ronnie hastened to add. 'But this place must cost a small fortune to run and that wouldn't even pay to heat the place. The fire in our bedroom has been burning since the moment we arrived.'

'And you should be grateful for that, Ronnie. Not casting aspersions.'

He bridled at her rebuke but it didn't stop either of them. 'Well, he and Sean are as thick as thieves. And I wouldn't be surprised if they were.'

'Thieves? You're calling Rafe and Sean thieves?' Neva glowered at them. 'I'll have you know that Rafe worries day and night about keeping this place going. He hasn't had things easy and you spreading rumours about him killing his wife doesn't help. And he didn't you know. She left and they're divorced. She's probably also enjoying Christmas cocktails somewhere right now. You really shouldn't talk about people unless you have something nice to say. It's not endearing, and it's not right.'

'Well, excuse us,' Cecil said. 'But we heard him say that you couldn't go to the old barn with him this afternoon because it's off-limits and no one's allowed there but him. Doesn't that make you wonder what he's trying to hide?'

It did, but she wasn't going to admit that to them.

'No. It makes me realise that I'm in someone else's home and I must respect their privacy. You seem to be forgetting that Rafe didn't have to let you come here. He could've told you to find somewhere else to stay. I would have. Rafe deserves credit for that. Not you two finding shady goings on where there are none. Now if you'll excuse me, I'm going to talk to Ethel and Queenie. At least they appreciate what Rafe and the Wynters have done for them, even if you don't.'

She had left them both open-mouthed and stormed over to the ladies who were sitting on the sofa laughing and giggling like girls.

'You look cross, dear,' Ethel said.

'I am. Those two are still slagging off Rafe, but they're happy enough to take his hospitality, eat his food and drink his drinks. Why do some people have to be so nasty?'

'Some people can't help it,' Queenie said. 'And sometimes life throws things at them and they feel angry and hurt and that makes them lash out at other people. We never know what makes another person who they are.'

'Still going on about him killing his wife?' Ethel asked.

'Yes. But not only that. They seem to think he's up to something with Sean. Oh. Not like that. Something shady, I mean. They don't know how he affords all this.' She waved her arm in the air.

'By working hard, making good investments and even better business decisions, I should think,' said Queenie. 'Luckily for him, and for us all, Rafe takes after his grandfather, Sebastian, not his father, Phillip.'

'Does he have a job? Other than running this place?'

Queenie shook her head. 'No. He did for a time. Some hot shot position in the City. But Wynter House is a demanding mistress. She wanted his attention full time.'

'That must cramp his love life.'

Neva fiddled with her glass, suddenly wishing she hadn't said that, especially as Ethel chuckled and winked at her.

'Got ideas in that direction, eh? I thought so. But I don't blame you. I'd be falling at his feet if I were a few years younger.'

'No. I like Adam.'

And she really wished she hadn't said that.

Ethel narrowed her eyes. 'You sure?' She shrugged. 'He's lovely too. But there's something about young Rafe.' She smacked her gums together. 'Something in those eyes. That smile. Not that he smiles nearly enough for my liking.'

'What's in the old barn?' Neva quickly changed the subject. Rafe's eyes and his smile were not a topic she wanted to dwell on.

Ethel and Queenie gave her and each other, startled looks.

'A barn's a barn,' Ethel said. 'Old or otherwise.'

'Then why is it locked? And why is it off-limits?'

'I think, perhaps, you've been listening to Cecil and Ronnie too much,' Queenie said.

'Perhaps because it's an old barn,' Ethel added. 'Perhaps it's falling down and it's locked for everyone's safety. Don't you go seeing shadows where there are none. Don't fall into that trap.'

'You're right. I'm sorry. That's probably what it is.'

But it wasn't and Neva knew it. The barn may be old but it didn't look as if it was about to collapse. Far from it. It looked as if it had been rebuilt or at the very least, renovated. Just like the stables, of which Neva had caught a glimpse. Although they were no longer used as stables. According to Judith, horses were an unnecessary expense.

'Neither Rafe nor Adam, and certainly not Olivia have much inclination to ride these days,' she had said, when Sasha had asked about horses. 'A decision was made not to replenish the stock when the last of the horses passed away. The stables now house chickens and ducks.'

Which was a shame because the stables were rather elaborate and looked far too grand for such a purpose.

The old barn was fairly elaborate too. At least the frontage was. There were some carvings above the doors, but Neva hadn't yet gone close enough to see what they were.

Ethel and Queenie knew more than they were letting on. She had seen the startled looks when she'd mentioned the old barn. One thing was for sure though: they were loyal to Rafe.

As was Adam. He smiled as he poured some wine for her and the rest of her family before passing the bottle along the table. 'We don't usually have wine bottles on the table, but we simply don't have enough staff. And getting temporary employees this close to Christmas was impossible. Believe me, poor Rafe tried and failed. He's not happy, even though I told him he shouldn't worry about it. Everyone will just muck in and help themselves.'

'He does take his responsibilities and his position very seriously, doesn't he?'

'He has from the moment our father died. He didn't really have a choice. Someone had to look after Olivia and me and I'm grateful every day that he did.'

'Does he know that?'

'What? That I'm grateful?' He gave Neva the oddest look.

'Yes. Sometimes we take people for granted. We assume they know how much they mean to us so we don't tell them. But if we don't, how will they know?'

'You think I take Rafe for granted?'

'No. I'm just asking if you've told him lately?'

'That I love him?' Adam grinned. 'Sorry. I'm being facetious. You're right, Neva. I should tell him more often. I'll tell him this evening after dinner. Although, if I'm honest, I was rather hoping to be doing something else entirely this evening. And not with Rafe.'

She didn't need to look into his eyes to know what he meant, and she tingled at the prospect.

'Yes. Ethel suggested we should all play cards. I assume that's what you meant.'

He gave an appreciative laugh. 'Of course it was, Neva. What else could I possibly have in mind?'

'I've no idea, Adam. But I may have one or

two suggestions.'

'You don't know how happy I am to hear that. I like a woman with a mind of her own.'

'Good. And I like playing charades. Perhaps we could do that. Sasha's surprisingly good at it. If she's allowed to stay up late tonight, that is.'

Adam laughed louder and one or two people, shot a look at him and Neva.

Including Rafe, Neva noticed, as she glanced in his direction. He was seated at one end of the long table, and when she glanced at Olivia, who was seated at the other end, the woman was glaring at Neva so intently that if looks could kill, Neva would have gasped her last breath.

Neva threw Olivia a quick smile and in response, Olivia banged her delicate, etched wine glass down with such force that all eyes turned to her as it shattered in her hand.

Chapter Twenty-One

Neva did not get a chance to play charades, or anything else with Adam, thanks to Olivia. Which given the woman's bizarre behaviour, was probably just as well. But it was all rather odd. Rafe hadn't seemed too pleased that Adam appeared to be having such a good time with Neva, either. But was he actually jealous? Or was there some other reason that he didn't like the idea of the two of them getting on so well? For Olivia to be cross enough about it to break a glass, though, was extraordinary, to say the least.

Perhaps Olivia didn't think Neva was good enough for her grandson. Even for just a fling. Class barriers might be coming down, but there were still plenty of snobs in the world, or people with delusions of grandeur. Working as a hairdresser had taught Neva that.

Countless numbers of her posh former

clients in London had sat in her chair, moaning about the unsuitability of their offspring's latest amore, while treating Neva as a friend and confidante. And you could bet your life that if one of those offspring had taken Neva home as their date, those same clients would have soon shown her the door. She had cut, coloured, blow-dried and coiffed the hair of some of them for the past twelve years and they'd told her all about the parties they'd held. But had any of them ever issued her an invitation? Nope. Not one.

Not that any of that bothered her. She didn't hold with snobbery of any sort. They might think their blood was blue, but when they were cut, it ran red like hers and everyone else's. And she had no time for anyone who thought they were superior to anyone else. What a person did for a living or where someone was born, didn't define them as a person; their actions did. And Olivia Wynter's actions had clearly defined her as a bit of a snooty cow.

But Neva could give her a run for her money, and if Olivia thought she could intimidate one of the Grey girls, she would soon find out she was wrong. Although it was probably best not to make any wedding plans with Adam just yet.

Neva smiled to herself as she hurried downstairs to breakfast the following day, still thinking about Adam. And also about Rafe and Olivia's reactions.

'You're looking pleased with yourself,' Rowan said, when Neva joined her family in the dining room. 'Did anything happen we should know about?'

Neva sat opposite her sister and grabbed a slice of her toast. 'Only that I had the best night's sleep I've had since we arrived in Wynterslcap. That bed is so comfortable that even my nightmares couldn't keep me awake.'

'Nightmares?' Dawn looked concerned. 'Have you been having nightmares, sweetheart? Is anything worrying you?'

'Only whether we should buy presents for everyone here, or whether we're still going home for Christmas. It's a bit unsettling not knowing if we're staying or going. The weather looks good today so will Rafe tell us to go home, after all?'

After Olivia's reaction, anything was possible, but that Rafe might send them home because of it, had only just occurred to her.

'He might, I suppose,' Dennis said, looking somewhat deflated. 'But after the amount of Sean's beer, Nigel and I drank last night, and the Baileys the three of you downed, I don't think any of us should be driving.'

'Good.' Sasha beamed at them all. 'Then we'll have to stay. Look! There's Rafe. Ask him Gramps. Ask him.'

As usual, Sasha wasn't particularly quiet and Rafe walked towards them, clearly having heard his name.

'Good morning. I hope you all slept well. Is there something you'd like to ask me?'

'Can we stay?' Sasha blurted out.

'Sasha!' Rowan snapped.

'Please!' Sasha pleaded, all big-eyed and pouty lips, ignoring her mum completely. 'Please! I love it here. And Daddy and everyone's drunk so they aren't allowed to drive, or they'll go to jail. And I'll have to spend Christmas on my own and that'd be horrid. Please!'

For a moment, Rafe looked doubtful, as if he wanted to say, 'No. Get your bags packed and leave right now. You've caused enough chaos already.' He darted a look at the windows, possibly to see if the sun was still shining, which it was, in a cloudless pale blue sky. And then he looked down the length of the table.

'We completely understand if you'd rather we leave,' Dennis was saying, but I think we would need to call some cabs because Sasha's right. Unfortunately, we did all have a bit too much to drink last night. That's our faults entirely. We should've considered the fact that we might be going home today. But sadly we didn't. Oh. But how's your grandmother's hand? No serious injury, I hope.'

'Yes,' Neva said. 'Please pass on our good wishes for it to heal speedily.'

Rafe suddenly smiled. 'Thank you. And thank you for asking. Olivia's fine. Just a silly accident. She's a little embarrassed about it. But anyway. It is Christmas Eve tomorrow and the roads are still impassable in places, according to the news and traffic reports. More so inland, as it happens. Which means you'd still have a difficult journey home. So if you all want to stay, then yes. Why not? You're all in your rooms anyway and a couple of nights won't make much difference in the scheme of things.'

'Yay!' Sasha jumped up and down and sung out to everyone in the room. 'We're staying for Christmas. We're staying for Christmas.'

Some people took that news better than others. Ethel and Queenie and most of the rest, looked almost as pleased as Sasha, although none of them was jumping up and down. Cecil and Ronnie on the other hand, did not. How would Olivia react when she heard the news? That thought brought an even bigger smile to Neva's face.

'Thank you so much, Rafe,' she said.

His smile faded slightly as he met her eyes. 'I thought you'd be pleased. I can see I was right.' He looked away but not at anyone specific, although his comments were obviously still directed at her. 'Adam's in the rose garden. There aren't any roses this time of year but there's an abundance of holly and ivy. He's helping Gavin gather some to decorate a few of the family rooms. We feel people may want to have some less formal areas in which to spend their time over Christmas rather than the drawing room, the morning room and this one. We don't usually decorate the family rooms, but he seems to think we should.'

'He's right,' Rowan said. 'You can never have too many decorations in my book. Or lights.'

'I'll pass that on. Now if you'll excuse me, I'm going into Merriment Bay and I need to be there by 9.30. Enjoy your day.'

'Thanks so much,' Dennis said.

'Drive safely,' Dawn added.

Neva watched him go.

'He's always so formal, isn't he?' Rowan said. 'So prim and proper. It must be hard work living like that every day. Or do you think it comes naturally to a man like that? I wonder if he ever lets his hair down. Adam seems much more laid back. Although still very proper and good mannered.'

'Excuse me,' said Neva, getting up and dashing after Rafe.

He was already at the front door when she caught up with him, and he was saying something to Sean and Carruthers. She hung back until he spotted her.

'The rose garden's behind the kitchen garden. Go through the dining room, down the stairs, turn left at the bottom and follow the corridor to the garden door. Once outside, simply follow the path. Or Archie can show you the way in a moment.'

'That's good to know. But I wasn't asking.'

A small frown creased his brow. 'Oh? Then what can I do for you?'

'You can take me with you to Merriment Bay. If that's not too much trouble. Unless you're taking someone else and there isn't room.'

It seemed he didn't know how to answer that and he stared at her for a moment or two. He then shot a look at Sean followed by one at Carruthers.

To her surprise, both men turned and walked away. Sean smiled at her and said hello; Carruthers did the thing with his brows and inclined his head ever so slightly in a bow and wished her a good morning.

'Um. Why do I get the feeling I'm going to be told off?'

Rafe's mouth twitched a fraction and there was a hint of amusement in his eyes.

'I have no idea, Neva. Have you done something wrong?'

'Apart from asking to go with you, no. Not as far as I'm aware.'

'I've got business there. I'm not sure how

long I'll be. It could take just an hour. It could take longer. If you want to go shopping, I'm sure Adam will–'

'Will you please give the Adam stuff a rest!'

He blinked as if she'd slapped him. 'Excuse me?'

'No, Rafe. I won't. I like Adam. Yes. But I'm not some silly girl. And I really don't need you to keep throwing him in my face. I don't know if you meant what you said in the library yesterday, but if you're jealous, you've got a funny way of showing it. Unless this is sarcasm. In which case, stop it. Because it's getting on my nerves. But if this is your way of showing you're interested in me, then frankly, you're pretty crap at it.'

Oh God. Had she said all that? All of it?

'I ... I ...'

'Rafe Wynter – speechless. That's probably a first. Forget the lift. I'll call a bloody cab.'

She stormed back towards the dining room. She had no idea what Rafe did because she didn't turn around to look.

Chapter Twenty-Two

Getting a cab wasn't as easy as Neva thought it would be.

For one thing, cabs from Merriment Bay had to cross the stone bridge in Wyntersleap and as both bridge and village were currently under a few inches of water, no cab was going to risk that. The only other way to get to Merriment Bay was all around the houses. Well, via a couple of other villages to be precise. Instead of being five miles, the roundabout route was fifteen. That was easily do-able, but it seemed there wasn't anyone who wanted to do it.

Much to Neva's irritation, when Adam saw her half an hour later and asked what was wrong and she told him – although not the bit about her conversation with Rafe – he offered to take her himself.

'I can't ask you to do that. You're helping

Gavin.'

'We've done the gathering bit. Now it's just the decorating and I'll make a deal with you. I'll take you to Merriment Bay if you'll help with the decorating when we get back.'

That was perfectly fair, but she could just visualise the self-righteous look on Rafe Wynter's face when he found out she'd gone with Adam, after all. She was about to say yes when Rowan appeared from nowhere.

'Did I hear you say you're going into Merriment Bay? Is there any chance I could join you?'

Adam's smile faltered for just a second. 'Of course. The more the merrier.'

'Really?' Rowan was clearly excited. 'How many people can you fit in a Range Rover?'

Adam tilted his head slightly to one side. 'Is this one of those jokes about elephants in a mini?'

Rowan looked at him as if he were mad. 'No. I was asking if there was room for Mum and Dad and Nigel and Sasha. And Tempest, too. Although if that's a deal breaker, I'm sure George would be happy to give her some more training. He's such a lovely man and so good with animals.'

'Err. Yes. Yes, there's room. And it's fine to bring Tempest too.' Judging by the expression on Adam's face, he felt as if he'd just been run over by a steam roller. 'I'll be ready to leave whenever you are.'

'Great,' Rowan said. 'I'll get the others and grab our coats. We'll be with you in less than five minutes.'

Twenty minutes later, the Greys, the Lanes, Tempest and Adam all piled into his vehicle and headed for Merriment Bay.

They took the scenic route: currently the only route possible, and for fifteen miles of countryside, Sasha pointed out every robin, every horse, sheep or cow and for some reason, every post box. Tempest joined in, barking at each sighting, whilst Rowan and Nigel discussed the pros and cons of Range Rovers and whether or not Adam was a very good driver.

'Should you be going so fast on such narrow lanes?' Rowan asked. 'You know the area of course, but if a horse had been around that corner it'd be sitting on your windscreen right now. And although it's a beautiful day, there're lots of puddles after all that rain.'

Adam slowed down until a tractor behind started tooting.

'I think you're in his way,' Nigel said. 'You may need to go a bit faster.'

Adam opened the window briefly and waved to the driver. 'It's a friend of mine, saying hello.' But he sped up again, just a little, even though the tractor turned into a gap beneath the hedges.

Dennis tutted in the front passenger seat. 'Leave the man alone. He knows these roads. We don't. Adam, you may want to get a bit further over to the left. Those bushes ahead on the right will get in the way of any oncoming traffic.'

On the back seat, Dawn hummed *Driving Home for Christmas*, one of the family's favourites, and Sasha, Rowan, Nigel and Dennis eventually all joined in.

Adam gripped the steering wheel tighter and screwed up his brows, as if in deep concentration. Either that or he was getting a headache.

Neva grinned at him via his rear-view mirror as she joined in with the Chris Rea song. At least her family were no longer commenting on his driving.

By the time they read the sign saying: *Welcome to Merriment Bay*, they'd even managed to persuade Adam to sing along with them, despite him repeatedly saying that he didn't know the words.

'We're here!' Adam said. He sounded more excited than Sasha. And from the way she was bouncing up and down on the back seat, she was very excited indeed.

'It looks beautiful.' Neva stared out of the window as they passed a large aircraft hangar to their left.

'That's the Merriment Bay World War II

Museum. It's small but it has quite a lot of interesting items. It even has a vintage Spitfire. Amias Wells takes people up in it, but it's not cheap.'

'I know,' Dennis said. 'It's going to be one of the first things I do when we move here.'

Adam looked at him, and then at Neva via the rear-view mirror. 'You're moving to Merriment Bay? All of you? When?'

Did he sound pleased? Or terrified? Neva wasn't sure.

'Dawn and I are moving down in early January. We're hoping Neva's going to be moving here around the same time. That's one of the reasons we rented the cottage. We tried to get something here but everything was booked. It was all a bit of a surprise to our children. We only told them on the day we all arrived. We were going to wait until Christmas Day but I'm glad now that we didn't. There's a salon and a flat that we're hoping Neva may be interested in.'

'I am here you know, Dad. And I don't think Adam wants to hear all our family plans.'

Adam grinned. 'On the contrary, I do. So you may have a place of your own down here soon, Neva?'

'If I like what I see and think I could settle here and make a go of the business, then yes.'

'Rowan and Nigel are staying in Surrey,' Dennis continued. 'But they'll visit us often. It's not really that far.'

'Look at that bay,' Rowan said. 'I bet that's a great place to be on a hot summer day.'

'And so is the Spitfire Café,' Adam said, pointing to a brightly painted building on an equally brightly painted, raised deck overlooking the bay. 'And the pub, The Hope and Anchor. That's got a garden that also overlooks the bay. It's a wonderful place to come on a warm night to sit and listen to the sound of waves gently lapping at the shore and look up at a star-filled sky.'

'Aren't you the romantic?' Rowan jested.

'You have no idea.' Again he took a backward glance via the mirror and this time he also winked at Neva.

They passed a few houses on the right and a massive, beautifully decorated Christmas tree before crossing a raised bridge over the river that flowed out into the sea.

'Is that still River Wynter?' Neva asked. 'It doesn't look anything like it does in Wyntersleap.'

'That's because it's lost its impetus in the reservoir, and because it's wider from the reservoir down to the sea. In the summer, people take kayaks from the reservoir, down the river and out into the bay. Where would you like me to drop you?'

'Anywhere here will be fine,' Dennis said. 'Are you going to come with us, or do you have plans of your own?'

Adam hesitated for a second before pulling up outside an Italian restaurant called Bella Vista. 'I think I'll leave you by yourselves for a while and let you do your family stuff, if that's OK. Rafe's here at our bank for a meeting. I'll grab a coffee with him. What time do you want to go back? There's no rush so please don't feel under any pressure. I know several people here so I can go and shoot the breeze, as they say.'

Dennis looked at his watch. 'It's 10.15 now. We'll go and look at the salon and flat first. I know it's Monday and it's not Christmas Eve until tomorrow but the agents might be closing early and they've got the keys. The office is just along there. Horton & Wells, estate agents, so this is perfect. After that, we'll nip round to take a look at our new home and then just have a quick wander.'

'Oh. I'll drop you at the estate agents then.' Adam inched further along Coast Road and pulled across it to stop right outside.

'I want to do some last-minute Christmas shopping too, if that's OK, Adam?' Neva said. 'But it shouldn't take me longer than an hour.'

'There're several shops along here,' Adam said, 'and Merriment Bay Market is at the end of this row. At this time of year it's a Christmas Market with lots of stalls selling festive goods, and a couple of other attractions. I won't spoil the surprise. Shall we say we'll meet up in the café there at 12.45? Just in time to get home for lunch. Or I'll give you my number and you can text me when you're ready to leave.'

'No need for that,' Dennis said. 'We'll be there at 12.45 on the dot. We Greys and Lanes are always punctual.'

'Remind Rowan of that, will you, Dad?' Neva said. 'We had to wait twenty minutes for her this morning.'

'Don't blame me.' Rowan rolled her eyes. 'Nigel couldn't find his phone.'

'I really hope you like the salon and the flat, Neva,' Adam said.

'So do I, Adam. Thanks so much for bringing us. Have fun. We'll see you later.'

'I'm missing you already,' he said.

He probably was. But not in a good way.

He was no doubt relishing the prospect of some peace and quiet.

Chapter Twenty-Three

Neva loved both the salon and the flat the minute she saw them. The two-storey building fronted Coast Road and was on the corner of that, and Main Road leading off it. It was just a short walk from the estate agent's offices and they had actually driven past it, but Dennis had wanted to keep it a surprise until they stood outside. Main Road separated it from Bella Vista, the Italian restaurant where Adam had originally planned to drop them.

A large gold-painted pillar separated the entrance to the salon and the bright blue door to the flat upstairs. Neva and her family decided to view the salon first. It was closed at the moment, because the owner had gone to Spain for Christmas.

Two large picture windows either side of a central glass door which had a tinkling bell above it, fronted a spacious reception area with a desk, shelves with product displays, and a sumptuous multi-coloured sofa and a gold leaf, metal and glass, coffee table, scattered with magazines.

The salon itself extended back for some way, giving plenty of space for the row of three retro black faux leather chairs in front of three black dressing-table type units each with a grand, gold-leafed framed mirror sitting on top. Opposite those, were a line of five realistic-looking orange trees which separated the cutting and styling area from three wash basins with three reclining chairs, again of black faux leather. Behind all this were two doors, each leading to beauty rooms. One had a treatment table that matched the salon chairs; the other, had a large massage chair and add-on foot bath for pedicures and a couple of table and chairs for manicures.

One thing was apparent. If Neva took this on, she was going to need some staff. If only Jo hadn't just started a new job, got engaged, and moved to Upminster. They could've had such fun running this place together. And they could've built themselves a good business too. Oh well. What was meant to be would be. She'd have to find herself someone just like Jo. But that was never going to happen. There was no one on the planet who could ever take the place of Jo.

'I love it, Mum and Dad. It needs a bit of a

touch-up. Those bright red walls for example could do with being a much softer colour. I love red walls, but not in a space like this. And not when you can see the sea from here. And those black tables should be lighter. I'm going to bring the outside in and make this place a haven of relaxation and tranquillity. But the gold leaf's staying. I also love a bit of glitz.'

'We're so pleased you like it,' Dawn and Dennis said, beaming at her.

'Sounds like you've already moved in,' Rowan said. 'Obviously Grey Building & Design will do any work you need. At a discounted rate.' She winked at Neva and smiled.

'Haircuts all round?' Neva offered, laughing.

'That should do nicely. You've got a deal.'

'Can I have my haircut now?' Sasha asked. 'I want to look pretty for Christmas Eve tomorrow.'

'Not here, sweetie,' Neva said. 'But I'll do it back at the house. And that's given me an idea. I'll have to have a word with Rafe when we get back.'

But that wasn't a particularly delightful thought. Not after the last thing she'd said to him.

The flat was equally lovely. And what was even better was that there was a semi-hidden door leading from the salon into the long hallway that led from the main front door on the street to the foot of a flight of stairs. At the top of those, was another door and inside, a fairly spacious hall. As the building was situated on a corner, at the end of the small row of shops and flats, it had windows to the front and side, which meant the kitchen at the side was not only large, but light and bright and airy. To the left of that was a good-sized bathroom, and to the other side of the kitchen, was a large sitting room with two French windows leading out onto small balconies; one at the side and the other at the front. They were only wide enough to house a small table and at a push, two small chairs, but at least it was some outside space and each provided idyllic views over the bay and the English Channel. Neva could picture herself sitting in the evening, a glass of wine in one hand, a good book in the other. Or possibly just being one with the world and admiring the view. Also to the front were two fairly good-sized bedrooms with stunning views out over the sea and glimpses of the bay to the left.

'When can I move in?' She beamed at her parents.

'Sod you,' Rowan said. 'When can *I* move in?'

Sasha, who had been hanging over the iron railing surrounding one of the balconies, probably calculating the drop, yelled, 'Swear jar!'

Decision made, they returned the keys to the agents and set the wheels in motion to finalise the deal. The owner was intending to emigrate to Spain, so the salon came with all fixtures, fittings and furnishings. Neva wouldn't even need to buy anything to get started. She already had her stock. It was just a case of moving in and unpacking. And suddenly, she couldn't wait. The next chapter of her life was about to begin.

From the agents, they went to see Dawn and Dennis' new home. It was a mere stone's throw from the salon, but when Sasha picked up a stone to try, Neva stopped her.

'It's an expression, sweetie. Not a suggestion.'

The Grey family home in Surrey was a large Edwardian detached house. Not large compared to Wynter House of course. Compared to that it was a doll's house. But this new home was completely different. For one thing it was modern; and by the look of it, designed and built by an architect, who was possibly either drunk or on drugs at the time if the odd shapes and angles were any indication. For another, it was virtually smack bang on the beach. OK, there was a narrow access road called Channel View Lane separating it from the shingle, sand and sea, but other than that and a small drive and front garden, the front door opened onto a wide expanse of beach.

Inside, it was even more up-to-date. Everything from the front door lock to the vacuum was high-tech and remotely controlled. Shutters at the windows were voice activated, as was the TV. Even some of the kitchen appliances and gadgets started on command. There was also a lift despite the fact the house only had two storeys, but it also had a roof terrace, so technically, it had three floors.

The four bedrooms all had en suites, and the showers looked like something you'd find on some futuristic planet. Each bedroom had a view of the sea and the master bedroom had views to the front and the side, overlooking the bay in the distance. On the other side of a long hall were a study, a small library, another family bathroom – this architect was definitely a fan of good hygiene, and the lift. Beside the lift was a staircase leading up and down and also to the large, open roof terrace which had plants, various sun loungers, chairs and tables, and astonishingly, a hot tub in which to sit and view the stars.

'You can keep your flat,' Rowan said. 'I'm living here.'

'It's fantastic,' Neva agreed. 'But it's the complete opposite of what I was expecting. You like older properties usually.'

'True,' Dennis said. 'But we simply couldn't resist this house from the moment we saw the details. And we're not getting any younger. We may need all the help we can get. This has all the mod cons and we hardly need to lift a finger.'

She grinned at him. 'Ask Carruthers if he's looking for a new job, and you won't even have to do that.'

The back garden wasn't large, just fifty feet or so in length and behind the fence was a border of trees and an area of grass and shrubs that eventually met Coast Road. But who needs a back garden when your front garden opens onto the whole world? Or at least, the English Channel. And besides, there was that incredible roof terrace.

Once they'd all had a good look around, they wandered back along Coast Road towards the small shopping arcade where the Christmas market was in full swing. There were rows of stalls selling everything from gifts to wrapping paper; from mulled wine to freshly baked mince pies.

There was even a small ice rink. One that could be erected and dismantled pretty much anywhere. It was an ice cube compared to the iceberg-sized one at Somerset House, but it had lights and music and laughter, just like that rink had.

To one side of the rink was an outdoor café selling hot drinks and hot snacks, served by some pretty hot-looking men and women, all dressed as Santa's elves. And at one of the tables, sat Adam and Rafe.

'Look!' yelled Sasha. 'It's them.'

For a second it looked as if Rafe was considering making a run for it. He sat bolt upright and cast his eyes around as if searching for the nearest exit. But he stayed put and even managed a sort of smile as Neva and her family approached. Adam beamed at them, although he also sat upright as if preparing for the worst.

'Hello you two,' Dawn said, waving and smiling. 'Isn't this wonderful? A real winter wonderland. Oh my. Or should that be a *Wynter* wonderland as you two handsome young men are here?'

'It's very festive,' Rafe said, his cheeks a pale red, although whether that was due to the cold or from embarrassment wasn't clear.

'I'll get us all drinks,' Dennis said. 'Rafe? Adam? Would you like another.'

'I'm fine, thanks,' Rafe said.

'No thanks,' said Adam, grimacing as he peered into his tall, heat-proof glass mug. 'One merry mint hot chocolate is quite enough for me.'

'I need to pee,' Nigel said, dashing off towards the signs that had male and female toy elves hanging by their fingers from the words: Ladies and Gents.

'What's the verdict on the salon and flat, Neva?' Adam asked, getting to his feet along with Rafe and pulling up chairs for everyone to sit.

Rafe gave both Adam and her a questioning look.

Neva sat down. 'They're both perfect. More than I could have ever hoped for.'

'You'll be moving to Merriment Bay in the near future then?'

Now Rafe look stunned and his lower lip dropped.

'You're moving to Merriment Bay?' There was a hint of something akin to desperation in his tone.

'Yes. It seems I am. Along with my Mum and Dad. We'll all be moving down in January.'

'Next month?'

'Unless someone's changed the calendar and switched January to the summer. Yes. Next month.'

He glared at Adam. 'You knew about this?'

Adam grinned. 'I only heard about it when I gave them a lift here this morning. I was going to mention it, but I thought I'd wait and see if Neva was going ahead with it first. Besides, I didn't want to spoil the surprise.'

'We're not moving here,' Sasha said, pulling her sulky face, before suddenly brightening. 'But we'll be coming to visit, so we'll come and see you and say hello. Maybe we'll even come and stay with you too.'

'No, we won't, Sasha,' Rowan said, rolling her eyes, before smiling at Rafe. 'Don't worry.

We won't inflict our delightful daughter and our dog on you after this Christmas.' She ruffled Sasha's curls and laughed.

'You're welcome any time,' he said.

Neva wasn't sure whether she was the most surprised by that, or if it was Rowan, Adam, or even Rafe himself.

'Can we go skating, Mummy?' Sasha tugged at Rowan's hand.

'I'm too old and tired. Ask your aunt.'

Neva pulled a face. 'Me on skates? Really? Has hell frozen over? Surely you remember the devastation we caused when we were in our teens and went rollerblading in the park?'

Rowan burst out laughing. 'Oh! I'd forgotten that. But it was a long time ago.'

'And what? You think my skating skills could only have improved with time and absolutely no practice whatsoever? I like watching people skate. I don't want to be a participant.'

'Oh go on. It's Christmas.' Rowan nudged her arm, still laughing.

'Yes. The season of peace and goodwill to all men. Not the season of murder and mayhem. Thanks. But no.'

'I didn't have you down as a woman who's scared to take risks,' Adam said, grinning mischievously.

'I'm not. But I am a woman who knows that risks should only be taken once you've weighed up the pros and cons and calculated that more good than bad is likely to be the result. Nothing good could possibly come out of me putting on a pair of skates.' Neva laughed and shook her head.

He leant forward. 'I will if you will.'

She leant forward too. 'No. But you're more than welcome to take my place.'

'Will someone please skate with me?' Sasha pleaded.

'OK,' Adam said, getting to his feet. 'I'll do it.'

Sasha slipped her hand in his and with a pleading look at Neva, he was dragged to where the punters were putting on their skates.

Neva glanced at Rafe. He looked as if he were deep in thought and several miles away. Even when she said his name twice, he didn't respond. Finally, she clicked her fingers in front of his face.

'Hello-o. Calling Rafe Wynter. Come back to planet Earth.'

He flinched. 'I'm sorry. What?'

'I want to ask you something.'

He stiffened visibly. 'Ask away.'

'It's Christmas Eve tomorrow and there's a staff Christmas party, isn't there? For former and current employees.'

'Yes. But of course, given the situation, everyone who's staying at Wynter House is invited.'

'Oh. That's very kind. Are you sure?'

His brows drew together. 'Yes. Wasn't that what you were asking? I thought I'd already made that clear.'

'That we were invited to the party? No. You hadn't. And I don't ask to be invited somewhere. I prefer to wait to be asked.'

'I'll try to remember that. I really thought I'd extended the invitation to everyone. I'll have a word with Judith as soon as I get back and make sure everyone knows.'

'Good. What I wanted to ask is whether you would mind if I gave everyone at Wynter House, who wanted one, a wash, cut and blow-dry in time for the party tomorrow? Or whatever they want. Or a manicure, pedicure, or whatever. I do those too.'

'I'm not sure I understand. Why would I mind?'

'Because you might not want me taking over a room somewhere and effectively turning it into a hairdressing and beauty salon. Although I wouldn't have to, would I? There's already a grand salon in Wynter House. I heard Taryn say earlier that she was taking coffee to Olivia in the grand salon. That would be perfect. I promise I won't make a mess.' She looked him in the eye and grinned broadly.

He blinked several times and took a second or two to respond. When he did, his voice was halfway between surprised and patronising.

'I'm afraid Olivia would have a heart attack if I allowed that. You see the grand salon isn't actually a–'

'Oh bloody hell, Rafe. Give me some credit. I know I'm just a hairdresser, but I'm not completely thick. I know what a grand salon is, and I know it's got nothing to do with cutting hair. It's just another posh name for a room for entertaining guests. Although why your house has to have three such rooms, and yet not that many guests, is beyond me. And none of them has a TV, but that's neither here nor there. It was a joke. Do you know what one of those is? It's a comment, story or quip intended to make people laugh. I won't give up my day job and try to become a comedienne then.' She gave an irritated sigh.

'I'm sorry if I don't understand your sense of humour sometimes, Neva. But I can assure you I'm well aware that you're not "thick". You're obviously an intelligent and career-focused woman who knows her own mind. And also clearly a woman who knows how to get what she wants.'

'OK. Don't overdo it.' She threw him a little grin.

He grinned back, albeit with a hint of sadness. 'Once upon a time, Wynter House was filled with guests. Kings and Queens have stayed there. Those days are long gone though. And it's probably just as well.'

'I bet you wish you didn't have guests now, either. Seriously though. What about a utility room or something? You must have somewhere you can stick me to do a few washes, cuts and blow-dries. And paint a few nails. You can even put me in the cellar, if you like. Although not if there're spiders. I'm terrified of spiders. And not if there's any chance I might get locked in. I'm not as brave as Sasha.'

The grin now spread across his face and he shook his head. 'I don't think I've ever met a woman quite like you.'

'Is that a good thing or a bad thing?'

Did she detect a twinkle in his eyes?

'It could be either. It could be both. It's a question I've been asking myself since the moment we first met.' The twinkle and the grin both vanished and he stood up abruptly. 'I have to go. I'll speak to Archie and Judith. We'll find you somewhere for your hairdressing.'

'Thank you, Rafe,' she said, as he disappeared into the throng of happy, laughing people without so much as a backward glance.

And the minute he had gone, it started snowing.

Chapter Twenty-Four

Snow continued to fall at a steady pace and by the time Sasha and Adam had finished skating and they had driven back to Wynter House, the grounds of the estate were a vista of pristine white, broken only by a few tell-tale signs of robins and other garden birds going about their daily business.

After lunch, George took Tempest, Boris and Duchess out to play, and Sasha and Neva went too. The grounds didn't look quite so pristine after that. But everyone had fun. George helped Sasha and Neva build a huge snowman and he taught them some commands to use on Tempest as well as the other two dogs. All three dogs obeyed him immediately but when Sasha and Neva tried the same commands, the dogs seemed to think obeying them was optional.

There had been no sign of Rafe at lunch,

but Adam had been very attentive and he even joined Neva and Sasha outside and had a snowball fight, which he clearly let Sasha win. The more time Neva spent with him, the more she liked him. One thing did surprise her though, as she told Jo later when she called.

'I don't know why, but I'd assumed Adam worked here along with Rafe. He doesn't. He's an investment banker in the City. He lives in London from Monday until he comes back here on Friday evening. He says he's "got a little place in town" that goes with his job, which probably means it's one of those swanky, company apartments several of our previous clients used for their affairs.'

'Hmm. Not sure I like the sound of that. But just because he wears the T-shirt, it doesn't mean he plays like the rest of the team. Now give me an update on what's been happening.'

Neva told Jo everything and when she got to the bit about being in Rafe's bedroom, Jo got very excited until Neva explained.

'Olivia definitely sounds weird. Do you honestly think she broke the glass because Adam was flirting with you?'

'I don't know. I'm pretty sure I won't be on her Christmas card list though.'

Neva told Jo all about the salon, the flat and Merriment Bay.

'Oh, Neva. It sounds like heaven, and Merriment Bay sounds lovely. I'm so happy for you. I hope you took lots of photos. Send me some when you get a chance. And I take back what I said about you needing more than two weeks to sort out your life. It's only been a few days and it seems everything is falling into place. And now it's snowing too. You're going to have the perfect Christmas. I just know you are.'

'I don't know about that. But it's certainly getting there. I'll send you some piccies later. I'll send some of this place too. I don't know why I didn't think of that before. But enough about me. How're things with you and Charmaine?'

'She's still alive, so I suppose that's something, right? But it's touch and go, believe me. Especially now I can't even hide in the shed. She can follow my tracks in the snow! And Rob seems to be constantly arguing with his sister, which is driving me insane. If we run out of Baileys, well, let's just say, you'll be hearing about me on the evening news. I'd much rather talk about you and those sexy-sounding brothers. Have you made up your mind which one you want in your Christmas stocking?'

'I don't think it's as simple as that. But there's a party tomorrow night and who knows. Something might happen then.'

'Make it happen. It's Christmas and you know what that means? Mistletoe! Make sure there're bunches of it everywhere. That way you're bound to bump into one or other of them under a sprig or two. And they're not allowed to say no to a kiss under the mistletoe. It's bad luck.'

'I'll do that and let you know how it goes. I've got to go now and help put up some decorations. Call you tomorrow. Love ya.'

After ringing off, Neva, along with her family, spent the rest of the afternoon helping decorate a couple of the 'family' rooms in Wynter House. These were smaller and cosier than the rooms Neva had seen so far, and the furniture and furnishings gave the impression that these rooms were lived in. Really lived in. Like any other sitting room in any other house. Only larger and with more expensive ornaments. One even had a TV. So the Wynters were fairly normal after all. Thank goodness for that.

Taryn also helped and instead of listening to Christmas music from a playlist, Neva and the others were treated to Taryn's melodious voice as she sang all their favourite songs and carols. She encouraged everyone to join in, and they did so cheerfully. Even Cecil and Ronnie, to Neva's great surprise.

In one of the rooms there was a piano and now that they were in the swing of it, Cecil and Ronnie proved they had hidden talents. And after a few glasses of mulled wine, made by

Penny and served in huge, silver punch bowls, people weren't just singing – they were dancing.

'Is it Christmas Eve already?' Rafe queried, standing at the door, a smile on his face.

'Come and join us,' Neva said, as she danced with Adam.

Rafe's smile disappeared. 'I'm afraid I can't. But I did want a quick word.'

She gave Adam an apologetic smile; he gave her a mock bow, and she walked over to Rafe.

'Can't dance? Or simply don't have time right now?' She smiled up at him.

'I can dance. Especially with the right partner. But Sean's waiting for me downstairs. I merely came to tell you that further to our conversation, Judith's found a room. When you've got a moment to spare, no doubt you'll have a word with her and she can show you where everything is and help you set up your things.'

'Thank you. Isn't the snow beautiful? It really feels like Christmas now, doesn't it? Have you been a good boy this year?'

What on earth was she going on about? Was she so desperate to keep him talking that she'd say something as stupid as that? Yep. From the expression on his face, he was thinking something similar.

'Excuse me? Have I ...? Oh I see. Another

one of your quips.' He looked thoughtful for a moment. 'I suppose that depends on one's definition of "good", doesn't it?'

'Does it? Is there a grey area? No pun intended as my surname is Grey. You know what I mean. Surely you're either good, or you're bad?'

'Over the course of a year, it's possible to be both. Several times. It's possible to be both in one day. But now I'm being pedantic. On the whole, I think I've been good. Although as it's not yet Christmas Eve, there's still time for me to be bad. I'm beginning to think that might be a good idea.'

He gave her the most devilish smile she had ever seen.

And if that was anything to go by, she had to agree.

Rafe Wynter being bad might be a very good idea indeed.

Chapter Twenty-Five

There was no sign of Rafe at afternoon tea and Neva was a little disappointed. He didn't show up for drinks at 8.p.m., and his seat at the head of the dining table was empty at dinner that night. So was Olivia's, but Neva didn't care about that.

Adam was not quite so attentive, or as flirtatious as he had been but he did sit next to her at dinner and they chatted about what was planned for Christmas Day.

'We have breakfast a bit later, at 9.a.m. That's to give Penny and Roger some time on their own. We're going to do that as usual. Then Olivia goes to the chapel and after that we have coffee and mince pies. Again, that'll remain the same.'

'How far's the chapel? Is that in Merriment Bay?'

He grinned at her. 'No. It's towards the

back of the house.'

'This house? You've got a chapel in your house?'

He laughed. 'Doesn't everyone? Only joking. Yes, we do. Several houses like ours have their own chapel.'

'Do you have your own priest or whatever?'

'No. But we do have one we can call and he'll come here to officiate if we need him.'

'I've got an electrician like that. Sorry. I'm not religious. And the electrician's my best friend's fiancé. Anyway. Did your priest officiate at Rafe's wedding?'

'Rafe's wedding? What makes you ask about that?'

Neva shrugged but heat spread across her chest right up to her cheeks.

'Just curious.'

He gave her a doubtful look. 'Rafe got married in a Registry Office in Oxford. I'm not sure Olivia has forgiven him yet for that. But as she didn't approve, and flatly refused to attend, it didn't matter to him where the ceremony was held.'

'Blimey. He must've loved Pippa very much to go against Olivia.'

'Pippa? You know her name?'

'Rafe told me the other day. And about the divorce. Why are you so surprised? Is it hot in here or is it just me?'

'It's not hot. Perhaps you're getting a cold

or something. Shall I get you some tablets?'

'No thanks. I'm sure I'm fine. But you didn't say why you're surprised.'

'Oh. Because Rafe never talks about her to anyone. And never as Pippa. Her name's Phyllida. Only people who knew her, or those he trusts, refer to her as Pippa. When was this? When did he tell you about her, I mean?'

'Um. Yesterday. I was in the library and Rafe stopped to talk. I made some silly remark about him needing a wife to support him, or something like that, and he said a wife was the last thing he needed. Then he told me about Pippa.'

'Yesterday?'

'Yes. Not that long after we'd had breakfast. You were all dashing about but Judith said there was nothing I could do to help so I wandered into the library. You've got a fabulous collection. Why have you got such a strange smile on your face?'

Adam shook his head and gave a little laugh. 'It's not a strange smile. It's a happy one. I'm glad Rafe opened up to you about Pippa, that's all.'

'Adam?' Dawn leant towards him across the table. 'Does Penny get a day off?'

'Penny? Our cook? Yes, of course. We're not slave drivers, Dawn.' He winked at her. 'Why do you ask?'

'Because I've been wondering, what with

so many people staying for Christmas and you saying that Rafe had tried to get more staff but couldn't, what will happen on her day off?'

'I'm sure Rafe and Judith have got that covered. Don't worry. We won't let you go hungry.'

Dawn tutted, even though Adam still smiled.

Neva jumped in. 'I think what Mum was asking was whether there's anything we can do to help? She's not worried about us not being served food each day.' Neva laughed and shook her head. 'We're not used to having people wait on us, so Mum was offering, in a roundabout way, to do some cooking, or at the very least, lend a hand.'

'Yes. That's exactly what I was doing. It doesn't seem fair for all of us to just turn up and expect poor Penny to cook for us, even if Taryn's helping. And bearing in mind there's breakfast, lunch, afternoon tea and dinner. When does she ever sit down?'

'I hadn't thought about it. But I'm sure Rafe and Judith have.'

'Well, I think we should help. Especially as there's the party tomorrow night. Shall I speak to Penny, or do I need to discuss it with Rafe or Judith first? I don't want to cause offence.'

'Leave it with me. I'll have a word and get back to you by breakfast at the latest.'

'Mum's an exceptionally good cook, Adam,

so you've got nothing to worry about on that score.'

'That's not what worries me. It's what Olivia will say if she finds out. I was hoping for a quiet Christmas,' he said, screwing up his face.

'So was I, Adam. But I think that ship sailed shortly after we arrived on Friday.'

Cecil and Ronnie got up from their seats and sauntered towards Adam.

'Do you know where Rafe is this evening? We were hoping to have a word.' Cecil had a contrite expression on his face, as did Ronnie.

'He's ... out.'

'Oh?'

They all looked at Neva. She shouldn't have sounded so surprised.

Cecil continued: 'Do you know when he'll be back?'

'Not really, I'm afraid. He'll be at breakfast tomorrow. Can it wait until then? Or is it something I can help you with?'

They exchanged looks and nodded at one another.

'We wanted to thank him for what's he's done for our Persephone.'

'OK. I'll pass that on.'

They exchanged more looks.

'You have no idea what we're talking about, have you?'

'Sorry. No.'

'The lead,' Ronnie said. 'Persephone's a house cat. We don't let her out at the cottage in case something dreadful happens. Like falling in the river.' He gave Neva a meaningful glance.

'Since we've been here,' Cecil said, 'the poor treasure's had to stay in her basket or sit on our laps. Rafe said we could take her to our bedroom, which we did. But she likes to be with us during the day, too, so it's been difficult.'

Ronnie beamed. 'Until today. Rafe got us a cat lead in Merriment Bay this morning but felt it needed some adjustment. It was just cotton webbing, which is far too rough for Persephone's delicate skin. He asked George and Ethel and Queenie to work their magic and we're all so thrilled with the result. They made some padding out of red silk and the softest sheep wool and sewed it over the webbing. Persephone loves it! We've been strolling all over the house with her this afternoon.'

Cecil and Ronnie clapped their hands together in glee.

'Why didn't you thank him when he gave it to you?' Adam asked, which was exactly what Neva was thinking.

'Oh he didn't give it to us,' Cecil said. 'Ethel and Queenie did. They said it was an early Christmas present from Santa. But Ethel took us to one side at drinks this evening and told us what Rafe had done. We're so grateful, we feel we owe him an apology, not just our thanks.'

Ronnie nodded. 'And to think, we suspected him of being a drug dealer. And Sean too.'

'A drug dealer?' Neva shrieked. 'Where on earth did you get that idea?'

She shook her head in disbelief. First they'd called him a wife-killer, then they thought he and Sean were thieves, and now, he and Sean were drug dealers. They were truly unbelievable.

'It's not so far-fetched,' Cecil said, defensively. 'Since we've been here, he's been in and out of that old barn at all times of the day and night. We've seen him.'

'I'll pass on your thanks, as I said.' Adam got to his feet. 'And I can assure you, gentlemen, neither Rafe nor Sean is dealing drugs. Now if you'll excuse me, I need to go and check on Olivia. I'll see you later, Neva.' He gave her a friendly smile and a not so friendly one to Cecil and Ronnie.

'Well,' Cecil said. 'We were only saying what we've seen with our own eyes.'

Neva sighed. 'But a drug dealer. That's a bit much even for you two, isn't it?'

Ronnie tutted. 'You wouldn't be so quick if you'd smelt what we had when we happened to be passing the place this morning. There's definitely something going on in that old barn. And although we're giving him the benefit of every doubt, after what he's done for

Persephone, he wouldn't keep it locked if it wasn't something he wanted to hide.'

'I agree,' said Cecil. 'But we can't stand here gossiping. We need to take Persephone for an evening stroll.'

They looked like kids at Christmas, which in a way, they were. But it made Neva think, and she knew she wouldn't sleep tonight until she'd had a look.

'Mum, Dad, everyone.' Once she'd got their attention, she gave them a wan smile. 'I'm getting a bit of a headache. I'm going for a stroll outside. I'll see you in the morning.'

'But it's snowing, sweetheart. And probably freezing too.'

'I'll be fine. Good night.'

She walked slowly until she was on the other side of the door then she raced upstairs, threw off her dress and tights, pulled on jeans and a jumper, put on her boots and grabbed her jacket. She made her way downstairs and dashed out the front door.

The cold hit her instantly, catching her breath, and fine snowflakes landed silently on her head and clothes. The lights from the house, together with the fairy lights on the bushes and in the trees cast rainbow-like reflections onto the glistening snow. She crunched her way around the side and checked that no one could see her before switching on the torch on her phone.

She almost lost her footing a couple of times as she ran across the snow to the old barn and darted around the back, out of sight of the house. She could hear a sort of rumbling. And voices. Soft mumbling only but she was certain one was Rafe. She was getting used to the sound of his voice and could even tell if he was cross, or pleased or confused. He seemed to be cross most of the time when he was speaking with her.

Using the beam of her torch, she searched for a gap or a hole but couldn't find one. She walked around to the other side but still made sure she was out of view of the house. She was about to give up when she saw it. A small hole, near the ground. She bent down, banging her head against the wood and cursing at the arrow of pain. It felt as if she'd hit something sharp but she had no idea what it could be. Unless he had booby-trapped the place.

She laughed at her ludicrous notion and got onto her knees, bending her back and resting on her elbows to try to peer through the hole. Eventually, she lay down flat on her stomach. She had a bit of a view but not very much. There was a large copper container with long metal tubes going in and out. To the right of that were large, glass, almost urn-like jars containing various different coloured liquid, to near those, several large carton-type boxes. She spotted Sean, taking a handful of something from one of the cartons. He shook it and it seeped through his fingers like heavy duty green-brown ash.

Oh my God! Had Cecil and Ronnie been right, after all? Were Rafe and Sean drug dealers? She had never taken drugs in her life, but didn't cannabis look like that? She'd seen pictures of it somewhere. It wasn't as bad as heroin or some of the other drugs on the street, and it had medicinal qualities, or so many people believed. But it was still a drug. And by the looks of all the cartons she could see, and that massive copper container, plus those jars, whatever it was, they had a lot of it.

'Can I help you with something?'

She rolled over onto her back and tried to push herself upright but her jacket caught on something and she couldn't move.

'I didn't hear you coming!' She sounded like a mouse. A frightened mouse.

'Evidently.' Rafe shone his torch at her.

Drug dealers killed people. But Rafe wouldn't do that, would he? Although he did have a missing ex-wife. God. Why was she thinking about that now?

He reached out for her and she instinctively recoiled.

'I'm not going to hurt you, Neva. I'm going to help you up. You're soaked. You've been lying on the snow. And I think your jacket's caught on a nail.'

'Oh. Um.' She reached to her side and managed to free herself. 'I was looking for ... my locket. I've lost it. It means the world to me. I thought it might be here because I saw Tempest with something in her mouth earlier and–'

'Do you honestly expect me to believe that? Apart from the fact you don't have a locket.'

'How do you know?'

'Because I would've seen it around your neck.'

He held out his hand

'They'll hear me if I scream.'

He raised his brows. 'I don't doubt it. But why would you scream? There's really no need for that.'

'I didn't see anything.'

'I'm sure you didn't. Give me your hand.'

She backed closer to the side of the barn. Her bottom was freezing but what else could she do?

'Oh! For heaven's sake!'

He grabbed her with one hand and lifted her to her feet. She fell against him and caught the faintest scent of lavender. Or sandalwood. Or something else. Cannabis probably. A trickle of warmth ran down her forehead.

'You're bleeding! You've cut your head.' He pulled a handkerchief from his pocket, and with one arm wrapped around her back, he pulled her closer and wiped away the blood. 'I don't think it's serious but we'd better get Penny to take a look. She's a first-aider. Come with me.'

She held back and shook her head. 'I'll go on my own. You go back to whatever it is you were doing. Which I know is nothing bad or anything.'

He frowned. 'You think I'm doing something I shouldn't in the barn?'

'No.' She shook her head again.

'Oh, Neva. It's nothing illegal, I can promise you that. It is something I want to keep a secret for as long as possible though. Especially from Olivia. I can't tell you what it is yet, but you'll laugh about this when you find out. Now please, let me take you to the house.'

He sounded so genuine, so sincere. Should she believe him? Could she?

'I can go on my own.'

'OK. If that makes you feel more comfortable, do that. I'll stay here until I see you're safely back inside. And go to see Penny right away. That was probably caused by the same nail that caught on your jacket, and some of them are ancient and rusty. You'll need the wound cleaned just to be on the safe side. Promise me you'll go to Penny.'

She nodded. 'I promise.'

'Good night then, Neva. I'll see you in the morning.'

'Good night.'

She ran to the house as fast as she could, without slipping, but she did keep her promise. The minute she got inside and closed the door safely behind her, she went to see Penny. He hadn't killed her so that was a good sign. Although he might when she was alone in her bed.

'Pull yourself together,' she said out loud. 'If he was going to kill you he would've done it already.'

Then she laughed at her ridiculous behaviour.

As if Rafe would be a drug dealer? He'd gone out of his way, not just to buy a cat a lead, but to also make the damn thing more comfortable for the feline. And for two people for whom he had no reason to do anything nice. Was that really something a criminal would do?

Chapter Twenty-Six

Neva awoke to a winter wonderland and she couldn't quite believe her eyes when she looked outside. A heavy covering of snow weighed down the branches of the trees and she could only just make out the roof of her car. Some of the other cars, like Rafe's and Adam's were more visible but even they were snowed in. It was just as well it was Christmas Eve and that no one at Wynter House had to go anywhere in particular.

It was also a good thing that, after getting some TCP dabbed on her wound and the all-clear from Penny last night, she had asked Nigel, Rowan and her dad to bring all her hairdressing equipment and stock and her beauty supplies indoors.

Judith had arranged for her to use the old washroom which was opposite the kitchen and due to its size and position, was no longer used as such. It was clean and fairly bright, thanks to its high windows, and although the floor was old flagstones, Judith had arranged for one or two rugs to be placed here and there.

There were two large sinks against the wall, thankfully connected to both hot and cold running water and to which Neva could fix her shower attachment. And, more importantly, there was a massive fireplace, which although it was of plain stone, threw out as much heat as the fires upstairs.

A Christmas tree that looked a lot like the one Neva and her family had installed at the cottage but with decorations that definitely weren't theirs, had even been put in one corner. They had already retrieved their own decorations from the pile of boxes they had helped to move on Sunday.

There was a small sitting room beside the kitchen, diagonally opposite the washroom and Judith had suggested that if people needed to wait between their treatments, say for colour to develop or for curlers to do their thing, they could use this room. It was a room Penny used, if she needed to put her feet up for a minute or two without having to trudge along the corridor to the main, staff sitting room farther away from the kitchen. But she said she was more than happy to share for the day, especially as she was going to be one of Neva's clients, and also because Rowan and Dawn would be helping her and Taryn and Judith and Wendy in the kitchen.

Neva showered, dressed and dashed downstairs. She couldn't wait to get started. But first she was looking forward to a hearty breakfast, and to seeing if Rafe said anything about last night. She was feeling a bit embarrassed by her foolish behaviour and hoped he wouldn't bring it up. He was unlikely to do so as he wanted to maintain his secrecy, but she was desperate to know what it was he and Sean were doing in the old barn. And why was it called 'the old barn'? She had yet to see a new one and the only other outside building was the stables-turned-chicken and duck house. But that was by the by.

Rafe was chatting to her mum and dad when she walked into the dining room and he smiled the moment he saw her.

'Morning all.' She tried to sound as casual as possible as she smiled at Rafe and her parents.

'Good morning, sweetheart,' Dawn said. 'How's your head this morning?'

Rafe's smile faltered. He no doubt assumed she had told her parents everything.

'The headache's completely gone, thanks. I'm glad I decided to go for a short stroll, followed by an early night. But I caught my head on a branch or something and gave myself a little cut. It's fine though. Penny sorted me out with some TCP and a couple of painkillers, just in case.'

There was a questioning look in Rafe's eyes but his smile was back in place.

'Dawn and Rowan have kindly offered to make lunch and afternoon tea today, in addition to giving Penny and Taryn help with the catering for this evening. Dennis has offered his services moving chairs and tables into the ballroom, and I've heard several people eager to avail themselves of your skills, Neva. I'm very grateful for everything you and your family are doing to help make everyone's stay here a pleasant one.'

'It's the least we can do.' Neva smiled at him.

'Especially as you've said we should stay for the duration of our holiday,' Dennis said, smiling cheerfully. 'That really is going above and beyond, and we intend to do more than cook a few meals and move a few chairs.'

'We're staying? For New Year too?' Neva looked directly at Rafe.

'Unless you'd rather not.'

'Neva loves it here as much as we do,' Dennis said. 'Now please don't take this the wrong way, Rafe, but Nigel and I are builders and I couldn't help but notice there're a couple of things here that need a bit of attention. If you've got the necessary supplies, we'll happily fix one or two of those for free.'

Rafe looked shocked. But not unpleasantly. 'I couldn't ask you to do that, Dennis. You're here on holiday. Your assistance today will be more than enough.'

Dawn laughed. 'They don't know the meaning of the word, Rafe. No matter where we go, the pair of them get itchy hands after a few days, and start fixing things. Even if it's just a loose screw. You'd actually be doing us all a favour. They're like bored teenagers if they're not kept fully occupied.'

'And I'm not suggesting we take on the big repairs. I don't mean to be rude about your gorgeous home but I know what old houses are like. There's always something that needs replacing, repairing or rebuilding.'

Rafe had told Neva the very same thing, so he could hardly take offence, and fortunately he didn't because he smiled.

'Constantly,' he said, and he even gave a little laugh. 'That means a great deal to me, Dennis. You and your family are so kind. Gavin and myself do what we can, as does Adam, when he's here, but we're no experts, and good, reliable builders are a rarer find than a golden goose these days. I'd appreciate your advice on a couple of matters that need some attention.'

'Perfect. After breakfast we'll move the tables and chairs and then we'll give you a shout and you can tell us what you need.'

Rafe looked genuinely pleased, but Neva

wasn't so sure Rowan would be and she held her breath when Sasha, followed by her parents, came stomping in looking as if she'd just been told off.

'Thank heavens for that.' Rowan rolled her eyes when Dennis broke the news to his daughter and Nigel. 'We weren't here for more than ten minutes before Nigel was pointing out that this needed doing and that needed doing. And how hc'd love to get his hands on the damaged section of wood panelling in the grand hall because he knew exactly how to make it look as good as new. And by that of course I mean, centuries old but no longer damaged. It'll be lovely to get a bit of peace and quiet.'

She glared at Sasha. Something had clearly happened.

Nigel frowned and gave Rafe an apologetic smile. 'I wasn't criticising or anything. It's just that I can't stop myself from noticing these things.'

'No need to explain. I understand completely. I sincerely appreciate your kind offer of help and I welcome your thoughts and comments.'

Neva laughed. 'You may regret saying that, Rafe.'

He smiled at her but there was a hint of sadness in his eyes. 'I may regret a few things over the last few days, Neva. But I don't think this will be one of them. If you'll excuse me, I need to have a word with Archie, but I'll come and find you later, Dennis and Nigel, if that's OK.'

'Absolutely.'

'Why did Rafe look sad?' Sasha asked, as he walked away.

'Did he?' Dennis said. 'I thought he looked rather pleased.'

'Not when he looked at Neva, he didn't. Have you been naughty too, Neva?'

'Not that I'm aware, sweetie, but sometimes we can do things without realising the effect they may have on other people.'

Rowan tutted and did the eye-roll. 'You're eight, Sasha. And sometimes you talk a lot of nonsense. Come and have some breakfast and then we'll have to find something to keep you out of mischief today. Neva's going to be busy doing everyone's hair and Granny and I are helping in the kitchen. If your Daddy's going to be working, we need to find someone to look after you. I wonder if George is free again today?'

'He did look sad.' Sasha crossed her arms and pouted. 'And I'm eight. I don't need looking after.'

'As you've been demonstrating so clearly since we arrived. Let me see. You got yourself locked in the secret passage and Rafe had to organise a search party, wasting hours of everyone's day. Last night you disappeared into the attic because you were convinced you saw a ghost head in that direction. You scared poor Judith half to death when you jumped out at her. You're lucky she brought you back to us and didn't shut you away in that attic. And you excelled yourself this morning with your stunt on poor Carruthers and that hand. You should be grounded, and when we get home, you will be. And don't laugh, Neva, because that just encourages her.'

Neva bit her lower lip but it didn't stop the spurt of laughter.

'Did you really jump out at Judith? And what's this about Carruthers and a hand? Oh come on, Rowan. You have to tell me.'

Nigel shook his head. 'Sasha bought some things with her pocket money in one of the shops in Merriment Bay, and one of those things was a life-like, child's hand. This morning she came downstairs long before we even got up and she asked Carruthers to show her where the library was. Being the butler that he is, he did, and she put her hand in his, only it wasn't her hand, of course. Then she pulled him, and the hand came off in his.'

Sasha giggled. 'It was *soooo* funny, Neva.'

Neva could imagine his face. Those eyebrows of his must have done a bit of a dance at the very least.

'It wasn't,' Rowan snapped. 'The poor man

almost had a heart attack.'

Neva was still laughing when she asked, 'How do you know? You said you weren't up.'

'But Ethel was. She saw the whole thing and told us all about it.' Rowan slapped butter on her toast as if she were smacking the bread with her knife.

'I didn't have Ethel down as a tell-tale or a spoilsport.'

'Spoilsport? Oh, she thought it was even funnier than you do. She told us because she thought we'd find it hysterical too. We didn't. She said she thought he was going to die of shock when Sasha 'held' his hand, and then when it came off in his, Ethel said he looked as if his brain had exploded and he would drop dead on the spot. He let out a strangled yelp, and stumbled backwards, as if he thought he'd actually pulled Sasha's hand off.'

Sasha giggled louder and clamped her little hands over her mouth to try to hide her amusement.

'Sorry, Rowan,' Neva said, 'but I'd have given anything to see his face.'

'You might not feel that way if he tells Rafe and Rafe decides we've caused nothing but trouble and it's time we left. It's just as well Dad and Nigel have offered to help. That might at least make him think twice.'

'I don't think Rafe would throw us out over a little practical joke, sis. Besides, he's already told us we can stay for the New Year too.'

'Yippee!' Sasha bounced up and down on her seat. 'I'll be able to find all the ghosts and I've got lots more jokes to play on ...' She let her voice trail off, took a large mouthful of toast, and beamed at Neva.

Chapter Twenty-Seven

Neva couldn't help herself. The moment she saw Carruthers in the hall shortly after breakfast, she gave him a cheerful smile and asked if he could give her a hand.

He actually made a little gasp. Just a tiny one but she definitely heard it. Then he did his thing with his eyebrows, cleared his throat, pushed his shoulders back a fraction more than they already were and said, 'Of course, Miss Grey. I do beg your pardon. Neva. How may I assist you?'

Without thinking, she gave him a playful slap on his arm and smiled.

'I'm sorry, Carruthers. I don't need any help. I was only teasing.'

Again, the eyebrow thing and another little gasp but he composed himself admirably and added a small bow.

'If you'd like a haircut, I'll be in the old

washroom downstairs. Have a good day. And happy Christmas Eve.'

'Thank you. And to you, M-Neva.'

Neva watched him stride across the hall as a voice to the side of her made her jump. She looked round and saw Rafe, but not right away. He was leaning against the door frame of the library, and had been partially obscured from her view by the wide branches of the Christmas tree in the hall and where she was standing. There was a sardonic smile on his face and his arms were loosely crossed. It was the first time she'd seen him look a little laid back. It suited him. So did the light grey jumper he was wearing with his jeans. It brought out the blue in his eyes.

'You do know you've just destroyed his equilibrium for the day, don't you?'

'You've heard about Sasha's little trick then?'

His eyes twinkled and it looked as if he was trying not to laugh. 'I have. Ethel told me. But that wasn't what I meant. I was referring to your offer of a haircut.'

'Oh? Why would that destroy his equilibrium? Doesn't he like having his hair cut? He always looks so immaculate.'

'Exactly. And that's the point. He'll now spend all morning worrying whether he looks as if he needs to have his hair cut. For a man like Archie, that's a very serious matter.'

Neva grinned. 'I see. Then next time I bump into him I'll tell him he doesn't.'

'Thank you.'

He smiled at her as he eased himself away from the frame and his arms relaxed at his sides. He walked out into the hall and towards the front door.

'What about you, Rafe?'

He turned. 'What about me?'

'Would you like a haircut?'

He grinned at her. 'Are you saying I need a haircut? Or are you also trying to destroy my equilibrium? More than you have already.'

'More? How have I done that? Oh. By us all being here, you mean?'

'No, Neva. That's not what I mean.'

'You're talking about last night then, aren't you? I'm sorry.'

'Not just about last night. I was thrown off balance the moment we met. And I think you're well aware of that.'

'Neva?' Rowan came rushing into the hall. 'Oh, Rafe. You're here too. Have either of you seen Sasha? She's disappeared again. One minute she was standing beside me, the next she was gone.'

'She's on the front lawn with George,' Rafe said. 'I saw them from the library window. They're taking the dogs for a walk. Although in these conditions, I think it's more of a tumble than a walk. She's perfectly safe with him.'

Rowan breathed a sigh of relief and slapped her hand against her chest.

'Yes. He's a lovely man. That girl will be the death of me. I'm telling the pair of you right now, don't even think about having kids. They'll give you nothing but worry and sleepless nights. Oh. I didn't mean together, of course.' She gave a burst of laughter and hurried back the way she came.

Rafe was giving Neva the strangest look and a crimson flush rushed over her.

'My family can be so embarrassing at times. I'm sorry. I don't know why she said that.'

'As it happens, I've been thinking about very little else, and worry and sleepless nights are things I'm clearly going to have to get used to.'

What did he mean by that? Was he saying he had been thinking about having kids? Or that he'd been thinking about how embarrassing her family could be?

'You've had worries and sleepless nights for most of your life, haven't you? I mean, about this place. Looking after this house. You know what I mean.'

'I have. But I'm accustomed to those concerns. Lately, I've found myself thinking about things that have taken me completely by surprise. And I'm not quite sure what to do about them.'

'Oh? What sort of things?'

Was he saying what she thought he was? If he liked her – really liked her – why couldn't he just say it?

A crease formed between his brows. 'Are you saying you don't know?'

She slowly shook her head and took a deep breath. As far as she was concerned, the chemistry between them right now made the Big Bang look like a firework fizzling out.

'Rafe. I know I told you the other day that I'm not completely stupid, but to be quite honest, sometimes I have no idea what you're talking about. Are you saying you like me? Or have I totally misunderstood the looks and the smiles? I know I said you were pretty crap at this but I'm not very good at it either. If you do like me, please just say so and save us both a lot of time and doubt. Because ... although God knows why, I think I may like you.'

He didn't really get a chance to say anything. Sean shoved open the front door and burst into the hall, shouting for Rafe at the top of his voice.

'I ... I have to go, Neva. But we'll resume this conversation later.'

'Bloody hell, Rafe. Why do you always have to be so prim and proper? Fine.'

She turned and stormed off along the hall, ignoring Sean's apology for the interruption, and the fact that Rafe called her name twice.

Why couldn't the silly sod just come after her? Was that really too much to ask?

Especially after he'd given her a look that was so full of passion, she wanted to rip off their clothes and have sex right there in the hall.

But she mustn't think about that. She had people's hair to cut and style.

Besides she could hardly have passionate sex with Rafe in the hall of Wynter House.

She couldn't even begin to imagine how Carruthers would react to that.

And neither could Jo, when Neva called her to have a good moan.

'Perhaps he'd stand there, all straight-backed and wait until you'd finished, then ask if there was anything sir or madam required. But you can bet those eyebrows would be going like the clappers.'

'Yeah. I wish I knew what was going on in Rafe's head though. I'm absolutely convinced he really likes me. Most of the time. Sometimes I think he wishes we'd never met. But he hasn't said anything about liking me or, possibly being in danger of falling in love with me, or anything really, since our conversation in the library. And because I've never dated anyone from his sort of background, I don't know what to do. Is he always going to be so stiff upper-lipped?'

'It's not his upper lip you need to worry

about,' Jo joked. 'So you've decided he's the one you like after all, have you? I thought you might. Why don't you just do the mistletoe thing like I suggested?'

'Because there's never any about when we're together. And yeah. I like him. I think I like him a lot. Which is actually really annoying.'

Jo laughed. 'I can imagine. You could always carry some mistletoe around with you. Or just grab him by the collar and give the man the most passionate kiss possible. Not even Rafe could resist that. I told you. Do it tonight at the party. If you don't, I'll come down there and damn well do it for you.'

'Rob would love that. Speaking of which. How are things going?'

'Not brilliantly. I tried to have a word with him about the jumpers, the whole Charmaine thing and the rows with his sister, oh, and about him suddenly not wanting to get off his arse, and he told me I was being unreasonable. That it was Christmas and he was on holiday. That he and his sister often rowed but it didn't mean anything, and that his mum had gone out of her way to make me feel part of the family. I don't know if it's me or him. But I do know that this isn't going as I hoped. I'll see how it goes and give it until the New Year.'

'And what then? What if nothing changes?'

'Then it's not meant to be and I'll have to

end it.'

'Seriously? Four years is a long time and you've just got engaged. Everyone goes a bit crazy over Christmas. Things might settle down again once life's back to normal.'

'I hope so. But if it doesn't, I'll be looking for a new job and a place to live.'

'Oh Jo. I'm so sorry. I hope it does work out. Um. But if it doesn't. I do happen to know where there may be a job going for such a talented hairdresser like you. It even comes with a room in a flat overlooking the sea. Of course, you would have to share with someone, but I believe she's a lovely girl and very easy to get on with.'

'Really? I heard she was a bit of a weirdo. And a silly tart who won't kiss the man she's crazy about. But I hope you mean it, Neva. Because ever since you told me about that salon, the flat and Merriment Bay, I haven't been able to get it out of my head. And you know what. I think that's the problem. I'd rather be there with you than be here with Rob and his family. Which tells us both all we need to know about my relationship, I think.'

'Are you serious?'

'I think so. But it's hard. As you say, it's been four years. I want to make sure before I throw it all away. The truth is though, the whole proposal thing was a bit of a wake-up call. I was more excited about getting the new job than I was about getting the ring. You know that. And if getting engaged didn't really thrill me, should I honestly be living here and thinking about getting married?'

'Oh, Jo. Are you sure it's not just because it's Christmas? And because of what's been happening, you've been thinking about your parents? It is true though. You were nowhere near as excited about the engagement as I'd thought you'd be.'

Jo sighed. 'If the silly sod hadn't got down on one knee in the middle of the dining room at The Ritz, I think I might have said no. But all I could think about was how embarrassed he would be. And how much the whole evening had probably cost him. And I did love him. I do love him. I'm just not sure I love him enough. These last few days have made me realise that. If I did, even Charmaine wouldn't bother me. Unless there's some sort of miracle between now and the New Year, I really think this is over.'

'I'm so sorry, Jo. Is there anything I can do?'

'You can kiss that bloody Rafe Wynter. Someone should be having fun this Christmas. And I promise, if I do come down, I won't get in the way of you and Mr Prim and Proper. Oh. But as you've decided it's Rafe you want and not Adam, the brother's going spare, right?'

Jo was clearly hurting but she wasn't the

type to wallow in self-pity. Making jokes was her way of dealing with any problems she may have.

Neva laughed. 'Yes. But I don't think Adam's your type. Although wouldn't that be great? We're getting ahead of ourselves though. Let's not forget Rafe hasn't even said he likes me yet, let alone that he wants to have a relationship with me. And even if he does say he likes me, it could just be lust and all he wants is a quick fling. Why does this stuff have to be so confusing?'

'He does like you and I think he wants a relationship. He doesn't sound like a man who just wants a fling. Not from the things you've told me. And it doesn't matter about Adam. There's bound to be someone in Merriment Bay I fancy.'

It sounded as if Jo had already made up her mind, and Neva felt a little sorry for Rob. Come the New Year – or possibly even before, Rob Ashford was going to be history as far as Jo was concerned.

But she couldn't help but feel happy at the prospect of being reunited with her best friend. She and Jo would be moving out of their flat in London in January, and moving into their flat in Merriment Bay, not long after that. Until then, they could stay at her parents' new house.

Chapter Twenty-Eight

Other than a quick lunch break, Neva didn't stop and she was on her feet from the moment she sat Ethel down and washed and curled her hair, until the minute she brushed the cuttings from George's shoulders. There was a steady procession of people throughout the day and, other than the fact that she was in an old washroom in the downstairs corridors of a stately home, the comings and goings, gossip and laughs, were just as they would be in any other hairdressing salon.

Rowan, who along with Dawn, was helping in the kitchen, even made tea, coffee or hot chocolate for each of Neva's clientele, and they were given the mince pies and biscuits Dawn had made at the cottage, to munch on while they waited.

The gingerbread house Dawn and Sasha had made took pride of place at afternoon tea, but Neva didn't stop for that. Sasha brought her a piece together with a couple of other cakes Dawn and Rowan had made in Penny's kitchen.

One big surprise of the day was when Carruthers appeared, late in the afternoon, gave a little cough and a bow and asked if he could possibly prevail upon Neva to provide him with a slight trim.

She assured him that nothing would give her more pleasure, and when he left, he smiled at her for the first time since she'd arrived, but it only lasted a moment and he was back to his usual self. Neva had never been so nervous in her life. Even when she had given Adam a "bit of a tidy up" as he called it, she hadn't felt like that.

This was until ten minutes after George left, just as Neva was about to clear up, and Rafe stood in the doorway. He leant against the stone wall, looking just as relaxed as he had this morning, and rather annoyingly, twice as sexy. His face was slightly flushed as if he'd either been doing some physical work, or he'd been running. His hair looked damp and rather dishevelled as if billowed by the wind. And his dark blue eyes sparkled with excitement.

'I don't believe I've ever seen so many happy and impeccably coiffed people in Wynter House. Words like 'wonderful' and 'talented' and 'genius' are being bandied about.

And everyone's comparing fingernails and toenails. Even Archie is pleased. And believe me, that's high praise indeed.'

'You sound surprised.'

'Do I? I'm not. Not at all.'

'I'll tell you something that may surprise you.' She tried to force herself to keep calm. But she was fighting a losing battle. 'I've never been so nervous as I was when I gave Carruthers a trim.'

He grinned at her. 'You must be exhausted. People have been in and out of here all day.'

She met his eyes and rested her chin on the top of the broom handle. 'Yes. In fact, the only people I haven't had in this chair today are Olivia ... and you.'

A slow smile crept across his face. 'I don't think Olivia will be availing herself of your skills, and as much as I would be delighted to do so, you've had an extremely busy day and it looks as if you're clearing up.'

She straightened up, tossed the broom to one side and patted the back of the chair.

'Nope. I was simply preparing for my next customer. Sit down Rafe and tell me what you'd like me to do.'

For a moment it looked as if he was going to turn and run but he walked to the chair, flashed her another smile, and sat down.

'Anything you want, Neva. I'm in your hands.'

'You may regret that. What if I decided to dye your hair purple?'

He glanced at her over his shoulder. 'Would it suit me?'

'Don't tempt me.' She tapped his shoulder with her fingers and felt how firm it was. 'What have you got in your hair? It looks like ...'

Oh God. He'd obviously been in the old barn again. She picked out a couple of bits of dried something or other and tossed it on the floor.

'I'll wash it later,' he said.

'We can wash it now. Come over to the sink.'

She walked to the far wall and waited for him to join her. He hesitated, but finally pushed himself out of the chair and strode towards her.

'Where do you want me?'

He was doing this on purpose. He must be. And it was working. She was getting hot, bothered and very turned on. She stood on her tiptoe, slid one hand into his hair, and shoved his head forward as fast as she could, grabbing the shower attachment with her other hand and turning it on.

'Stick your head in the sink. Please.'

Before he could say a word, he was bending over one of the large stone sinks and having his head soaked with lukewarm water.

Neva had given everyone who had their

hair washed, a quick head massage. It was one of the things she always did, having checked with each of them to make certain they would like one.

She didn't bother to ask Rafe. Knowing him, he'd say no. But as she rested the shower attachment beneath the tap and leant forward and massaged shampoo into his hair, his shoulder pressed against her breasts and his hand brushed against her thigh. Instead of moving away, she moved closer, pressing into him far more than was necessary and leaning her body against his side. Her fingers kneaded his skull and she closed her eyes, unsure who was enjoying the experience the most. Him or her. The fire roared in the hearth opposite but the heat she was feeling had nothing to do with the flames in the grate.

'Oh God, Neva,' he moaned softly. 'That feels so good.'

'Tea, coffee or hot chocolate?' Rowan asked, from the doorway.

Neva jumped, knocking Rafe sideways and sending the shower attachment shooting out of the sink, resulting in an arc of water over Rafe and herself. She grabbed the attachment and quickly turned off the tap, but her hair was dripping and Rafe had water and shampoo running down his face and jumper.

Rowan gave them both an odd look before throwing them each a towel.

'Well?'

'Well what?' Neva asked, blushing from the tips of her toes.

'Tea, coffee or hot chocolate?' Rowan looked directly at Rafe and smiled.

He wiped shampoo from his eyes and dabbed at his jumper. 'Nothing for me thanks, Rowan. I've just had some water.'

'Right. Well, I think Rafe's your last for today, and as we've prepared everything for tonight, if you don't mind, I'll nip upstairs and start getting ready for the party.'

'That's fine,' Neva said. 'We won't be long.' She turned to Rafe but she couldn't look him in the eye. 'Sorry about that. She's been making drinks for everyone all day and she must've seen you come in. Um. I need to finish washing your hair and give you a bit of conditioner.' She waited by the sink until he stepped back in front of her.

He didn't say a word, but she could feel him looking at her intently as she pretended to busy herself with the shower attachment and the taps. He eventually bent down over the sink and she held his head still so that she could wash out all the shampoo. Now she stood as far from him as she could and her back was aching by the time she rinsed out the conditioner.

'Back to the chair, please.'

She still didn't look at him but he was definitely looking at her. She towel-dried his hair and ran a comb through it, picking up her scissors and snipping away where necessary. She closed her eyes tight as she ran her fingers through it, this time not because she was enjoying it but because she was trying so hard not to. She needed to do this to make sure she had cut the hair evenly and she opened her eyes once she was certain she could touch it without melting on the spot.

He's just another client, she told herself. He's just another client. If she repeated it enough times she might believe it. But she sighed with relief as soon as she had finished.

'All done,' she said, gingerly brushing the cuttings from the towel around his shoulders and watching hundreds of dark brown strands of *him* fall to the floor. She would pick a few of those up when he had gone.

'Thank you, Neva,' he said, getting up from the chair. 'I don't think I've ever had a haircut quite like this one.'

She grabbed the broom as quickly as she could and began sweeping the floor, avoiding the hair she had just cut.

'It was my pleasure. But I think I should tidy up now, and get upstairs. I believe there's a party starting in just over two hours and I need every second of that to get ready if I'm going to look at least half decent.'

He took a step towards her and she quickly moved the broom and herself further away.

'I think you look much better than half decent right now.'

She laughed but it sounded more like someone being strangled.

'That's because you've had shampoo in your eyes. Make sure you rinse that out again when you get upstairs, and if there's any irritation, have a word with Penny and get some eye drops or something.'

'We're not going to continue our conversation from earlier then? Or talk about what happened just now?'

She coughed in surprise. 'It's been a long day, Rafe. I really need a shower. Can we discuss it later?'

'Of course. Thanks again for ... everything. I'll see you tonight at the party.'

'Yep. That's a date. No! I didn't mean ... That is, what I meant was–'

'It's OK. I know exactly what you meant. I'll see you at 8. And Neva. I wish it was a date.'

He was gone by the time she realised what he'd said.

Chapter Twenty-Nine

Neva had never taken more than about forty-five minutes to get ready for anything in her life, and that time included showering, doing her hair and make-up and getting dressed. And she would have loved to have continued the conversation with Rafe in the wash room. But she was being honest when she had said she needed a shower. She'd been on the go since breakfast and what with the heat from the fire and the hairdryer, together with all the colourants and shampoos, she wasn't quite sure of the 'scent' she may be giving off.

The way things had been going, anything could've happened in that room. Having slightly whiffy armpits was not what she wanted if she and Rafe were going to be having an intimate conversation about their feelings; kissing; and definitely not if they were going to go the whole hog and have sex. Plus, as much as she wanted him – and God, did she want him – she would prefer their first time not to be in an old wash room with a couple of stone sinks and flagstone floors. And the possibility of Rowan popping back to check if they wanted a hot beverage. Or worse, Carruthers appearing in the doorway just as they got to a particularly passionate bit.

Tonight, for the first time in her life, it actually *did* take her more than two hours to get ready.

That was partly because the minute she was sure Rafe was out of earshot, she phoned Jo and told her all about the shampoo massage incident. Then she'd rushed upstairs and collapsed on the bed, twisting and turning and imagining all the things that might have happened if Rowan hadn't come in at that precise moment.

After that, she'd jumped in the shower, and spent longer than usual because she couldn't stop thinking about running her hands through his hair earlier and how wonderful it had felt.

Spraying perfume under her arms and deodorant on her wrists and neck had delayed her even more, and once she'd washed that off, it took several changes of clothes before she finally plumped for the first dress she'd put on. It was one of Jo's and Neva hadn't realised she had packed it in her holdall by mistake. It wasn't the type of dress she would usually wear, but somehow tonight, it felt right.

It was deep purple with delicately embroidered silver thread around the edges of the low sweeping neckline and three-quarter-length sleeves. The tight-fitting bodice of crepe at the front and sheer, purple organza at the back had tiny flashes of glitter, sparkling here and there. The skirt floated from her waist and danced around her hips and thighs when she moved; more sheer, glittery organza over tight-fitting crepe, and thankfully hiding the fact that her stomach definitely wasn't quite as flat as she would have liked.

She took a selfie and sent it to Jo, waiting an agonising five minutes before a row of emoji hearts, excited faces, faces with tongues hanging out, popping eyes and several thumbs-up preceding the words: *sex tonight* and a stream of exclamation marks, beeped in reply.

Her hair was swept up in a loose bun, and taking Jo's earlier advice, she fixed a sprig of mistletoe into the side. If anyone approached that she didn't want to kiss, she'd quickly take it out. Shimmering purple fingernails and matching toenails and a pair of high heeled glittery black sandals completed the ensemble and when she took one final glance before heading downstairs, even she thought she looked pretty good.

Rafe was standing near the Christmas tree in one corner of the room, deep in conversation with Olivia but he turned as Neva sashayed as best she could into the ballroom. By the expression on his face and the look in his eyes, he thought she looked pretty good too, but he stayed exactly where he was and soon returned to his conversation with his grandmother.

Cecil and Ronnie looked Neva up and down and gave her a low wolf-whistle. Ethel and Queenie both gave her a thumbs-up and even Sean and Gavin threw her admiring looks. Her family all did a double take and smiled. Sasha told her she looked as beautiful as a model in a magazine; a massive exaggeration but quite something for an eight-year-old into ghosts, vampires and zombies. Sasha, once again wore the zombie princess outfit Neva had bought her, but thankfully, on this occasion, without the festering blister.

Dawn and Rowan, along with Penny, Taryn, Wendy and Judith had excelled themselves in the kitchen: the buffet for the evening was fit for Kings and Queens – and zombie princesses. There were platters of turkey, of festive ham, and of smoked salmon. A whole, clementine and vodka-baked salmon. Coronation chicken scones, halloumi fries, spiced mini Scotch eggs, sausage and fennel seed swirls, quail's eggs, devilled eggs, cocktail sausages wrapped in bacon and plain ones too, accompanied by bowls of fresh horseradish, honey and mustard, homemade mayonnaise and various other dips and sauces. There were prawns dressed with a lemon and dill sauce, prawns in paprika and chilli, and plain prawns. There were freshly made pâtés, sole goujons, and much more besides. The cherry, chocolate and hazelnut Pavlova, Christmas cheesecake, Wynter Pudding trifle – one of Penny's secret recipes, a massive Christmas cake, and various mini cakes and other tempting treats were more than enough to satisfy anyone with a sweet-tooth. And another gingerbread house, this one a replica of Wynter House, took centre stage.

Adam appeared by Neva's side and handed her a glass of champagne.

'You were right. Your mum is a very good cook. And may I say how sensational you look tonight? I'm afraid you'll have to make do with me for a while. Olivia is chewing Rafe's ear off.'

'Oh. Any idea why?'

'I'm not sure I should say, but Rafe will tell you anyway. He told her tonight about what he's been doing in the old barn.'

Neva almost spilt her champagne. 'Really? And? What is he doing? It's nothing illegal, is it? No. Forget I said that. Of course it's not.'

'Rafe should be the one to tell you, Neva. Not me. But no. It's definitely not illegal.' He gave her an odd look. 'When we first met, that rainy day on the road, which seems so long ago now but is only a few days, I thought you and I might have some fun together.'

She met his eyes. They were nowhere near as dark as Rafe's. Or, now that she thought about it, anywhere near as gorgeous.

'So did I, Adam. But the thing is—'

'I know what the thing is, Neva. And he's standing over there talking to Olivia when he should be here, benefitting from this stunning view. But may I ask you something?'

'Um. Of course.' She was blushing from head to toe.

'It's not just lust, is it? Do you think it could be love?'

She met his eyes. 'For him? Or for me?'

He smiled and shook his head. 'I already know what it is for him. He's my brother and sometimes I think I know him better than he knows himself. What is it for you? I suppose you might think it's none of my business, but he was hurt very badly by a woman once, and I'd rather not see that repeated.'

'Pippa, you mean? But that was years ago. Hasn't there been anyone else since her?'

'No one serious, no. And only two other relationships. But they didn't last. I sort of forced him into them and I could tell from the start his heart wasn't in either. He tried. I'll give him that. But he's not like me. Rafe doesn't do things by halves. He takes after Olivia in the romance department and I sometimes think he doesn't really understand the meaning of the word, 'fling'. Rafe's not the type. Unlike me.' He winked at her. 'When Rafe falls for someone, you can pretty much guarantee he's in it for the long-haul. But I'm getting the feeling you don't want to answer my question.'

She shook her head. 'It's not that I don't want to answer. It's that I'm not sure what to say. This whole thing has taken me by surprise. I never expected to feel like this. To be completely honest, I've never felt this way about anybody in my life before I met Rafe. And I wasn't looking for a relationship right now. I'll be starting a new business and moving to a new town. Romance was the last thing on my mind. A fling with you would've been nice, and I did think that might happen. But now I know I don't want that. And what I do want, really frightens me. You asked if it's lust or if I thought it could be love. I suppose I'd have to say, it's definitely lust. But it's also love. And I don't *think* it could be love. I *know* it is. I'm just not sure what to do about it.'

He beamed at her, and took her glass out of her hand. 'Then come with me, Neva Grey, because I know exactly what you should do about it. You should tell someone else exactly what you've just told me. Only perhaps leave out the bit about considering having a fling with me. Under the circumstances that may be better left unsaid.' He linked her arm through his and walked her towards Olivia and Rafe.

Olivia glowered at her. Rafe darted looks between Adam and her and back again, furrowing his brows as if he didn't know what was going on but was dreading they were going to tell him they had just become an item or something.

'We're having a conversation, Adam,' Olivia said, ignoring Neva completely.

'I can see that, Olivia, but with the greatest love and respect, I think Rafe's been talking with you for far too long this evening and he and Neva have rather a lot to discuss.'

Rafe looked stunned. 'We do?' Then a huge smile spread across his mouth. 'Yes, we do. Excuse me, Olivia. Perhaps we can pick this up later. Although, having said that, I've a feeling I may be busy. I'll talk to you tomorrow.'

'Rafe!'

Rafe ignored her and held out his hand to Neva, looking her directly in the eye, and the twinkle in his eyes and the smile on his face made her realise Adam was right. Adam took Olivia's arm, and turned her in the opposite direction.

'Shall we?' Rafe said, looking as if he'd been given the best early Christmas present ever.

Neva beamed at him and put her hand in his. 'I'm not sure exactly what you're asking me, Rafe, but whatever it is, the answer is yes. Absolutely. Without a shadow of a doubt.'

Chapter Thirty

Neva woke up and stretched. It was Christmas Day. And last night, her Christmas wish had come true. No. All her Christmas wishes ever, had come true. She turned over onto her side and ran a finger down the length of Rafe's cheek.

'Are you awake, Rafe?' she whispered.

A satisfied smile crept onto his lips and he wrapped one arm around her, pulling her closer. 'I don't think we ever went to sleep, did we?' He slowly opened one eye and then the other, the smile getting bigger and sexier all the while.

'Who needs sleep?' she said, running her finger further downwards beneath the covers of Rafe's four-poster bed.

'I do, if you expect me to keep up with your insatiable demands.'

'Oi,' she gave him a playful slap. 'If anyone

was insatiable last night, it was you.'

He reached out a hand and stroked her cheek, taking her chin between his finger and thumb and easing her towards him as he lifted his head to hers, kissing her on the lips as if he would never let her go.

Finally they eased apart. 'It's Christmas Day,' he said. 'Merry Christmas, Neva.'

'Merry Christmas to you, too, Rafe. And thank you for my present.'

He looked confused. 'I haven't given you your present yet. Or was that sarcasm?'

She shook her head. 'No sarcasm. If last night wasn't my present then I've clearly been a very good girl all year because believe me, being with you and waking up in your bed is the best present you could give me.'

He smiled and his eyes were filled with love. 'The same goes for me. I must've been a very, very good boy. Although last night, you were a very bad girl, Neva, but in a very good way.'

'Look who's talking! I was worried you'd be all prim and proper, but there was nothing very prim about the wonderful things you did last night, although they were all very proper. Very well done, that is. We could go on like this all morning. But you know what, Rafe. Actions speak louder than words. And it's still very early, so we've got plenty of time before breakfast.'

He pulled her close again and looked into her eyes. 'I've never felt like this about anyone before, Neva. Not even Pippa. I'm ecstatic but I'm also a little bit terrified. Scared I'll do something to mess this up. I know you and I have only just met and I know some people will think this is crazy, but I'm in love and I don't care. I want you to see what's in the old barn. I don't want to keep any secrets from you. That's why I had to tell Olivia about it last night because in all good conscience, she had to know before I told you. You'll understand why later.'

'I understand anyway, Rafe. She's your grandmother. Your family. And I've only just come into your life. Whatever it is you're doing in there, at this moment in time, it's only right that Olivia knows first. But I think you should know. You'd have to do something unbelievably bad to screw this up. Because something that feels this right can't possibly go wrong. And just in case you're in any doubt, I'm in love too, and I don't care what anyone thinks either.'

He beamed at her. 'Weren't you saying something about actions speaking louder than words? The old barn can wait. It's been there for centuries; it's not going anywhere.'

He kissed her again and it was some considerable time until Neva got to see what was in the old barn, but when she did, she laughed with joy.

'Gin! You're distilling gin? To an old family recipe?'

Rafe nodded. 'One of the Wynters, from generations ago, was a distiller but he was also a gambler and he lost the whole thing on the turn of a card. My grandfather, Sebastian, Olivia's husband, found copies of the recipes that distillery used. He bought this 300-litre copper pot still shortly after he met Olivia. Traditionally, they're all given names by every distiller. This copper pot still is called Olivia. Don't laugh. Grandfather did that as a compliment. He adored her. They adored one another, so everyone says. Not just Olivia.'

'I know. Ethel and Queenie said the same. But why would you keep this a secret? It's perfectly legal to have a gin distillery, isn't it?'

'Yes. Anyone can have one, within reason. But there's an awful lot of red tape, licences, regulations and such, so it takes a lot of time and patience just to get the go ahead. We had to wait almost eighteen months to get our licence. And that's before you even begin distilling. Then comes all the tests and trials to find the best recipe, the perfect blend, the exceptional flavour. That's what all these cartons are. They're filled with hops and herbs, berries, seeds, roots and fruits. Juniper of course, that has to be used to classify it as a gin, but we use lavender for example, not to add flavour as you might expect, but to add a creaminess to the blend. We've got blackberries, strawberries, cloves, samphire, elderberry, citrus fruits. It's all a matter of testing and trying to get it right. And those huge glass jars, which are called carboys, contain several ingredients in liquid form. Sebastian's recipe was good, but today's palates demand more intricate flavours. More depth. That's what we've been working on. When Sean interrupted our conversation, it was to tell me he was certain we'd got the perfect blend. It was one we've been working on for a while and it was finally ready. He was far too excited to wait to try it. We'll have other flavours too, but this one's the one we both felt the most passionate about.'

'I understand. So what happens now? Now that you've perfected that one?'

'We bottle it and hopefully sell it and then make more blends. Let me show you the label for this first one.' He took her to a laptop on a table in one corner and brought up a picture on a screen. It was a white background with Wynter House at the top, looking exactly as it does, but in an illustrated form, and Wyntersleap Falls and River Wynter below it in shades of blue and white, looking just as magnificent as they did in reality, with what looked like splashes of water on the label and etched into the pale grey-blue bottle.

'Wyntersleap Gin. Distinctively dry gin

from the waters of River Wynter.' Neva read the label. 'Is that true? Do you use the water from the river? Is that allowed?'

He nodded. 'We use the water from a natural spring that's a tributary of River Wynter, so yes.'

'So why the secrecy? You didn't say. And I think this is fantastic!'

'Because when Grandfather died, Olivia boarded this place up and said it was strictly forbidden for anyone to come in here again or to touch anything here. I decided to go against her wishes, nearly two years ago now. And I didn't want her to know because if Sean and I failed, we'd have upset her for no good reason. But Grandfather had a real passion for gin, Neva, and it made no sense to leave this sitting here doing nothing when there was a chance it could actually be making us some money. Gin is big business these days, and although fads come and go, it's been around for centuries and it'll be around for centuries after I'm dead and gone. Olivia rarely ventures outside these days, and she never comes to this barn, but we didn't want her to get word of it from anyone else. The staff know, and Ethel and Queenie, too, but they're all sworn to secrecy and would never betray my trust.'

'I'm astonished. Impressed. Thrilled it's nothing illegal.' She grinned at him and he pulled her into his arms. 'There's only one problem. I don't like gin. Only joking. I love gin. So are you going to let me try some?'

'Absolutely. And if this business takes off, I'll buy another copper pot still, and I'll name it, *Neva.*'

She gave a little gasp. 'Are you saying you adore me, Rafe?'

He tilted his head to one side and looked deep into her eyes.

'Do you really need to ask? Because if you do, you're right. I really must be crap at showing how I feel.'

He kissed her and she had no doubt.

'You're far from crap at it, Rafe,' she said, her voice husky from the kiss and her heart beating wildly as she looked into his eyes. 'I assume the barn door also locks from the inside, doesn't it? Because I'm going to show you how I feel, and I don't want anyone bursting in until I'm certain you have absolutely no doubt about that at all.'

He took her hand and, beaming at her, they went to lock the barn door. After that, she led him to the sofa in one corner.

'Merry Christmas, Rafe,' she said.

'Merry Christmas, Neva. I'm thanking my lucky stars that you came to spend Christmas at Wynter House, and I'm praying you'll want to spend every Christmas here from now on.'

'Try and stop me, Rafe. Come hell or high water, rain, power cuts or floods, I'll be spending every Christmas at Wynter House. And I'll be loving every minute of it, because I'll be here with you.'

MERRY CHRISTMAS!

Coming soon

Merriment Bay series

Coming Home to Merriment Bay

The Merriment Bay series and the Wyntersleap series are interconnected with several characters appearing in both. However, each series can be read alone.

A Note from Emily

Thank you for reading this book. A little piece of my heart goes into all of my books and when I send them on their way, I really hope they bring a smile to someone's face. If this book made you smile, or gave you a few pleasant hours of relaxation, I'd love it if you would tell your friends.

I'd be really happy if you have a minute or two to post a review. Just a line will do, and a kind review makes such a difference to my day – to any author's day. Huge thanks to those of you who do so, and for your lovely comments and support on social media. Thank you.

A writer's life can be lonely at times. Sharing a virtual cup of coffee or a glass of wine, or exchanging a few friendly words on Facebook, Twitter or Instagram is so much fun.

You might like to join my Readers' Club by signing up for my newsletter. It's absolutely free, your email address is safe and won't be shared and I won't bombard you, I promise. You can enter competitions and enjoy some giveaways. In addition to that, there's my author page on Facebook and there's also a new Facebook group. You can chat with me and with other fans and get access to my book news, snippets from my daily life, early extracts from my books and lots more besides. Details are on the 'For You' page of my website. You'll find all my contact links in the Contact section following this.

I'm working on my next book right now. Let's see where my characters take us this time. Hope to chat with you soon.

To see details of my other books, please go to the books page on my website, or scan the QR code below to see all my books on Amazon.

Contact

If you want to be the first to hear Emily's news, find out about book releases, enter competitions and gain automatic entry into her Readers' Club, go to: https://www.emilyharvale.com and subscribe to her newsletter via the 'Sign me up' box. If you love Emily's books and want to chat with her and other fans, ask to join the exclusive Emily Harvale's Readers' Club Facebook group.

Or come and say 'Hello' on Facebook, Twitter and Instagram.

Contact Emily via social media:
www.twitter.com/emilyharvale
www.facebook.com/emilyharvalewriter
www.facebook.com/emilyharvale
www.instagram.com/emilyharvale

Or by email via the website:
www.emilyharvale.com